A Simple Song

Books by Melody Carlson

Double Take

Just Another Girl

Anything but Normal

Never Been Kissed

Allison O'Brian on Her Own—Volume 1

Allison O'Brian on Her Own—Volume 2

LIFE AT KINGSTON HIGH

The Jerk Magnet

The Best Friend

The Prom Queen

A Simple Song

a novel

Melody Carlson

Revell

a division of Baker Publishing Group
Grand Rapids, Michigan

© 2013 by Melody Carlson

Published by Revell
a division of Baker Publishing Group
P.O. Box 6287, Grand Rapids, MI 49516-6287
www.revellbooks.com

Printed in the United States of America

Library of Congress Cataloging-in-Publication Data is on file at the Library of Congress, Washington, DC.

ISBN 978-0-8007-2225-8

This is a work of fiction. Names, characters, incidents, and dialogues are products of the author's imagination and are not to be construed as real. Any resemblance to actual events or persons, living or dead, is entirely coincidental.

The internet addresses, email addresses, and phone numbers in this book are accurate at the time of publication. They are provided as a resource. Baker Publishing Group does not endorse them or vouch for their content or permanence.

13   14   15   16   17   18   19   7   6   5   4   3   2   1

1

Katrina knew it was wrong to sing purely for pleasure. Sure, it was permissible to sing a lullaby when rocking a baby to sleep. It was even acceptable to sing simple songs while working in the garden if it helped to get the weeds pulled and if no one was around to hear. Music, she understood from the Amish Ordnung, was mainly meant for worship. But even in worship, one had to be careful because it was sinful to sing too loudly—or too beautifully.

She'd learned that embarrassing lesson more than ten years ago when she'd allowed her voice to soar up joyfully during a hymn at church. Only seven at the time, she believed she was worshiping God with her whole heart. But her spirits plummeted back to earth when she discovered such vibrant singing was both sinful and vain.

"God does not want you to draw attention to yourself like that," her daed somberly told her afterward. He claimed he had heard her singing above the others even though he was clear over in the men's section on the other side of the barn. "Your voice is not for your own enjoyment, Katrina. And it is vainglory to distract others with it." His discipline for her selfish display was being forbidden to sing for an entire month. That was a long month indeed. Because the truth of the matter was, Katrina loved to sing.

Yet Katrina did not feel like singing today. In fact, she barely raised her voice at all during the hymn. And she did not understand why her grandfather had encouraged singing at her grandmother's funeral service. Music was never allowed at funerals, and there would probably be talk of it all over their settlement before the week was out. Even the minister had seemed shocked when Daadi Yoder humbly announced that it was his wife's dying request to sing that particular hymn at her burial. It wasn't even from the *Ausbund* hymnal.

Katrina blinked back tears as she watched the smooth pine box being lowered into the grave. Despite his injured spine, Katrina's father had made the coffin for his mother, starting on it the very same day that she died, just three days ago. Although grieving was meant to be private, Katrina had witnessed her daed crying as he sanded the pine smoother than a coffin need be. However, the tears might have been from the pain in his back too. The poor man had been unable to walk or stand the next two days and had barely been able to get out of bed and dress in his black suit today. She'd witnessed the pain carved into his brow as he'd bowed his head to pray.

With tear-filled eyes Katrina turned away, gazing out over the countryside as she waited for the men to fill in Mammi's grave. Looking past the somber dark line of buggies and horses, her eyes came to rest on the fertile green fields, broken by an occasional fence line or big red barn and plain white house. Dairy cows grazed peacefully over at the Millers' farm. Just an ordinary spring day in Holmes County. Except that Mammi was dead. Katrina still couldn't believe it. Mammi had always been one of Katrina's favorite people. Katrina would dearly miss her grandmother and her sometimes peculiar ways.

As Katrina listened to the minister finishing his speech by saying how they had all been created from dust and were privileged to return to dust, she realized that he'd hardly said a word about her departed grandmother. It only made Katrina feel worse to think that now she'd never have the chance to know her mammi better. Especially since she'd always suspected there was some untold story attached to Mammi. Although Mammi never spoke of it, Katrina knew that she'd left the English lifestyle long, long ago. Preferring the simple life, she'd been baptized and married Daadi. But the question Katrina had always wanted to ask was, *Why? Why did she choose one world over another?* Now it seemed unlikely that Katrina would ever hear that story.

"Can you believe your grandfather did that?" Cooper asked Katrina. She had chosen to walk back to the farm, hoping it would give her a chance to deal with her emotions, but she was touched when Cooper had offered to go with her. Cooper wasn't officially courting her yet, but some people thought it was just a matter of time. However, Daed would be quick to remind her not to put her buggy in front of her horse. The question of joining the church was supposed to precede any discussion of marriage.

"Did what?" she absently asked.

"Had us sing that hymn." Cooper adjusted the brim of his straw hat, tipping it down to shield his eyes from the noonday sun.

She nodded. "*Ja*, that was odd. But then my grandmother was a bit odd."

"I heard my grandmother saying that you are just like her." Cooper made a chuckling sound, which he tried to conceal with a cough.

"Just like her?" Katrina turned to peer curiously at him. "I am like an old gray-haired woman, am I?"

He looked embarrassed. "I'm sorry. I shouldn't have said that."

"It's all right. But I would like to know what your grandmother meant by that comment."

"She meant that when your grandmother was young, she looked and acted like you."

"Your grandmother knew Mammi back then—back when my grandmother first came to our settlement?"

"Sure."

Katrina's curiosity was aroused now. "What else did your grandmother say?"

"Not much."

"How did she say Mammi looked and acted?" Katrina was not ready to let this go.

"Like you."

"Cooper." She shook her head in disappointment, feeling the strings from her white *kapp* swishing against her cheeks. "Is that all you can tell me?"

"That's all I know of it. If you want more information, perhaps you should speak to my grandmother."

"Perhaps I shall." Katrina held her head high as she walked, hoping to send him the message that she was dissatisfied that he hadn't shared more freely with her.

"See," Cooper pointed at her. "You're acting just like your grandmother now. I've seen her do that very thing. My mamm would call that 'acting superior.'"

8

Katrina felt worried. "Do you think I act superior, Cooper?"

His lips curled in a smile. "I think you *are* superior," he said quietly.

She glared at him now. "That you would say such a thing!" She stormed off, hurrying on ahead to where her aunt was walking by herself.

"Aunt Alma," Katrina said as she linked arms with the older woman, "how are you doing on this sad day?"

Aunt Alma looked at Katrina with red-rimmed eyes. She had obviously been crying. "Not too well, I'm afraid."

"I'm sorry," Katrina told her. "I'm sure you will miss your mamm more than I can imagine."

Aunt Alma nodded. "She was my best friend."

Katrina knew this was true. Aunt Alma had never married, never left home. And even though Uncle Willis and Aunt Fannie lived in the same house, Aunt Fannie had never been very friendly with Aunt Alma. But then Aunt Fannie was not too friendly with many in their family. Sometimes Katrina wondered why Uncle Willis had married such a woman.

"I was just wishing that I'd known Mammi better," Katrina admitted. "I never dreamed she would pass away so suddenly."

Aunt Alma sighed. "Nor did I. She was only seventy-four. Daed is eighty-eight and still as healthy as a horse."

"Can you tell me more about Mammi?" Katrina said suddenly. "I mean, you knew her so much better than I did. I'd love to learn more about her . . . and how she came to live here. You were a little girl when she came to the settlement, weren't you?"

"*Ja*. Even though I know Mamm wasn't my mother by birth, she was the only mamm I ever knew, and she always treated me as if I were her very own." She sniffed. "I will be so lonely without her."

Katrina pulled her arm more snugly around Aunt Alma's. "Don't worry," she told her. "I'll still come over to visit."

Aunt Alma looked surprised. "Even though your mammi isn't here?"

"Certainly!" Katrina smiled at her. "I will come to see you." Aunt Alma seemed encouraged by this as they turned to walk down the long driveway that led up to the family farm. Many carriages were parking along the drive and over by the big red barn. Already family members were clustered in front of the house. Others were milling about, everyone dressed in black—women huddling together in their white *kapps* and men off to the other side in their yellow straw hats—all waiting to assemble together and share a meal. The dinner was meant to be a celebration of God's goodness in providing Mammi with eternal life. However, Katrina did not feel like celebrating.

"I would be glad to tell you all I know of Mamm." Aunt Alma spoke quietly as they came into the yard. "But it will have to be later, Katrina. Fannie expects me to help serve dinner."

"I know." Katrina looked over to where men were setting up tables outside. Fortunately the weather was fair today. "I'm working in the kitchen too."

"Perhaps you can help me to clear out Mamm's things after dinner. Daed asked me to handle this for him. I'm sure there isn't much to be done, but we can talk as we work together."

"*Ja*," Katrina eagerly agreed. "I would like to help you."

Aunt Alma paused by the rosebush near the back door,

turning to look at Katrina. She had fresh tears streaming down her plump, ruddy cheeks. "Your friendship is very dear to me, Katrina. As you know, your daadi is a man of few words. It will be very quiet now."

Katrina reached out to hug her. "You still have me, Aunt Alma."

Her aunt nodded, then after adjusting the strings on her *kapp* and drying her face with her hands, she went into the kitchen. Soon they were all busily working to heat up casseroles, fill baskets with rolls, carry out plates and cutlery, and get everything ready for the big dinner. Katrina was thankful to be busy and grateful that her best friend, Bekka, had come over to help as well.

"You girls better eat before there's nothing left," one of the older women finally told them. So they filled their own plates with the limited selection of foods, but instead of eating outside with the other women, they cleared a spot on one end of the kitchen table and huddled together, bowed their heads in prayer, and then began to eat.

"I'm sorry about your grandmother," Bekka told Katrina. "I meant to come by your house and tell you after I heard the news, but we had a big order to package and ship before Saturday."

"It's all right," Katrina assured her. "It's been very busy here too."

"I know you were close to your grandmother." Bekka patted Katrina on the shoulder. "I'm sure you will miss her."

Katrina simply nodded, breaking a roll and spreading some butter over it. The women were starting to wash dishes now, and the kitchen was getting noisy again. Out the kitchen window, Katrina could see that most of the diners were finishing up. Children were playing. Adults stood about, conversing. It wouldn't be long until this "celebration" dinner would be over and everyone would go home to their chores. Katrina spied Cooper and his family, who looked like they were getting ready to leave too.

Bekka nudged Katrina with her elbow, tipping her head toward the window. "I heard you and Cooper had a fight today," she whispered.

Katrina wrinkled her nose. "It wasn't a fight."

"I heard you stomped off in anger."

"We simply had a little disagreement," Katrina quietly explained.

"A lovers' quarrel?" Bekka had a teasing glint in her eyes.

"A what?"

Bekka shrugged. "It's something I heard on the computer once . . . an old movie line."

Katrina shook her head. She wondered about how much time her best friend spent on the computer—supposedly working on orders for her family's soap and candle business. Katrina was aware that Bekka watched movies in the little lean-to storage room that doubled as an office. Sometimes Katrina worried that Bekka was a little too worldly. But instead of responding to her friend's silly comment, Katrina stuck her fork into Mamm's special potato salad, taking a big bite as if she were truly ravenous, when in truth, all the food tasted like sawdust today.

"Will you come to the group singing on Sunday night?" Bekka asked as she was getting ready to go home with her family.

Katrina glanced over to where Mamm was just bringing in a new load of dirty dishes. "I don't know, but I don't think so," she said quietly. "I doubt that I'm allowed . . . so soon after a death in the family."

"*Ja*. You're probably right. But we will miss you." Bekka hugged her. "See you soon, I hope."

As Katrina went over to help with the dish washing, relieving Aunt Alma from the task of drying, she tried not to think about how much she would miss the group singing. After all, she reminded herself, how could she want to sing while grieving for Mammi? Besides that, she still felt somewhat conflicted when it came to group singing. As much as she loved the informal socials where young people were allowed to visit and make music together, she always felt guilty at the weekly event. Not only for singing with abandon but for enjoying the music so much.

This was just one more thing about Amish religion that puzzled her—it seemed contradictory. Daed had warned her to be cautious when it came to music, and yet she had been allowed, even encouraged, to go to the group singing. Her first time there, she'd been shocked to discover some of the young people actually brought musical instruments to these gatherings. She'd assumed that the Ordnung forbade the use of musical instruments, but some of the young men had pulled out harmonicas and banjos—one fellow even brought an accordion once. She shook her head as she set a small stack of clean white plates in the cupboard. So confusing. Yet as much as she questioned these things, she was afraid to tell her parents. What if they made her stop going?

Katrina had been old enough to attend group singing for only a few months now, but it had quickly become the highlight of her week. Still, she found it hard to believe that group singing was actually allowed in her settlement. It made no sense on so many levels. Yet she understood that it was related to *rumspringa*—a time when youth were encouraged to discover where they were going spiritually. She also knew that parents secretly hoped their teenagers would form romantic relationships at these gatherings, and that these relationships would lead to courtship, and that courtship would lead to commitment—both in marriage and in the church. It was simply a means to an end.

Mostly Katrina went for the music, although it was at group singing that she had first caught Cooper Miller's eye. She certainly liked the boy well enough. He was lively and witty and smart—not to mention handsome with his golden curls and sparkling blue eyes. Plus he had a nice, deep singing voice, and to her surprise he seemed to take pleasure in the music as much as she did. However, she concealed her pleasure better than Cooper. Because of her father's correction, she was cautious about enjoying music in an obvious way. As much as she loved singing with gusto, she still felt uneasy about it afterward. Yes, conflicted described it.

"You've done your share of kitchen work," Aunt Alma told Katrina as she brought Katrina's younger sister, Sadie, to replace her. "I think Sadie is eager to help now."

Sadie didn't look nearly as enthused as Aunt Alma claimed, but Katrina gladly relinquished the tea towel to her. "Don't break anything," she warned her, remembering how clumsy Sadie sometimes was at home.

Sadie gave Katrina a smoldering look that would've earned her a lecture if Mamm or Daed had seen it. Katrina shook her head, then turned back to Aunt Alma. "Is there anything else I can do to help?" she asked.

"I would appreciate it if you would give me a hand upstairs."

"Certainly." Katrina gave Sadie a warning glance, which her sister ignored. Then Katrina followed Aunt Alma through the front room, where Daadi was sitting by the woodstove with some of his men friends, and up the narrow staircase.

The sounds of their footsteps echoed down the upstairs hallway, and for a moment Katrina had the distinct feeling that Mammi was about to appear before them dressed in the same white garments she'd been buried in. Aunt Alma paused at the end of the hall, standing by the door that led into her parents' bedroom as if she felt something too. Exchanging grim looks, they both just stood there a moment. Then Aunt Alma reached for the doorknob.

Katrina had been in that bedroom only once that she could remember. She'd been about ten, and because Mammi had been sick in bed, Katrina had been invited to come keep her company. But it felt like trespassing to go in there now.

Aunt Alma slowly opened the door, and the squeaking hinge sent a chill down the back of Katrina's neck as she followed her aunt in. To her relief there was nothing amiss or unusual about this dimly lit room. Like the others in the house, it had well-worn wooden floors and sparse furnishings. Aunt Alma went over to the tall, narrow window next to the bed and pulled the pale muslin curtains open, letting the spring sunlight flood in and making the room more cheerful. Katrina knew that some of Mammi's more conservative neighbors had questioned her use of curtains, wondering what she had to hide. But the curtains had remained in place for so many years that they looked as if they might fall apart if handled too roughly.

Katrina glanced around, taking in the neatly made bed with one of Aunt Alma's quilts on top and the straight-backed wooden chair next to the small, plain dresser. As usual, a few items of clothing hung on pegs near the door. Truly, it seemed Mammi's things could not include much to sort through, although Katrina appreciated being asked to help.

"It's down here." Aunt Alma kneeled down on the faded rag rug that Mammi had crocheted many years ago—another luxury that some of her neighbors would probably question. She bent over, letting out a groan as she stretched to reach something beneath the bed.

"Here, let me help you." Katrina got down beside her, and together they tugged out a small wooden trunk covered with dust. "What is this?"

"It was your mammi's." Aunt Alma sat down on the chair with a tired sigh. "I believe my daed made the box for her shortly after they married. I barely remember it. But this morning he reminded me of it. He said that everything inside of this belonged to her."

Katrina knocked on the lid, seeing that it was nailed tightly shut. "What are we supposed to do with it?"

"Open it."

"How?"

To Katrina's surprise, Aunt Alma produced a hammer that she must have concealed beneath her apron earlier. "With this."

Katrina felt a rush of excitement. "Are we *allowed* to open it?"

Suddenly Aunt Alma glanced at the open bedroom door with a worried look.

"Do you want me to close it?" Katrina asked.

Aunt Alma somberly nodded.

With her curiosity growing, Katrina hurried to the door,

and after peering down the hallway to be sure that Aunt Fannie wasn't lurking nearby, she quietly closed it.

"Daed asked me to deal with this box for him." Aunt Alma knelt down again, and using the claw end of the hammer, she pried out a nail and then another. Almost afraid to breathe, Katrina watched her aunt with wide eyes until finally she removed the lid and set it aside.

2

"Oh, my!" With the hammer still in her hand, Aunt Alma sat back on the chair, pushed a gray strand of hair back into place beneath her *kapp*, and let out a sigh.

Katrina stared into the box at something made of fabric. It looked like an odd sort of patchwork, but the shapes were irregular and the fabrics were strange. Some were colorful prints, others were shiny, some were velvety, and there were even ribbons and lace sewn in. "What is it?" Katrina asked.

"Take it out and see," Aunt Alma told her.

Katrina carefully removed what looked to be some sort of garment. Standing and holding it up to its full length, she saw that it was a very colorful patchwork sort of dress that reached nearly to her ankles.

"How interesting." Aunt Alma reached over to examine the fabric. "Someone put a lot of work into making this."

Katrina laid the dress upon the bed, then removed a square piece of flat cardboard. It had a faded photograph of three people on the front and the words *Windy Grove* on top. In smaller letters it said *Willow Tree* on the bottom. Inside was a black, round disk. "Do you think this is a phonograph record?"

she asked her aunt. "I've read about such things, but I've never actually seen one."

Aunt Alma just shook her head. "I have no idea."

"How old were you when Mammi married your daed?"

"About five."

"How long ago was that?"

She sighed. "Well, I'm nearly fifty. So it was about forty-five years ago."

Katrina was doing the math in her head. "So that would've been the late 1960s, and Mammi must've been around twenty-nine then."

"*Ja.*" Aunt Alma nodded. "That sounds about right."

"*Willow Tree . . . Windy Grove,*" Katrina read the words aloud. "I wonder what that means."

"Look at that woman there," Aunt Alma said suddenly. "Do you know who I think that is?" She reached for the record cover now, studying the image closely. Holding it up, she looked at Katrina in astonishment. "Unless I'm mistaken, that young woman is your mammi."

"Are you serious?" Katrina stared at the smiling, dark-haired woman in disbelief. Was it possible her gray-haired mammi had ever looked like that?

"Can't you see it?"

"See what?" All Katrina saw was a long-haired, pretty young woman in a long, brightly colored dress, and two bearded men standing on either side.

"She looks just like you."

Katrina blinked. "Really?"

"*Ja.*" Aunt Alma turned the cover over, peering at the words on the back. "Starla Knight," she declared. "Knight must've been Mamm's maiden name before she married Daed."

Katrina nodded. "*Ja*. Her first name was Starla. I remember it because it was kind of a strange name."

"She gave your daed a bit of a strange name too," Aunt Alma mused.

"Frost?" Katrina thought for a moment. "I guess it is strange . . . but I'm used to it. Daed always says it was because it was such a cold morning when he was born."

Aunt Alma nodded. "It was."

"Starla Knight . . ." Katrina ran the words over her tongue. "It's so pretty. It almost sounds like *starlit night*."

"Do you think she was part of some sort of musical group?" Aunt Alma asked with wide eyes.

Katrina felt a strange rush running through her. "Was Mammi a singer?"

"She did have a beautiful singing voice," Aunt Alma said quietly.

"You heard her sing?"

"Only a time or two . . . and only when she didn't know I was listening. I caught her singing in the garden once. And one time when she was hanging the wash. It was so beautiful I wanted to hear more, but when I asked her to sing for me, she flat out refused. She scolded me and told me to never speak of it to anyone. And I never did . . . until now. I do hope she'll forgive me for telling you."

"I'm sure she will. Mammi was always a very forgiving soul." Katrina was fascinated as she continued looking through the box, finding an odd pair of boots and some other strange items, as well as some envelopes and papers. But nothing interested her as much as the mysterious phonograph record.

"What are you going to do with these?" she finally asked her aunt.

"I don't know. Daed just wanted me to get rid of them. He even suggested I burn them. Mostly he doesn't want anyone to see them. Particularly your daed."

"Burn them?" Katrina clutched the dress and record protectively. "Please don't."

Aunt Alma frowned. "No, I don't want to do that."

"Why would Daadi want to burn these?"

"He said he was worried that at his age, he might pass on suddenly like Mamm did." Aunt Alma's brow creased. "He was concerned that Fannie might be the one to clean this room and find this box . . . and, well, you never know how that could end up."

Katrina did know. Aunt Fannie was a talker. No secret was safe with that woman. But even worse, Aunt Fannie acted like she was better than the rest of them. She was quick to judge and condemn others without having all the facts. Katrina could only imagine how Aunt Fannie would react if she saw the contents of this box . . . or the implications that seemed to be contained in it.

"May I keep these things?" Katrina asked hopefully.

Aunt Alma nodded. "*Ja*. I think your mammi would like that. I know I would like that. As long as you can keep your daed and the rest of your family from seeing them."

"I can do that." Katrina hoped she could.

"Let's bundle them up in something," Aunt Alma suggested.

"*Ja*. I don't want anyone to see me carrying this out."

Aunt Alma removed a pale blue dress from a peg on the wall. "This was her favorite dress. You can have it too. Wrap it around everything you want to take, and if anyone asks, you can tell them it's just some old clothing your mammi left to you."

With the mysterious items safely wrapped in her mammi's dress, Katrina was about to go.

"Wait." Aunt Alma put her hand over her mouth. "I just remembered something else."

"What?" Katrina watched as her aunt opened the bottom dresser drawer, going through what appeared to be Mammi's underclothes. Katrina hoped she wasn't going to make her take those too.

"Here." Aunt Alma was unrolling a piece of white cloth to reveal something small and rectangular.

"Is that a cell phone?" Katrina peered curiously at what looked like a hand-sized electronic device but unlike other cell phones that she'd seen.

"I don't know for sure." Aunt Alma uncurled a yellowed cord. "But Mamm sometimes had this with her when she thought she was alone." She pointed to the round piece at the end of the cord. "This went in her ear, but she didn't want anyone to see—"

Just then there was a loud knock on the door, and Aunt Alma placed her back to the door as she bundled up the little box and thrust it at Katrina.

"Who is in there?" Aunt Fannie demanded. "Open this door!"

Katrina shoved the small package into her large bundle, wrapping it snugly under the blue dress as Aunt Fannie pushed open the door.

"It's only us," Aunt Alma calmly told her, although her cheeks were flushed and her pale blue eyes were glittering with excitement.

"What are you two doing in here?" Aunt Fannie looked suspiciously from one to the other. "And why was this door blocked?"

"I was simply standing in front of it," Aunt Alma said.

"What is that?" Aunt Fannie pointed at the bundle in Katrina's arms.

"Those are the things Mamm left to Katrina."

"To Katrina?" Aunt Fannie narrowed her eyes. "I never heard a word of this."

"Ask Daed to explain it to you," Aunt Alma firmly told her. "I am simply obeying his instructions."

Aunt Fannie pressed her lips tightly together. She knew better than to question her father-in-law since he was still the head of their household. "Well, it does seem odd," she said finally, "for Mamm to leave her things to Katrina like this." She peered at the bundle. "But I don't know if that surprises me. Mamm was always an odd one."

Katrina exchanged glances with Aunt Alma.

"Mamm is not here to defend herself." Aunt Alma spoke sharply to her sister-in-law. "And one should not speak ill of the dead." She waved her hand. "Certainly not in the departed's own room."

Aunt Fannie looked slightly flustered now.

"If you'll excuse us," Aunt Alma continued, "I have chores to attend to, and I'm certain that Katrina is needed at home."

"*Ja.*" Katrina nodded eagerly. "That's right." She tossed Aunt Alma a grateful look, then hurried out the door and down the hallway. Slipping quietly down the stairs and out the back door, she cut behind the house and down the fence line alongside the recently planted cornfield, and she went directly home.

To her relief, her family wasn't home yet. After taking her precious bundle up to the bedroom she shared with Sadie, she was unsure what to do. Looking around the small room, she knew there was no place to hide all these things. And as much as she loved her spirited and precocious fourteen-year-old sister, she wasn't sure she trusted her with Mammi's secrets. Although Sadie, like Katrina, was only related to Aunt Fannie by marriage, she did seem to have some of the same personality traits—including a loose tongue at times. What if Sadie told her friends about Mammi's mysterious box of items?

Thinking of Sadie's friends reminded Katrina of her most trusted friend. Bekka was blessed to have a room of her own now that her older sister, Louisa, had married. Not only did Bekka have a private bedroom, but because she helped with her family's soy candle–making business, she also had more freedom than most of Katrina's friends.

Katrina was about to leave for Bekka's when she realized Sadie might've gotten wind that Katrina had inherited some things from Mammi. Aunt Fannie might be talking about it in the kitchen right this minute. Katrina decided to leave a few things behind, including the strange patchwork dress and boots as well as Mammi's favorite old blue dress. She put them in the bottom drawer of the dresser she shared with Sadie, knowing that although it was supposed to be Katrina's drawer, it would only be a matter of time before Sadie discovered them. Hopefully the strange items wouldn't invite too many questions—and if they did, Katrina would simply explain that they were from Mammi's life before she left the English and joined the church. What was so unusual about that?

She bagged up the rest of the things in a canvas shopping bag, left Mamm a note in the kitchen promising to be back in time for evening chores, and took off toward Bekka's house. Once again, she cut across the fields, carefully walking the fence lines to avoid stepping on the tender sprouts that were just coming up all over. In a month's time all this acreage would be lush and green with produce, and by summer's end, it would be ready to harvest.

Although Daadi owned this acreage, they all called it the family farm. But because Uncle Willis, born to Daadi's first wife, was ten years older than Daed, he had taken over managing it years ago. Still, they called themselves partners, and up until the tractor accident several years ago, Daed had always worked hard. Now he felt sorry that he was unable to do his "fair share," but fortunately Katrina's two older brothers, Drew and Cal, were strong and fit and both seemed to love agriculture. Much more so than Uncle Willis's only son. Thomas had no interest in farming and was currently trying to start a business. Because Drew and Cal did most of the farm work, Katrina expected that Daadi would make them partners in the farm someday—hopefully in the not too distant future because Drew, who'd been baptized a few years ago, wanted to ask his girlfriend, Hannah, to wed. Hannah taught school but would gladly give it up to marry Drew. Especially if Drew inherited part of the farm.

Katrina could see Bekka's house now. It had once been a farmhouse too, but their land had been divided and Bekka's father had taken the smallest parcels. Now instead of growing produce like his brothers did, Bekka's father grew mostly herbs and flowers that the family dried and used to make candles and soaps. They'd started out by selling their goods to local shops but had eventually expanded into a larger business that shipped candles and soaps all over the country. As a result, Bekka had learned how to run a computer, and she handled most of the orders herself.

Katrina suspected she'd find Bekka working on the computer in the office, which was actually just an old root storage room attached to the back of the house. A few times Katrina had helped her print mailing labels, but most of what Bekka did, Katrina didn't fully understand. Sometimes she wondered if Bekka wasn't just pretending to work.

"Hello?" Katrina called as she tapped on the door. "Bekka?"

"Oh?" Bekka looked startled as she turned off the monitor, concealing whatever she had been looking at on the screen. "Katrina, what are you doing here?"

"I need your help." Katrina glanced around the small, crowded room. One wall had a shelf full of car batteries that Bekka used to power the computer. Another wall had the printer and paper supplies against it. The third wall, where Bekka worked, had a small desk with her computer and a telephone that was only used for business.

"Help with what?" Bekka eyed her canvas shopping bag. "What have you got there?"

Katrina closed the door. "Something I don't want Sadie to see."

Bekka came closer, peering curiously into the bag.

"I don't even know what all of it is." Katrina began to unload the contents, setting the various items on a cleared-off space next to the computer. "This all belonged to my grandmother." She told Bekka what had happened upstairs in her grandparents' house, perhaps making it seem more exciting than it was—if that was even possible.

Bekka's eyes were huge now. "Your grandmother was a singer in a band?"

"Well, I'm not sure that it was a band exactly." She held up the record cover. "But it seems she was musical. I mean, this is a record, after all. That suggests music."

"Willow Tree?" Bekka got a thoughtful look. "That does sound like the name of a music group."

Katrina frowned. "How would you even know?"

Bekka's fine brows arched mysteriously. "I have my ways."

Katrina pointed to the computer with a knowing look. "You mean *that*?"

Bekka shrugged.

"You do use it for more than just your family's business, don't you?"

She gave Katrina a sheepish smile. "Let's just say it's my window to the world."

"But you shouldn't be doing—"

"My parents don't care . . . At least they don't care until I get baptized. Then they'll expect more of me." Bekka turned the monitor back on. "Right now they don't mind as long as I get my work done. And I *always* get my work done."

The darkened screen slowly came to life, exposing a colorful image of funny little figures that suddenly started moving about.

"That doesn't look like work to me," Katrina pointed out.

Bekka laughed. "That's a game, silly."

"Oh."

"Let's google Willow Tree and—"

"Google?" Katrina was confused.

"It's a way to look things up," Bekka explained as she tapped some keys and clicked on some things so quickly that Katrina couldn't even follow it. "There," she said, pointing to a photo that looked similar to the record cover. "Willow Tree . . . folk trio . . . Willy Brown, Laurence Zimmerman, and the sweet vocals of Starla Knight—"

"That's her—my mammi. *Starla Knight*."

"Says here that they recorded a single hit titled 'After the Storm' in early 1966. Their only album, titled *Windy Grove*, was released later that same year. And then Willow Tree broke up in early 1968."

"That must've been right before Mammi came to live here in our settlement."

"How do you know?"

"Aunt Alma told me."

"Let's see if we can find them on YouTube."

"You what?"

"YouTube." Bekka waved one hand dismissively as she used the other to frantically click buttons. "I found it! Listen— listen—this is Willow Tree." She clicked again, and suddenly, right there in black and white, a young-looking woman with long, dark hair and two bearded men, each with a guitar, began to sing—right out of the computer.

Katrina stood there transfixed by the sound of the woman's voice—so clear, so pure, so beautiful. By the time the song ended, Katrina had tears streaming down her face, and she wasn't even sure why. But when she looked at Bekka, she felt a strange sense of relief to see she was crying too.

"That was your mammi!" Bekka said with passion. "You must be so proud."

Katrina gave Bekka a worried look. Pride was not an admirable trait, and Bekka knew it just as well as Katrina did. "I am amazed," she admitted. "I had no idea."

"Let me see if I can find another song," Bekka said enthusiastically.

By the time they had listened to three songs, Katrina was so overwhelmed that she had to sit down on the stool next to Bekka's office chair. "This is incredible." She shook her head.

"Do you know what's even more amazing?" Bekka said suddenly.

"What?" Katrina let out a slow sigh, still trying to take all of this in.

"You are just like her."

"Like who? Mammi?"

Bekka pointed to the frozen image still on the screen—the dark-haired young woman smiling happily with a guitar-playing young man on either side of her. "Her. Starla Knight. You could be her twin."

Katrina made a nervous laugh.

"I don't mean looks, although you do resemble her. I mean your voice, Katrina. It is just as good as Starla Knight's."

"Oh, no, of course it's not." Katrina waved her hand.

"It is!" Bekka insisted. "I've heard you sing. Everyone in group singing has heard you too. They might not say it to your face, but everyone there thinks your voice is beautiful."

Katrina felt the same old guilt all over again. "But that's not right," she said quietly.

"Why isn't it right?" Bekka demanded. "God gave you that voice, Katrina. I want to know—what is wrong with using it?"

Katrina had no answer for her. All she had were questions. Lots and lots of questions.

3

As badly as she wanted to, Katrina couldn't stick around and talk to Bekka about all the questions racing through her mind right now. Instead she asked to stash her bag of mysterious treasures in Bekka's "office." Naturally, Bekka agreed.

"I promise to keep my nose out of it," Bekka said as she tucked the bag into a space behind a big box of paper, "as long as you promise to come back and show me everything that's in it."

"Don't worry," Katrina assured her. "I haven't even had the chance to go through it all myself. That reminds me"—she reached back into the bag, feeling around for the little bundle and pulling it out—"do you know what this is? I don't think it's a cell phone, unless it's some old one."

Bekka examined the small box and cord and read the words on the front. "Realtone . . . Transistor . . . Want me to look it up?"

"*Ja*. If you don't mind."

Bekka pushed more buttons. "Oh, it's a radio," she told Katrina. "A small portable radio that was popular in the 1950s and 1960s."

Katrina turned one of the knobs, and suddenly—to her amazement—music was coming out of the little box. "Listen to this." She held it up.

"It must be an old-fashioned iPod."

"An I what?"

"Never mind." Bekka studied it. "I wonder if it's valuable."

"I don't know, but Aunt Alma said that Mammi sometimes had it with her. She put this thing in her ear." She looked around for a place to stick the end of the wire into, and after finding a hole that fit, she stuck the little round piece into her ear. "I can hear it," she told Bekka.

"It really is just like an old-time iPod." Bekka nodded knowingly.

Katrina wanted to ask her how she knew about all these things but then realized it was due to "working" on the computer.

"Do you want to leave that with the bag?" Bekka asked.

"No." Katrina shook her head, not wanting to part with what was pouring into her ear at the moment. "If Mammi could listen to this, then so can I."

Bekka gave a firm nod. "*Ja*. We're always being told to follow the examples of our elders. That's what you are doing."

Katrina grinned at her. Then she tucked the little radio up into her sleeve so no one would see it, told Bekka thank you and goodbye, and left for home. Once again, she cut along the fence lines, but she walked more slowly this time. It was wonderful to walk through the beautiful green fields with the blue sky and smatterings of clouds overhead—all the while listening to this beautiful music. Even when a man's voice came on after a song finished, talking about the singers and other things, she didn't mind. By the time she got home, she knew that she was listening to WODZ, the station that played the golden oldies twenty-four hours a day. It comforted her to think this was the same station that Mammi must've listened to when she was alive.

Katrina made it home in time to tend to her evening chores and to help Mamm and Sadie fix supper. She'd found a spot to hide her radio, up high on a shelf in the garden shed, and she felt it would be safe there since she was the primary gardener. She decided that if she was found out, she would simply tell the truth. Mammi had left the radio to her, and she was only following Mammi's example.

As she'd suspected, her parents did not approve of her or Cal going to the group singing out of respect for Mammi's passing. "Not for at least a month," Daed proclaimed when Cal asked the next morning. Of course, Drew wasn't concerned since he no longer went, and for some reason he was still allowed to visit Hannah at her home on Saturday night after the farm work was done. But Cal, like Katrina, was disappointed. Still, they knew not to argue with Daed. Especially when Daed was feeling particularly poorly. It seemed his back was worse than ever. Katrina overheard her parents quietly talking about some kind of medical surgery that might help him, which had to mean Daed was even worse than he let on. Of course, when the subject of money and how they would pay for it came up, the conversation had ended abruptly. "We will never have that kind of money," Daed had told Mamm. "Don't mention it again."

A shadow of sadness hung over their entire household. Mammi was gone. Daed's back was never going to get better. And there would be no group singing for at least a month. Despite the sunny spring weather, the Yoder home seemed draped in sorrow.

Katrina's secret escape from all this grimness was getting to listen to Mammi's radio. She could hardly believe it when, on Saturday night, the song "After the War" by Willow Tree was played. She was so excited that she nearly jumped up from where she'd been sitting by the irrigation pond, ready to run to tell her family this news. But then she remembered: this was her secret. However, as she listened—and to her amazement—she discovered she could kind of remember the tune as well as some of the words. She could almost sing along—or at least hum.

For the next week, Katrina listened to the radio so much that she had to replace the boxy little battery twice. Fortunately, her father always kept a big supply of batteries of all sizes in the pantry, and she found some that fit there. She told herself she would purchase more to replace the ones she was using the next time she went to town. In the meantime, she was so enthralled with the music on the radio that she did all her chores—and more—with enthusiasm. After a while Mamm actually became suspicious.

"I am grateful that I have such a hard-working daughter," she told Katrina after she'd offered to hang the wash, which was supposed to be Sadie's chore. "But I am wondering why you are being so helpful."

Katrina felt an all-too-familiar twinge of guilt. "It's just that I like being outside," she told Mamm. And this was true. "The weather has been lovely."

Mamm studied her closely. "Is that all?"

She shrugged. "I know how Sadie gets all clogged up and sneezes after being outdoors at this time of year."

Mamm nodded. "*Ja*, that's true enough." She smiled. "You are a good girl, Katrina."

Naturally, her mother's praise made her feel even more guilty. But as soon as she turned the radio on and stuck the plug in her ear, she forgot all about her guilt. It was as if she couldn't stop herself. Listening to this music was incredible, and it was becoming her window to the world—like Bekka had said about the computer. She also realized that the radio station played a lot of the same tunes again and again, and after a couple of weeks, she had learned many of them by heart.

"I'm sure you've been missing Bekka," Mamm said to Katrina as she came into the house after working in the garden on a Friday afternoon.

Katrina nodded. "She and her family should be back from the gift show by now," she told Mamm. "I hope it went well for them."

"Maybe you want to go visit Bekka and find out," Mamm said.

"You don't mind?"

"You deserve it, Katrina. You've been working so diligently. Ever since Mammi died, it seems you work harder than ever."

Katrina just looked down.

"In fact, I spoke to your father about it. I told him that it seemed unfair to keep you and your brothers from the group singing. You're all working so hard. Your father agreed you can go now."

Katrina smiled. "Thanks, Mamm!"

"Go and see your friend. Sadie can help me fix supper tonight."

Katrina was so happy, she decided to take the road to Bekka's house this time. Even though it would take longer, it would give her more time to listen to the radio. It would also give her the chance to walk past Cooper's house. She hadn't seen him since the day of Mammi's funeral, and she was starting to feel worried that he might've forgotten her by now. Especially since she had been unable to go to the group singing, and she knew lots of other pretty girls who liked Cooper would have been there. For all she knew, Tricia Green might've turned his head by now. But she hoped not.

Listening to the radio put a lilt in her step, but since she didn't see anyone on the road, she didn't think it mattered. But when she noticed a particular boy cutting across a certain farmyard toward her, she pulled the plug from her ear and tucked it back into her sleeve as she returned to a normal walking pace.

"Katrina," Cooper called out as he scaled the fence and hurried over to join her. "I haven't seen you in a long time. How are you doing?"

"I'm as well as can be," she said somberly. "After Mammi's passing."

He gave her a sympathetic look. "*Ja*, I know now how close to her you were. I apologize if I said something to offend you the day of her funeral."

She gave him a small smile. "I apologize if I took offense, Cooper."

His eyes lit up. "Where are you headed?"

"To the Lehmans'."

He smiled. "Mind if I walk with you? I need to pay Peter a visit." Peter was Bekka's older brother and Cooper's best friend.

She shrugged. "Sure, if you want to."

"The Lehmans were in Cleveland this week. Selling soap and candles at some big fancy show where shop owners from all over the country come to buy," he told her.

36

She nodded. "*Ja*, I know."

"They had to ride the bus to get there."

She nodded again. "*Ja*, I know."

"Peter said they had six heavy crates full of samples to take with them and—"

"*Ja*, I—"

"Is there anything you don't know?" He laughed.

"Well, Bekka is my best friend," she reminded him.

"*Ja*, I know."

Now she laughed. "I know something you don't know."

"What's that?"

"My parents are letting me and my brother go to the group singing this week."

"That is good news!"

She grinned. "I have missed it."

"And we have missed you."

She gave him a skeptical look.

"It's true. No one sings as pretty as you, Katrina. Everyone says so."

She felt her cheeks warming. "Thank you. But they should not say that."

As they reached the Lehmans', Cooper looked intently into her eyes. "I look forward to seeing you at the group singing, Katrina."

She smiled. "And I look forward to being there." Then she hurried back around the house, hoping to find Bekka "at work" in her office. To her relief, Bekka was there. And this time she actually seemed to be working.

"We got so many orders," Bekka told her. "It's unbelievable. My family is going to have to work so hard to fill all of them."

"But isn't that a good thing?"

"*Ja*. But it will keep us busy." Bekka looked up from her computer. "What are you doing here anyway?"

"Mamm let me have some free time." Katrina looked behind the box of paper to make sure her bag was still there. "But if you're busy, I can come another—"

"No, you can keep me company while I enter these into the computer," Bekka told her.

"If you don't mind, I'd like to go through Mammi's things," Katrina said.

"I was wondering when you were going to get back here to do that." Bekka chuckled. "I was about ready to go through them myself."

"I couldn't get away the first week," Katrina said as she opened the bag. "Then you were gone." As she pulled out the record, she told Bekka about how she'd been listening to the radio. "It's as if I can't stop," she confessed. "Sometimes when I know Sadie is asleep, I sneak it into my bed and listen there."

Bekka laughed. "You are worse than me and this computer."

"And I've been learning songs," Katrina told her.

"Really? What kinds of songs?"

"Most of them are from the sixties and seventies," she explained. "The station only plays old songs. But I love them." She sighed. "I love them so much I could just sing and sing." She stopped herself. "Except that I know it's wrong."

"Why don't you sing one for me?" Bekka asked as she plucked away at her keyboard.

"Sing one?" Katrina felt self-conscious now.

"Come on," Bekka urged. "I want to hear an old song."

Katrina tried to think of a good song. "All right, there is a group called Peter, Paul and Mary, and—"

"I think I've heard of them."

"Really?" Katrina was doubtful. "How do you happen to hear of all these singing groups? Do you listen to music too?"

Bekka gave her a sly look now. "I'm sure you've never heard of a TV show called *American Star* . . . have you?"

Katrina just shook her head. "No, of course not. Have you seen it?"

Bekka pointed to her computer. "I watch it on here."

"I know you watch movies, but the computer is a TV too?"

Bekka giggled. "Sort of."

"Oh." Katrina was surprised. There was a lot she didn't know about computers.

"This TV show is so great," Bekka told her. "Ordinary kids like you and me—well, except they're all English—anyway, they compete in singing. The winners get all this money. And sometimes they sing songs from groups like Peter, Paul and Mary."

"Really?" Katrina tried to imagine that but couldn't.

"So anyway, *ja*, I do know who Peter, Paul and Mary are. *American Star* did a tribute to them last season. They even showed old films of them singing."

Katrina just shook her head.

"Anyway, you were going to sing one of their songs."

"*Ja*. The reason I'll sing one of theirs is because the way they sound—the way they sing—reminds me of Mammi's group Willow Tree. But I've only heard Willow Tree a couple of times on the radio. Maybe three."

"You heard your mammi on the radio?" Bekka seemed truly impressed.

"*Ja,*" Katrina said with enthusiasm. "It was so amazing."

"Go ahead and sing." Bekka turned back to her computer. "I won't even look."

"All right. I'm going to sing 'Puff, the Magic Dragon,'" Katrina told her. "It sounds like a silly song, but it's actually a bit sad. I'm not sure if I got all the words right, but sometimes I make them up if I can't quite remember."

With that, she began to sing about the dragon that lived by the sea, the boy who loved him, and how the boy grew up and left the poor dragon all alone. She wasn't even sure if Bekka was listening or not. By the time Katrina finished, Bekka's fingers had quit flying over the keyboard, and she seemed to be staring intently at her screen at what looked like a customer's order for soap and candles. Then she spun around in her chair, staring at Katrina like she was staring at a ghost, and she looked like she was crying.

"What's wrong?" Katrina asked anxiously. "What happened?"

"Nothing is wrong." Bekka wiped her eyes. "It's just that it was so beautiful."

Katrina blinked. "You mean the song?"

Bekka nodded eagerly. "Katrina, that was the most beautiful thing I have ever heard. And I have heard a lot of people singing. I've been watching *American Star* for three seasons now."

"Oh . . ." Katrina waved her hand. "Well, that is a very pretty song, don't you think?"

"I don't just mean the song. It was great. But I mean your voice. I always knew it was beautiful. I just never knew it was *that* beautiful."

Katrina couldn't help but smile. "Thank you, Bekka."

"Your voice is so good that I know you could win a million dollars on *American Star*."

Katrina laughed. "I know you mean that as a compliment, but it will never happen, Bekka. Not in a million years."

"Maybe you should watch *American Star* with me," Bekka told her. "You might see what I'm talking about."

"Right now I just want to go through Mammi's things," Katrina told her. "And I know you need to work on those orders for your business."

Bekka nodded. "You're right."

"Will I bother you if I stay here and go through this stuff?"

"Not if you sing while you're doing it."

So, as Katrina sorted through the papers, some of which seemed to be words to songs and others of which seemed to be letters from record people, she sang what songs and words she could remember, often making up the missing words—and sometimes making both of them break up into laughter.

"What is going on in here?" Peter demanded as he opened the door and both he and Cooper suddenly burst into the tiny office.

"Go on," Bekka told him. "It's too crowded in here already."

"But I heard laughing," Peter told her.

"*Ja, ja,*" Bekka said. "Is there a rule against laughing while you work?"

"Are you working?" Peter asked.

"Look." Bekka pointed to her computer. "You can see that I am." She now pointed to Katrina. "And she is helping me."

Katrina had covered up her things with a box of loose papers and was now looking up at the guys with the most innocent face she could muster under the circumstances.

"Mamm said to tell you supper is nearly ready," Peter told Bekka.

"That means I'd better go home too," Katrina said.

"Me too," Cooper said cheerfully.

"Isn't that handy?" Bekka said with a teasing glint in her eye. "You can just leave those papers," she said to Katrina. "I'll put the rest of them away."

Katrina could tell by her tone that she meant Mammi's things. "I'll see you tomorrow," she said as she stood.

"Tomorrow?" Bekka looked confused.

"Katrina is coming to the group singing," Cooper said.

Bekka's eyes lit up. "It's about time they let you come back. I'm sure your mammi would agree it's been way too long."

Katrina just nodded. She wasn't entirely sure what Mammi would say or think of any of this. She reassured herself with the thought that Starla Knight would understand. Surely she would.

4

As Cooper walked with Katrina down the road, he started to hum one of the lighthearted tunes they had sung at the group singing. It was just a silly little song about a frog and a horse, but she could tell he wanted her to sing along. "Come on," he said finally. "Can't you just join in on the chorus?"

"Someone might hear us," she warned him.

"Out here?" He waved his hand to the fields all around them.

"Sounds carry."

"I don't understand you, Katrina. You have such a pretty singing voice, and I don't know anyone who is more worried about it than you are."

She considered telling him about the times she'd been chastised over her singing but decided not to.

"My grandmother told me something," he said in a slightly mysterious tone. "Something about your grandmother."

"What?" She stopped walking and turned to look at him.

"It seems that your grandmother was good friends with my grandmother's younger sister."

"What?"

"My grandmother said her younger sister—Great-Aunt Martha—was the one who first took your grandmother in."

"Truly?"

He nodded, pleased to have her full attention now. "My grandmother's family lived in a different settlement. And although my grandmother was already married and living over here when Great-Aunt Martha took your grandmother in, my grandmother knew about it. She met your grandmother back then."

"What else did she tell you?"

He shrugged.

"Come on, Cooper. Please tell me."

"I would tell you if I knew. Truth is, that's all I know."

She frowned.

"But my grandmother said that if you want to come visit and talk to her, she'll be happy to tell you whatever she knows."

"Do you think she really knows anything . . . I mean, anything that interesting?"

"She might."

Katrina thought about Aunt Alma. She'd been to visit her only once since the funeral. She could tell Aunt Alma was sad, but it had seemed to cheer her up to talk about Mammi. "Do you think I could bring my Aunt Alma to visit your grandmother?"

"I don't see why not."

"All right then." She nodded in agreement. "Tell your mammi that if she doesn't mind, I'll bring my aunt to visit her—the first chance I get."

Cooper grinned. "Great. I'll tell her."

She nodded toward her house. "Here we are. Thanks for walking me home."

"Anytime." He paused. "I know my grandmother will be home tomorrow. Just in case you and your aunt can make it."

"I'll keep that in mind." She waved and hurried up to her house. But when she peeked in the kitchen window, she could see that Mamm and Sadie hadn't even set the table yet. She decided to pop over to ask Aunt Alma about visiting Cooper's grandmother. She listened to her radio as she walked the fence line, and when she got there, seeing the front door was open, she went on inside just like she'd always done when Mammi was alive. She was barely in the front room when she heard the sounds of loud voices in the kitchen—arguing! Realizing she should've knocked, she was about to make a quick exit when she saw Daadi in his chair. She froze in place, then realized he was fast asleep and snoring.

"You can't let him keep taking advantage of you like that," Aunt Fannie was saying loudly. "He doesn't lift a finger for this farm, and yet you treat him like a full partner."

"Quiet," Uncle Willis said. "Daed and Alma will hear you."

"I don't care who hears me," Aunt Fannie said. "Frost is going to drain you dry, Willis. And it's not fair."

"But his boys are working and—"

"And you can pay them a fair wage for their labor," she continued. "But that's all you owe that family. It's wrong for you to take from our family to help someone who's not working. The Bible says if you don't work, you don't eat. Frost doesn't work, and he doesn't deserve to—"

"Frost has health problems, Fannie. You know that."

"Yes, I know that he's been saying that for years. But if he wants to, he goes out and builds something in his shop. He built his mother's casket, didn't he? And now that Mamm's

45

not around to protect her only boy, I say it's time to do some pruning on this farm before we all—"

"Hello, Alma," Uncle Willis interrupted.

"Is something wrong?" Aunt Alma's voice sounded small and worried.

"No," Uncle Willis said.

"Supper is nearly ready," Aunt Alma quickly told them. "I just ran out to pick some chives for the potatoes, and then I saw some—"

"Just let us know when it's ready," Aunt Fannie said loudly. "We'll be in the front room with Daed."

Katrina knew it was time to escape. She glanced quickly at Daadi, relieved to see he still seemed to be sound asleep, and quietly slipped out the front door and hurried around to the back door, finding Aunt Alma in the kitchen.

"Oh, Katrina." Aunt Alma smiled. "It's good to see you. You want to stay for supper? I can put on another—"

"No," Katrina said quietly. "I just came to invite you to do something with me tomorrow." She quickly explained about Cooper's grandmother. "Mrs. Miller will tell us what she knows about Mammi."

Aunt Alma's eyes lit up. "She will?"

"Can you come?"

"*Ja*, sure. Why not? I am a grown woman. I can go visit an elderly friend if I like, can I not?"

Katrina smiled. "I sure hope so."

"*Ja*, well, I better get supper on the table. You run along now, Katrina. Come by around ten tomorrow morning and we'll go visiting."

As Katrina hurried back home, she felt like she had a rock in the pit of her stomach. Aunt Fannie's words had been so cold, so harsh. How could she say such things about Katrina's daed, especially when he was in such pain all the time? What kind of unfeeling woman was she? What about practicing good Christian charity and love like they were taught to do? How could Uncle Willis put up with such animosity? And how was she going to tell her parents about this? Certainly they deserved to know.

As she went into her own house, where Sadie was setting the table and Mamm was removing a ham from the oven, Katrina decided it might be best to wait until after supper to tell her parents about what she'd heard. No sense in ruining a good meal. She knew it would crush her father. He hated being seen as weak or incapacitated and always tried so hard to keep up a strong front. When asked about his health, he'd always say he was "just fine" or "getting better every day."

But his family knew better. In fact, he was in so much pain tonight that he wasn't even able to come to the table. Katrina tried not to look at his empty chair as they sat down. She bowed her head with the others, silently praying as usual, but after she thanked God for his provision, she also asked God to help Daed get well. It was a familiar prayer, but tonight she prayed it with fervency.

When it was time to eat, she still felt worried for Daed as well as about the troubles brewing on the family farm. As a result, she didn't feel very hungry and only picked at her food.

"Are you all right?" Mamm finally asked her. "Feeling well?"

"I'm fine," she lied. Just like Daed.

"How are the Lehmans?" Mamm asked. "Did they sell a lot of candles and soap this week?"

Katrina filled them in on the happenings with Bekka's

family, answering a few more questions. Then the table got quiet again, and Katrina felt as if she couldn't stop herself from asking the question that was ready to leap from the tip of her tongue. "Is Daed ever going to get better?" she blurted.

"Oh, *ja, ja*," Mamm assured her. "He gets better all the time. He was just tired, that's all. Nothing to worry about."

Cal and Drew kept their eyes on their plates, and even Sadie looked perplexed by Mamm's casual reply. How could their family go on pretending that everything was perfectly fine? How could she?

"Truly, Mamm?" Katrina looked into her mother's gray eyes. "You honestly believe Daed is getting better?"

"I believe God will make him well." Mamm reached for the butter.

"But what if you're wrong?" Katrina demanded. "God doesn't heal everyone. What if Daed never gets better? And what if Uncle Willis decides that Daed is not able to partner with him on the farm anymore?"

"Oh, Katrina." Mamm shook her head. "Why do you go looking for trouble where there is none? The farm is your daadi's. He wouldn't let that happen. He loves your daed."

"Daadi is much older than Mammi . . . and she died. What if Daadi passes on too?" Katrina persisted. "Uncle Willis is the older brother. What if he decides to take over the farm for himself?"

Mamm shrugged. "Then the Good Lord will take care of us."

Katrina looked at her brothers. "What about Cal and Drew? What would they do if our family no longer had the farm?"

"Get jobs?" Mamm reached for the peas. "But don't worry. That is not going to happen. Daed is going to be better soon."

"It's been three years," Cal pointed out.

"And he's worse now than he was a year ago," Drew said solemnly.

"Oh, he's just worn out." Mamm lowered her voice. "And maybe he's grieving for his mamm too."

"But how would we live if we didn't have the farm?" Katrina asked.

"Maybe we'd learn to make soap and candles like the Lehmans." Mamm frowned at Katrina. "Now, that is enough talk about such things. Let us trust God and eat our supper in peace."

Although her brothers exercised more self-control than Katrina, she suspected they were just as concerned about this farm business as she was. She wondered how much they knew. Perhaps they had overheard Aunt Fannie talking like that before. Or maybe Uncle Willis's son Thomas had said something—especially since everyone knew that the apple hadn't fallen far from the Fannie tree.

Was it possible that her brothers were already making plans for another way to make a living? She knew that young men sometimes had to leave the settlement to find jobs. But her brothers had grown up working the farm. Agriculture was all they knew. Did this mean they would be forced to go out and work someone else's farm? And if so, what would become of her family?

It all seemed so unfair and unjust. What right did Aunt Fannie have to make such demands on a family she'd married into? And why did Uncle Willis even listen to her? Wasn't he the head of the household? And what would happen if Daadi passed away? The thought of him sleeping in his chair like that earlier, so completely oblivious to the conversation going on in his own home, was unsettling. How much worse would it be if he were really gone? And what about sweet Aunt Alma? Aunt Fannie probably only put up with her because of Daadi—although Katrina felt certain Aunt Fannie would miss all the work that Aunt Alma did around the house.

Katrina was tempted to go and tell her daed about all these things, but she knew it would only make him feel worse. It was hard enough for him to be laid up and in pain, but to learn that his injury could become his family's ruin . . . that would be too much to bear.

Thankful for her little radio, Katrina went out to do her evening chores of tending to the chickens and milking the cow, and it wasn't long until the tunes distracted her from her earlier concerns.

The next morning, Katrina worked quickly to complete her morning chores. She'd already asked Mamm if she could take Aunt Alma visiting. "I think she's lonely," Katrina explained.

"*Ja*, I'm sure Alma misses her mamm." She put her hand on Katrina's cheek. "You are a good girl to do that with her."

Of course, Katrina didn't feel like she was a very good girl as she listened to the radio on her way to get Aunt Alma, but her aunt was so pleased to see her that Katrina decided that she was actually doing a good deed. As they walked down a section of road with no houses, she even slipped the radio from her sleeve and showed her aunt how it worked.

"So that's what it was." Aunt Alma handed the earplug back to Katrina. "I wondered."

"I listen to the same radio station that Mammi listened to. They play songs called golden oldies, and I even heard Willow Tree a few times."

"From the record in the box?"

"*Ja*, but they don't play very many of their songs. I'd still like to hear that record."

"*Ja*, so would I."

"I listen to the radio whenever I can," Katrina admitted. "Doing chores or walking . . . even in bed after Sadie is asleep. Do you think that's wrong?"

Aunt Alma sighed. "I do not know. Maybe that is between you and God."

"I sing along with the songs sometimes." Katrina continued her confession. "I've even learned whole songs."

"What kind of songs?" Aunt Alma gave her a curious look.

"Do you want me to sing one?" Katrina could see the next house was still a fair distance away.

"*Ja*, please do."

So, once again, Katrina sang "Puff, the Magic Dragon," and when she finished, just before a horse-drawn buggy passed by, heading toward town, Aunt Alma was blinking back tears.

"That was beautiful, Katrina. Thank you."

"My favorite songs are the ones that tell stories," Katrina confided. "I don't like the songs that don't make any sense. Well, except that I like their tunes sometimes. I don't know what's the matter with me, Aunt Alma, but I just love music and singing. And I know it's wrong."

Aunt Alma didn't respond.

"I know Daed would be unhappy if he knew. So would Mamm. Maybe I should stop listening to the radio."

"I don't know the answer to that," Aunt Alma told her. "But I do know there are families who are not as opposed to music as our family."

"Why is our family opposed to music?" Katrina asked.

"I'm not sure. We know your mammi loved music."

"Yet you said she hardly ever sang."

Aunt Alma nodded. "That is true."

"Do you think it was because her voice was so beautiful?"

"Like yours."

"And she knew that it was selfish vainglory to sing with such a beautiful voice?"

Aunt Alma stopped walking and looked at Katrina with a creased brow. "I am sorry, but I do not know the answer. I do not understand why something so beautiful—something God has given you—how it can be wrong." She rubbed her forehead. "It makes my head hurt to think about it."

Katrina laughed. "I know. I feel just the same way."

Aunt Alma reached for her hand, holding it as they walked. "You and me—we are alike in some ways."

Now they were at the Millers'. Even if Katrina had been blindfolded, the smell of the dairy farm would have given it away. This farm had been in the Miller family for generations, but because Cooper was the youngest son, it was unlikely that he would inherit anything more than a job from it. She knew that Cooper loved woodworking, though. He'd told her that his dream was to become a cabinetmaker and that his Uncle Earl was considering taking him on as an apprentice. Unfortunately, his uncle lived in a settlement about thirty miles away. Katrina didn't like to imagine what she would do if Cooper went to live with his uncle. As sad as she would be to see him go, she didn't know if she could be happy living so far away from her own family. It would take most of the day just to make the trip there and back. No, that was something she didn't care to think about.

5

Before long, Katrina and Aunt Alma were seated on the porch with old Mrs. Miller. They worked together on shelling a basket of spring peas as they made polite conversation about the weather, inquired after Mrs. Miller's health, and heard her sympathy for Mammi's passing. Then the old woman set the bowl of peas on a bench and leaned forward to peer at Katrina with great interest.

"*Ja*, it is like I told Cooper. You are very much like your grandmother. You remind me of her when she was young. Even the way you speak is like her."

Katrina almost mentioned the youthful image of Mammi on the record cover but stopped herself. Not only were photographs forbidden, but to reveal that Mammi had been a professional singer—well, that would be inviting trouble.

"Katrina says you have a sister who knew my mother," Aunt Alma began.

"*Ja*, my sister Martha took your mamm into her home." She explained how Martha and her family lived in another settlement about thirty miles away. "Martha was still a girl at home back then. I had gotten married and was living right here." She smiled contentedly as she looked out on the green pastures and black-and-white cows.

"Is that the same settlement where Cooper's Uncle Earl lives?"

Mrs. Miller's pale eyebrows arched. "You know about Earl?"

"Only that he's a good cabinetmaker." Katrina felt her cheeks growing warm.

Mrs. Miller nodded. "*Ja*. Earl is Martha's oldest boy. Been making cabinets for twenty years. It's a good trade."

"I know Cooper would like to apprentice with his uncle."

"*Ja*, but that is a long way from home. Too far to travel each day. Cooper would have to live there with Earl." She peered curiously at Katrina. "It is not easy to leave your home . . . to live in a different settlement . . . but sometimes it is necessary."

"You did it," Aunt Alma said.

"*Ja*. But it is a sacrifice to leave your parents, your sisters and brothers—to leave them all behind and start a new life."

Katrina wasn't sure if Mrs. Miller was trying to give her a subtle warning or simply reminiscing.

"Do you remember much about my grandmother?" Katrina asked. "About where she had come from before she lived with your sister and your family?"

"Oh, *ja*, sure. She came from a neighboring district."

Katrina exchanged confused looks with her aunt.

"Are you saying she *lived* in a settlement?" Aunt Alma asked.

"*Ja*. I can't remember which one. I think it was up near Fryburg."

"So my grandmother was *already* Amish?" Katrina asked. "I thought I'd heard she was English."

"No, no. Your grandmother grew up Amish, but she went her own way for a while. About ten years, according to what Martha told me. But I never heard a word about it from Starla's own lips." Mrs. Miller shook her head. "Starla and I were friendly, but she never mentioned her past to me. Not once."

"But she grew up in an Amish home?" Aunt Alma still seemed confused. "Up near Fryburg, you say?"

"As best I can recall."

"She never spoke of family," Aunt Alma said quietly. "I always assumed her people were English and she'd left them behind to live here."

"Martha might be able to tell you more about that," Mrs. Miller said. "Although as I mentioned, she lives quite a distance away."

They talked a while longer, but it was obvious they weren't going to get any more information about Mammi. Besides, Katrina could tell Mrs. Miller was growing weary.

"Thank you for letting us come see you," Katrina told her, "but I think we should return to our homes."

"*Ja.*" Aunt Alma stood. "I must get dinner ready soon."

Mrs. Miller reached out for Katrina's hand, looking directly into her eyes. "Perhaps we should go visit my sister. I think Cooper could drive us there sometime. If I ask his father, I'm sure he will let Cooper go."

"That's such a long drive," Katrina told her. "Are you certain you would want to go?"

Mrs. Miller sighed. "I do miss my sister."

Katrina smiled as she gently squeezed Mrs. Miller's fingers. "Then I would be glad to go."

"I'll talk to my son." Mrs. Miller pushed herself up from

the chair. "Cooper can let you know." She pointed to Aunt Alma. "You might like to come along too."

Aunt Alma nodded eagerly. "*Ja*, if I can get away for that long, I would."

They said their goodbyes, and as Aunt Alma and Katrina walked back toward home, Katrina admitted how astonished she was to learn Mammi had grown up in an Amish home. "Knowing about her singing and the things in that box . . . I truly believed she was from an English family."

"What about the young men with her?" Aunt Alma said suddenly. "Do you suppose they were Amish too?"

"They did have beards, but that would mean they were married. Why would married Amish men be out making music like that? Besides, they weren't trimmed properly."

"*Ja*, that's true."

"I wonder if those men are still alive." Katrina saw the Lehmans' house up ahead now. "Aunt Alma, do you want me to walk all the way back with you, or do you mind if I stop to see Bekka?"

"I am fine to walk by myself." She patted Katrina's back. "You go and visit your friend."

"Bekka knows how to find out things. She might be able to help me find out more about Mammi." Katrina quickly explained about how the items from Mammi's box were being stored there. "For safekeeping."

"Thank you." Aunt Alma looked relieved. "I knew you would take good care of those things."

Katrina waved goodbye, then headed over to the Lehmans', going straight around back to where Bekka was actually working again. "I don't want to bother you," Katrina told her after they said their hellos.

"You're no bother," Bekka assured her. "I would love some company." She held up a box of order slips. "I have all these to enter into the computer, and it gets very boring."

"Not as much fun as playing games or watching that singing show."

"American Star." Bekka's eyes lit up. "They finally picked this season's winners—it's always a boy and a girl. Honestly, the girl's voice is not nearly as good as yours, Katrina."

Katrina waved her hand as she took out the bag so she could finish going through it and sat on the stool next to Bekka. "You just say that."

"Have you learned any more songs?"

"Sure. Lots of them."

"Please, sing one," she pleaded. "It will make my work go faster."

"I wish I could hear 'After the Wind' a few more times. I'd sing you that one. It's really pretty."

"'After the Wind'?"

"It's on this." Katrina held up the record. "Remember?"

"*Ja—ja!* That's right." Bekka jumped up from her chair. "I cannot believe I forgot about this."

"What?"

"When we were in Cleveland, after the conference ended, Peter and I did some shopping in a secondhand store." She pointed to the stool beneath Katrina. "I need that."

Katrina watched as Bekka moved the stool next to the shelf, climbing onto it to reach up to the top shelf and retrieve what looked like a small blue suitcase. "Help me with this." She handed the heavy case down to Katrina.

"What is in this?"

Bekka hopped down and took the case from her, set it

next to her computer, and removed the lid to reveal some kind of machine.

"Is that to play records?" Katrina asked hopefully.

"*Ja.*" Bekka pulled a cord out, plugging it into the power strip that was connected to a large battery pack.

Katrina handed her the record, so excited her hands were trembling. "I can't believe you did this, Bekka. Just for me?"

"I want to hear it too." Bekka slid the record down a small metal holder, then flipped a switch to make it start spinning. "The woman at the store showed me how it works."

Katrina watched with interest as Bekka moved another piece, saying it was the needle, although it looked like a stick. She set it carefully onto the outer edge of the record. There was a *click-click* sound but still no music. Katrina hoped it wasn't broken. And then, just like that, a song began to play.

Katrina closed her eyes to listen, soaking in each word, each note, each sound of the guitars playing. It was all so beautiful. When the song ended, she looked at Bekka with misty eyes. "Thank you so much!" But already another song was beginning to play.

By the third song, Bekka had returned to her computer, but Katrina, mesmerized by the music, could only sit and listen. She hardly moved until the needle had traveled all the way across the record. "That was so wonderful," she said as she moved the needle back to its resting spot. She turned the knob to Off and shook her head. "Mammi had a beautiful voice."

"*Ja,* she did." Bekka was still working at the computer. "But not as beautiful as yours."

"Now I know you're just saying that." Katrina took the record off the player and was reverently slipping it back into its case when she realized it had words and the little lines on the other side as well. "Do you think the back side plays too?"

"One way to find out," Bekka said over her shoulder.

Sure enough, the back side played too. But Katrina was getting worried over the time and knew she couldn't listen to every song. "I wish I could hear all of it, but I have to go," she told Bekka as she put everything away.

"I have an idea," Bekka said suddenly. "See if you can ride to the group singing with me and Peter tonight. Then ask if you can spend the night here afterward. By the time we get home, everyone will be asleep, and we can sneak back to the office and listen to it."

"What about Cal?" Katrina asked. "He usually drives me to the group singing."

"Invite him to come with us." Bekka's eyes twinkled merrily, and Katrina just laughed. Bekka had been eyeing Cal for some time now. Of course she would want him to join them.

As it turned out, the Yoders did ride with the Lehmans, picking up Cooper along the way. Peter had been allowed to use his parents' larger buggy, the one with a backseat where Cooper, Katrina, and Cal sat. And instead of just one horse, Peter had a pair of gleaming black Percherons pulling tonight. Katrina knew that pride was wrong, but she sensed that Peter was very well pleased with himself as he drove them through the settlement. She knew that the Lehmans' soap and candle business was prosperous, and she suspected the buggy and horses were a result of this.

"The group singing is at the Nashes' barn tonight," Peter told them. "Clear on the other side of the settlement . . . so we might be late."

"Let's start singing now," Bekka suggested, "to warm our voices up."

Cal looked a bit uneasy with this idea, and Katrina suspected that he, like her, still grappled with the idea of singing for enjoyment. What if Daed found out they were singing out here on the road?

But already Bekka was starting a song and Peter and Cooper were joining in as if nothing whatsoever was wrong. Katrina gave her brother an apologetic smile, and then she began to sing as well. By the second verse, Cal was singing too. By the time they came to the end of the tune, they were all singing boisterously.

"Very good." Bekka clapped her hands, then turned around and pointed to Katrina. "You should sing your dragon song."

"Katrina knows a dragon song?" Cooper asked.

Before she could respond, everyone—except for Cal—was begging her to sing the dragon song. She looked at Cal, and he just shrugged.

"Come on," Bekka urged. "It's such a pretty song."

So again Katrina sang "Puff, the Magic Dragon." When she finished, they all clapped and insisted she teach it to them. By the time they reached the Nash barn, they all knew the chorus. The barn was alight with lanterns, and it sounded like there were several musical instruments playing tonight. Katrina could hardly wait to get inside. Soon they were all clapping and singing along with all their friends.

They hadn't been there long before it was time to take a break and enjoy some refreshments. "Wait!" Cooper called out to the group. "Before you start the break, we have a song for you." Naturally, everyone was interested, clapping and encouraging Cooper to sing. "My friends have to join me," he said loudly. "Come on, Katrina, Bekka, Peter, and Cal. Come up here."

Bekka grabbed Katrina by the hand, pulling her up to the front. Katrina exchanged glances with Cal, but he didn't seem as concerned as he was earlier.

"The name of the song is 'Puff, the Magic Dragon,'" Bekka yelled out. "Feel free to sing along if you know it."

"Or you can just get your food if you want to," Peter added.

"Go ahead." Cooper nudged Katrina. "Start us out."

Feeling nervous but excited, Katrina began to sing the chorus. It turned out that several others knew the song too. After the chorus, which her friends had learned nicely, she realized she was the only one still singing, and she nearly stopped. But Bekka kept nodding her head as if to tell her to keep going, so Katrina continued to sing all the verses, and everyone joined in on the choruses. It wasn't until she'd finished the song—and everyone was clapping loudly—that she realized no one had gone to the refreshment table.

"That was great!" Cooper told her.

Even Cal slapped her on the back. "Well done, sis."

During the break lots of other friends came up to compliment her or thank her for singing. Naturally, this made her feel even more self-conscious. What would her parents think? However, when it was time to return to singing, she was asked to sing them another song—simply so they could listen.

"Come on," Cooper urged her. "Don't keep that voice to yourself."

The others clapped now, calling out encouragement. She went up front, and trying not to nervously twist the ends of her shawl, she told them that she liked songs that told stories. "I'm not sure, but I think this one is called 'One Tin Soldier.'

I had to listen to it quite a few times before I understood its meaning." It was one of the favorites of the radio station, and she'd probably heard it a dozen times by now.

The barn grew very quiet as she sang the opening words: "Listen, children, to a story . . ." She continued singing loud and clear, telling a story in song about a people who lived on a mountain and those who lived in the valley. For some reason the valley people were jealous, thinking that the mountain people had a great treasure buried up there. They insisted the mountain people should hand it over—or they would kill them. The people on the mountain offered to share their treasure, but the valley people refused. They wanted it all. So they went to war, killing all the mountain people. But when they pulled up the stone where the treasure was buried, all they found beneath it were the words "Peace on Earth."

When she finished the song, the barn was so silent she wondered if they all hated the song and her singing. "I'm sorry," she said quickly. "I know that was a serious song. But it reminded me of what we believe . . . our history . . . and . . ." She looked to Bekka for some help, but then she realized Bekka was crying. In fact, a number of people had tears in their eyes.

Cooper stepped up beside her now. "That was the best song I've ever heard," he said loud enough for everyone to hear. They all began to clap and cheer, begging Katrina to sing another song.

Relieved that they hadn't hated the song or her singing, she promised to sing another song after they did some more group singing. Before the night was over, Katrina wound up singing five more songs to her friends. When it was time to go, many of them begged to know if she would be back again next time. She promised she would try. But even as she promised this, she wondered, what if her parents found out?

6

"I don't see why you worry so much about what your parents think," Bekka said as they sat in the little office. They had just finished listening to the rest of the Willow Tree record, and it was well past one o'clock in the morning.

"We're supposed to respect and obey our parents," Katrina reminded her.

"You do respect and obey them," Bekka told her. "More than most kids."

"But my daed would not approve of me singing like I did tonight." Katrina was just finishing going through the last of Mammi's things, eager to open a sealed envelope she'd found. She hoped that it, like another envelope she'd just opened, might contain more photos of Mammi and her musical friends. She'd written "Willy and Larry and Starla" as well as the dates, all between 1962 and 1967, on the backs. When Katrina opened this envelope, she was surprised to see what looked like dollar bills. When she pulled them out, she was shocked to see that they were hundred-dollar bills. "Bekka!" she exclaimed, holding the fluttering bills in her hand. "Look at this!"

Bekka turned from her computer, where she'd been playing a game. Her eyes opened wide. "Where did you get that?"

"It was in Mammi's things." Katrina counted the bills. "Seven hundred dollars. Can you believe it?"

Bekka came over to watch as Katrina examined each bill carefully. "The dates are all before 1968. She must've put them in there when she got married."

"And left them there this whole time?"

Katrina just nodded.

"What are you going to do with them?" Bekka asked.

"I'll have to give them back to Daadi." Katrina wondered how she would manage to do this without attracting attention from someone else—like Aunt Fannie.

"Why?" Bekka asked. "I thought Alma gave all this stuff to you."

"She did, but we didn't realize there would be money." Perhaps Katrina could get Aunt Alma to help.

"Your grandmother was one mysterious woman." Bekka shook her head.

"*Ja*. Her story keeps growing bigger." Katrina thought of Aunt Alma again, knowing she would want to hear the music on this record. "Can I ask Aunt Alma to come to your office to hear Mammi's songs?"

"*Ja*. Tell her to come on over. I'm usually out here in the afternoon." Bekka let out a yawn, and Katrina realized how late it was. They began putting things away, and with everything turned off, they tiptoed into the house. Once they were in bed, Katrina listened to the sounds of the night. Bekka's even breathing signaled she was asleep, but Katrina was now wide awake.

So many thoughts and emotions were rushing through her

mind—guilt for singing, concerns for the family farm, curiosity about Mammi's past and the money, dreams of someday becoming Cooper's wife, worry that marriage would take her far from her family—it was like a herd of wild horses had been set loose inside her head. Finally, she slipped out of bed and retrieved her little radio from her bag, slid in the earplug, and eventually began to feel drowsy as she listened to the comforting sounds of music from decades past.

Katrina knew that Daadi might already be asleep by now. It wasn't that church was physically tiring, since they mostly sat, but the three-hour service did make for a long morning. Then there was the social gathering afterward, along with a light lunch. By the time Daadi got home, he was usually ready for a nap, but Katrina had asked Aunt Alma to keep him awake until she got there. Now she was hurrying along the fence line with seven hundred dollars pinned inside of her camisole, where it had been since this morning before church.

Aunt Alma greeted her on the porch. "Katrina, I told Daed you wanted to take a walk with him."

Daadi smiled as he emerged from the front room. "I would be honored to walk with you, Katrina."

"Thank you." She linked her arm in his, and together they went down the steps. As they strolled away from the house, she made small talk about the weather and the crops. Once they were a safe distance away, she began to speak more openly. "Daadi," she began, "I helped Aunt Alma clear away Mammi's things."

"*Ja.*" He nodded. "She told me. That seems fitting. I know I can trust you, Katrina."

"*Ja*. Of course you can." She pointed to a log bench. "Do you want to sit?"

He seemed unsure but then agreed. "You would think after sitting all morning in church, we would be tired of sitting."

As he eased himself down, she turned from him and unpinned the envelope of bills from her camisole. "There were interesting things in Mammi's box," she told him.

"I figured there would be."

"You mean you didn't actually know what was in there?"

"Didn't know . . . and don't want to know." He looked directly at her. "I don't mind that you know. You're like her in so many ways."

"So you don't want me to tell you about what was in the box?"

"That's right. When your mammi asked me to make her a box to put the things from her past in, she told me I could look if I wanted, but I said, 'No, thank you, everything I need to know about you is right in front of me.' So after she filled the box, she hammered the lid down tight, and that was the end of it."

"But you still didn't want anyone else to know about her past?"

He nodded firmly. "That's right. Her past was hers and hers alone. No one else needs to know."

Katrina bit her lip.

"Well, excepting you and Alma. I don't mind that you two know." He adjusted the brim of his straw hat to keep the afternoon sun out of his eyes. "But don't tell your father. Your mammi never wanted Frost to know about her past. He was her only child, and I think it was her way of protecting him."

"What if there was something in the box that would be useful to you?"

He looked doubtful. "Useful to me? Something that was nailed in that box all those years ago? I don't see how."

She held out the money. "This was in the box, Daadi."

He peered down at the bills with a surprised but troubled expression.

"I thought I should give it back to you."

He shook his head. "Nope. I do not want that money."

"What do I do with it then?"

"I don't much care." His expression grew stony hard, as if he was remembering something, and she wondered how much he really knew about his deceased wife's past. Was it possible he imagined it to be worse than it was?

"Then I will give it to Daed." She turned to pin the envelope of money back inside her dress.

"No. You cannot do that, Katrina."

"Why not?"

"Like I told you, your mammi never wanted Frost to know about her past. That is something I want to continue to respect. For her sake. And for his."

"But what about the money?"

"You can burn it for all I care." He pushed himself to his feet.

"Just don't give it to my father," she said quietly as she linked her arm in his again.

"That's right. And don't bring this up with me again, Katrina." His tone was as firm as Daed's was when he corrected his children.

"No, Daadi. I won't." She walked him to the house, saw him to his chair in the front room, then went on her way. She had no idea what she would do with the money, but she wondered if it could somehow help with Daed's back. She had heard Mamm saying how expensive his surgery would be. How far would seven hundred dollars go?

Her house was its usual Sunday kind of quiet. Sadie was reading in the front room. The brothers were nowhere to be seen. Daed was probably still flat on his back, just like he'd been the last several days. She found Mamm sitting outside next to her flower garden, just staring blankly at it.

"Hello," Katrina called out as she approached.

Mamm looked up. "You're back from visiting Daadi?"

Katrina nodded as she sat down on the bench next to Mamm. Without really thinking, she unpinned the envelope from her camisole and handed it to Mamm.

"What's this?" Mamm's eyes opened wide when she saw the contents.

"Seven hundred dollars."

Mamm looked at Katrina with a confused expression. "Where did you get it?"

"Daadi said I'm not supposed to tell Daed—or anyone really. But it's from Mammi."

"Mammi left this to you?"

Katrina paused, trying to think of a way to explain this dilemma while honoring both her grandparents' wishes. "I thought maybe it could help Daed get the back operation."

"That is generous of you, Katrina, but Daed's operation will cost more than twenty times this amount."

Katrina wasn't very fast at math, but she knew that meant more than fourteen thousand dollars. "Really?"

Mamm nodded, handing the money back.

"What should I do with this?"

"Save it for your future. I'm sure that's why Mammi left

it to you." She frowned. "And do as Daadi says. Do not tell anyone about this money. It will only stir up jealousy."

"Where should I keep it?"

Mamm got up and headed back into the kitchen, where she found a canning jar and filled it with red beans. "Slide the money down into the middle of the beans."

Katrina did as she was told. Mamm secured the lid, climbed onto a step stool, and tucked the jar far in the back of the top shelf of the pantry where it couldn't even be seen. "It will be safe there," she assured Katrina, "until you have need of it. For your future."

"Unless someone accidentally makes it into a pot of beans."

Mamm laughed. "Costly chili."

They walked back outside and sat back down on the bench. "Mamm, can I ask you a question?"

"You know you can."

"Why is it wrong to sing?"

"Wrong?" Mamm frowned. "It's not wrong. We just sang from the *Ausbund* at church this morning."

"I know. I mean the kind of singing where you enjoy the music."

"We let you and Cal go to the group singing last night."

"I know. But I don't think Daed really approves of that."

Mamm sighed. "Your father has some of his own ideas about singing."

"Some mothers sing lullabies to their babies," Katrina pointed out. "I've heard them. And some sing silly songs to their little children. But you never did that with us."

She nodded a bit sadly. "That is because your daed forbade it."

Katrina had suspected this. "Do you know why?"

Mamm shook her head. "It was one of the few things we disagreed upon. But he was the head of the household. I submit to him."

"Did your mother sing to you?"

"*Ja.* She did."

"I wonder if I will sing to my children . . . someday."

Mamm smiled. "They will be blessed children if you do, Katrina. I've heard you sing."

For some reason that made Katrina so happy that she felt tears of joy in her eyes. She hugged Mamm. "Thank you."

"I'm sorry I didn't sing to you as a child."

"I understand now."

"Remember, your father is simply trying to raise you children the way his parents raised him."

"I know. I just hope I can do it differently."

"That will depend on who you marry."

Katrina thought of Cooper now. She had never mentioned to her parents that Cooper was interested in apprenticing in a settlement more than half a day's journey away. She knew that Mamm would be distressed to think of Katrina living so far away.

"If it would make you feel better, you might want to talk to one of the ministers about singing. I know their views on singing are not as strict as your daed's."

Although Katrina felt somewhat comforted by her mother's words, she still suspected that Mamm would have been disappointed to see Katrina singing like she did for her friends last night. She hoped Mamm would never find out.

The next two weeks passed uneventfully. Katrina continued singing along with the radio as she did her outdoor chores. She continued to learn the words of more songs. She also continued to look forward to group singing nights and singing in front of her friends whenever they asked. And they asked a lot.

"You sang beautifully tonight." Bekka patted Katrina on the back as they rode home from group singing together. "I really loved that song about the man on the hill."

Katrina thanked her. Tonight she was sitting in the front of the buggy between Peter, who was driving the pair of gleaming black Percherons again, and Cooper, who was seated on her right. Meanwhile, Bekka was pleased as could be to sit in back with Cal. In fact, Cal appeared happy about the arrangement too.

Peter was whistling one of the tunes from earlier, and the horses' hooves were clip-clopping along in time. Katrina couldn't think of anywhere she would rather be right now. With a nearly full moon high in the sky and her friends all around her, all seemed right with the world. It was a moment she wished she could freeze in time.

"My grandmother tells me that I am to take us to visit Uncle Earl and Great-Aunt Martha," Cooper quietly told her.

"That's right. I nearly forgot about that."

"Is that the uncle who makes cabinets?" Peter asked.

"*Ja.*" Cooper nodded. "We might've scheduled a trip by now, but Mammi tripped on the porch steps and twisted her ankle last week."

"I'm sorry. Is it very bad?"

"She can't walk on it. But she did suggest that I could just drive you and your Aunt Alma over." He shrugged. "That is, if you still want to go."

Some of the urgency she'd felt before—longing to understand Mammi's past—seemed diminished now. Still, she was curious. It also would give her a chance to see where Cooper might be moving to eventually. "*Ja*, I would like to go. But perhaps we should wait for your grandmother to get better."

"*Ja*. We could wait. But I've been wanting to go visit my Uncle Earl for several months now. I need to talk to him about work . . . I need to make a decision about my apprenticeship." Cooper's eyes searched her face now, as if he wanted to know her thoughts on this. But how could she even begin to put such things into words, especially with everyone listening?

"I'm happy to go whenever it's best for you," she told him. "I'm sure Aunt Alma feels the same."

"Then let's plan on two weeks from today," he said. "That's the first weekend of June. Maybe Mammi will be better by then."

"The first weekend of June?" Bekka chimed in from behind. "I just heard that *American Star* is having auditions in Cleveland during the first week of June. Maybe on your way you can stop and try out for the show."

"Cleveland is not on the way," Katrina sharply told her.

"What is *American Star*?" Cooper asked.

"It's a TV show that Bekka sneakily watches on the computer—the computer that is supposed to be used for our family's business." Peter tossed his sister a scornful look as he continued driving the horses.

"Bekka watches TV?" Cal sounded genuinely shocked.

"At least it's not trashy TV," Bekka said, defending herself. "Just a bunch of people who can't sing half as good as Katrina. They compete for a cash prize. It used to be a million dollars to split between the two winners—a guy and a girl—but now I think both top singers win a whole million dollars each."

"A million dollars just for singing good?" Cal suddenly sounded interested.

"*Ja*. And the ones who make it into the top eight win money too," she told him. "I can't remember for sure how much each one wins. But I do know this: Katrina could win. Maybe even first place."

"Katrina could win a million dollars?" Cal asked.

"She sings that good," Bekka confirmed.

Katrina shook her head. "You cannot be serious. I would never have a chance against English people."

"But you have a good singing voice," Cal assured her. "Bekka thinks you could win."

"That is completely ridiculous." Katrina looked at Cooper, hoping he'd say something to help her out of this nonsense. But he was being quiet.

"She doesn't even have to win the top prize," Bekka told Cal. "I think the smallest prize is about fifty thousand dollars."

"That's more than enough for Daed's surgery." Cal nudged Katrina. "Maybe you should do this."

"Cal." She shook her head. "I'm sure there's never been an Amish person on that show, and besides the fact that I wouldn't have a chance, can you imagine what Daed would say?"

"You would have a chance," Bekka told her. "I've watched that show for three years. You are better than all of them."

"Even if all that was true, I would be shunned for doing something like this."

"You can't be shunned," Peter pointed out. "You haven't even been baptized yet."

"You know what I mean," she told him. "And my parents would be humiliated."

"Is it worse to be humiliated," Cal asked, "or to suffer

pain every day like Daed does? Besides, when it was all over you could come home and apologize."

"Yes," Bekka said eagerly. "Your parents have to forgive you if you apologize and repent."

"Then you could get baptized and join the church," Cal told her. "I would even get baptized with you. That would make our parents very happy."

"I don't know . . ." Katrina turned to look at her friend and brother. Couldn't they see how crazy this plan was? Had they all lost their minds?

"You've seen how much everyone at the group singing loves your music," Cal continued. Even in the dim lamplight of the carriage, she could see the longing in her brother's eyes. He was just as concerned about Daed and the situation with the farm as she was. "When you sing those story songs, Katrina, everyone really listens to you. I've watched their faces. I honestly believe it changes how they think about things. In a good way."

"That's true," Cooper said. "That first night—when you sang the tin soldier song—it was like being in church, only better."

Katrina didn't even know how to respond to that, but it touched her deeply. She promised her friends that she would think about trying out. "I'll pray about it too," she said as they dropped her and Cal off at their house. And that was exactly what she intended to do. She would pray, God would say no, and that would be the end of it.

7

Daed's back was worse than ever on Sunday morning. The whole house was awakened even before the sun came up by the sound of him shrieking so loudly it seemed as if he were dying. Katrina wondered if pain could actually kill a person.

"I will stay here with Daed," she told Mamm as they finished breakfast. "You need a break."

"One of the boys will stay too," Mamm said, "in case he needs help. He's too heavy for you."

"I'll stay," Cal offered quickly.

Mamm turned to Katrina. "Daed said he didn't want breakfast, but I want him to take one of those pills Dr. Warner prescribed, and he should have food with it."

"I'll take him up some oatmeal and applesauce," Katrina assured her.

"*Ja*, that would be good. The pills are in the cupboard next to the spices. Thank you."

As the others were leaving for church, Katrina was hurrying upstairs with Daed's breakfast and the bottle of pills. She knew the pills were for pain and very strong. She also knew Daed detested them. However, hearing him groaning down the hallway convinced her she might be able to persuade him.

"Daed?" she called out as she knocked on his door. "Breakfast."

His answer was a loud groan.

She pushed open the door with her elbow. "I know you're feeling poorly," she said as she set the tray on the dresser. "But Mamm says you need to eat. And you need to take a pill."

"Not hungry," he said stubbornly.

"Aw, come on now, Daed." She put her hands on her hips and looked down at him. Was it just her imagination, or had he aged a lot in the past few weeks? His hair, which was sticking out all over, was streaked with gray. Even his beard seemed faded. And his face was ashen—so much so that it sent a chill through her. This was serious. She opened the bottle and removed a pill, holding it before him with a glass of water. "Daed, you know this pill will help with the pain."

"Don't want it."

"*Daed.*" She held it out before him with her sternest expression. "Please, take your medicine!"

Daed actually blinked in surprise now, and despite his grimace, he almost seemed to be amused. But to her relief, he took the pill and popped it into his mouth, wincing as he reached for the water.

"Thank you, Daed." She took the glass from him when he had finished. "Now you need some oatmeal to go with it."

"Not hungry."

"I made it just how you like it, with applesauce and cream and honey and just a sprinkle of cinnamon." She dipped a spoonful and held it in front of him enticingly. "Come on, just a few bites."

He kept his lips tightly closed, reminding her of some of the toddlers she babysat for occasionally.

"Come on, Daed," Cal said from where he was standing in the doorway. "You know what will happen if you don't eat."

"That's right," Katrina said. "You will get sick to your stomach, and you'll vomit, and then you'll be in even more pain."

Daed's pale blue eyes flickered as if he was remembering, and then he opened his mouth, allowing Katrina to spoon-feed him about six bites before he shut his mouth, closed his eyes, and leaned back with a long, sad moan.

Satisfied that there was not much more they could do for him, Katrina picked up the tray and went out to the hallway where Cal was waiting with a creased brow. "He seems really bad," Cal whispered.

"I know," she said quietly as she continued to the stairs. Cal followed her back to the kitchen, lingering as she scraped the leftover oatmeal into the slop bucket for the pigs and then set the bowl with the other dishes that needed to be washed. She turned on the tap, waiting for the water to get warm and hoping that the propane tank had enough gas to run the water heater long enough to finish these. She had heard Mamm saying it was low.

"Did you notice how gray his face looked?" Cal was hovering near the sink.

She nodded, pouring in soap. "He needs to see the doctor."

"He needs that surgery."

"I know."

"What about what Bekka was talking about last night?" Cal put a hand on her shoulder. "What if you could do what she said? Win all that money?"

She pushed up her sleeves, wishing she'd thought to change from her Sunday dress before starting in on these chores. "Can you hand me that apron?" she asked.

He got Mamm's big blue apron and even helped to pin it on her.

"Katrina, you might have the power to make Daed well. That's not something you take lightly."

"Do you know what Daed would say if I told him I was going to go sing on a television show, Cal? You heard him screeching in pain this morning. Well, I'm sure he'd be hollering even louder if his daughter went out with the English and sang to win money."

Cal frowned, then slowly nodded. "*Ja*, you're probably right."

She began to wash a glass, shaking her head.

"But it's still *rumspringa* for you," he reminded her. "You're allowed to do wild things."

"Not that wild."

"I don't know. I've heard of districts where the youth do all kinds of things."

"Not our district." Suddenly she was thinking about Mammi—considering the things she had done and how she came back. "Unless . . ."

"Unless what?" he said eagerly.

"Oh, I was just thinking." She waved a soapy hand at him.

"What if we asked Daed?" Cal said hopefully. "We could tell him about this opportunity, and we could remind him that it's your *rumspringa* time, and tell him that this is something you *need* to do before you commit yourself to the church and get baptized."

She considered this. At least it was honest.

"You love to sing, Katrina. It seems to me this is something you need to get out of your system. Don't you?"

She turned to peer at Cal. Only sixteen months apart in age, she and Cal had always been close. Of everyone in the family, Cal seemed to know her best. Many times she had secretly prayed that he would fall in love with her best friend and marry her—and that would certainly please Bekka too. "You're right, Cal," she said slowly. "I do love to sing. But I feel guilty about it."

"That's only because Daed is so against it." Cal frowned. "But I don't know why. Lots of people don't think it's wrong to sing. Well, as long as it's not for vainglory."

"Vainglory," she said as she rinsed a glass. "That's the problem."

"But winning money to help Daed—is that vainglory?"

She wasn't sure, but by the time she finished the last dish, Cal had very nearly convinced her. "You're very persuasive," she admitted as she hung up the apron.

"Come on, Katrina, let's go speak to him now," Cal urged.

"He's probably asleep." She hoped he was.

"Let's go see."

They tiptoed up to Daed's room, and to Katrina's surprise, he was still awake and actually looked as if the pain pill had helped. "How are you doing, Daed?" she asked gently.

"Better," he told her.

"Aren't you glad you listened to Katrina and took your pill?" Cal said boldly.

"*Ja, ja*. That was a good thing." Daed let out a sigh of relief. "I am a stubborn man. I know."

"We want to talk to you about something," Cal began.

"*Ja?*" Daed looked at them with interest.

"We know you need your back surgery, Daed," Cal said in earnest. "And Katrina has a way to earn the money for it."

Daed looked skeptical, but he listened as Cal quickly explained the idea. Of course, Cal didn't get all the facts straight, but Katrina didn't think it mattered since she was certain that Daed would reject this crazy plan.

"It's Katrina's *rumspringa*," Cal said finally. "You know she loves to sing. This is something she needs to get out of her system . . . so that she can come back to us and commit to the church."

Daed's brows arched. "You want to be baptized?"

"She and I are both considering it," Cal told him. "But Katrina needs to do this first."

"You both want to be baptized?" Daed's voice was hopeful.

"I do," Cal assured him. "I want to get married someday too. But most of all I want you to get well first."

Daed's eyes softened as he looked from Cal to Katrina. She wasn't sure if it was Cal's persuasion or the medication. "I want to hear you," Daed said slowly.

"You want me to sing?" Katrina was shocked.

"*Ja.*" His eyelids looked heavy.

"Sing 'Puff, the Magic Dragon,'" Cal urged.

Right there in the little bedroom, Katrina began to sing. To her surprise, Daed's face lit up in a peaceful smile and he tapped his fingers on the quilt, listening as she sang the entire song.

"Beautiful," he proclaimed when she finished.

She was too stunned to react.

"So you give her your blessing in this?" Cal asked eagerly.

"*Ja, ja*, Katrina has my blessing."

"Daed?" Katrina peered curiously into his sleepy eyes.

"You are like my mamm, Katrina. *Ja*. Go and sing." Then he closed his eyes and began to quietly snore.

Katrina looked at Cal, wondering if she'd heard this right. But she could tell by her brother's huge grin that she wasn't mistaken. Together they tiptoed from the room and quietly slipped downstairs, but once they were back in the kitchen, Cal hugged her and let out a triumphant whoop. "We did it, Katrina. We got Daed's blessing."

She was still too shocked to react. "Does this really mean I'm going to do this?"

"You want to, don't you?"

She put a hand to her mouth, trying to suppress the wildly happy feeling rushing through her. "*Ja*," she exclaimed. "I do want to do this. I really truly do!"

For the rest of the morning, Katrina was so happy she never stopped singing. She sang as she finished the kitchen chores—even doing more than Mamm would approve of on a Sunday. Then she checked on Daed, who was still resting peacefully, before she went out to the garden and happily worked for a couple more hours, still singing.

Finally, she knew it was about time for the rest of her family to come home, and she went off in search of Cal. Finding him mending some harness pieces, she told him that she wanted to make a deal with him.

"Make a deal?" He looked up from the leather and metal in his hand.

"Yes. If I'm really going to do this—if I go try out for that show—I want you to manage things with Mamm and Daed."

"What do you mean manage?"

"I mean you got Daed to agree. Now I want you to explain the whole thing to Mamm and get her to agree too."

Cal nodded. "All right. I can do that."

"Good." She smiled. If anyone could pull this off, it was Cal. Of all the kids, he was the one with the best powers of persuasion.

When Mamm and the others came home, Cal rounded them up in the front room and explained their plan. Katrina watched Mamm and Drew—both of them looked completely stunned. Sadie, however, didn't seem all that surprised. In fact, she had a slightly knowing look on her face.

"I do not know what to say." Mamm just shook her head with an astonished look.

"Daed really agreed to this?" Drew asked for the third time.

"He did," Cal told him. Katrina nodded.

"We've been taught that *rumspringa* is a time to decide how we want to live the rest of our lives," Cal said somberly. "Katrina feels the need to sing."

"I've heard that she's been singing solos at group singing," Sadie said quietly.

Mamm looked surprised. "Is that true?"

Katrina murmured a yes, feeling the old familiar guilt.

"Everyone loves it," Cal told her. "They beg her to sing."

Drew looked distressed by this. "But what about vain-glory?"

Mamm held up her hands. "Katrina has free will. If she wills to do this . . . we cannot stop her."

"She can win money," Cal reminded them. "More than enough for Daed's surgery."

"How is he?" Mamm asked as if just remembering his earlier pain.

"Katrina took good care of him. He's resting well," Cal assured her. "And he really enjoyed it when she sang for him."

"You sang for Daed?" Drew looked at her in total disbelief. She just nodded.

"Why don't you sing for us?" Sadie said in a slightly teasing tone.

Mamm looked uncertain, but then she just shrugged. "*Ja*, why not?"

"Sing the tin soldier song," Cal suggested.

The room was quiet now. Katrina, feeling far more nervous than when she'd sung for the crowd in the barn at the group singing, stood and clasped her hands in front of her and quickly explained how this song was like a story. "It's similar to the story we've been taught at school about our history in Europe, when we were persecuted for believing in adult baptism and for being pacifists."

"Truly?" Mamm looked slightly impressed. "I want to hear this."

Katrina took in a deep breath, then began to sing: "Listen, children, to a story . . ." She put her whole heart into this song—imagining the sad, bloody scenes as she sang. When she stopped, the room was even quieter than before, if that was possible.

"Oh, my." Mamm wiped tears from her eyes.

"I've never heard anything like that," Drew admitted.

"Wow." Sadie looked at Katrina as if seeing her for the first time. "That was beautiful."

For some reason Sadie's reaction touched Katrina even more than the others'. "Thank you," she told her.

"See," Cal said with what Katrina hoped was not really pride. "Bekka watches this show all the time, and she says Katrina can win it."

Mamm stood. "I do not know what to say." She was headed

for the stairs but paused on the first step. "Your daed gave his blessing?"

Katrina just nodded.

Mamm shook her head. "I don't know what to say," she said again. "I can't give you my blessing . . . but I can't stop you either. It's your choice, Katrina."

"But what will our friends and neighbors say?" Drew asked with concern.

"They will say Katrina is on *rumspringa*," Mamm said sadly. "And we will tell them to pray for her . . . pray that she comes back to us . . . back to the Lord." She continued up the stairs with heavy-sounding steps.

Katrina never expected Mamm to be pleased about this. And she never dreamed both her parents would agree to such madness. Now that neither of them appeared determined to stop her, she felt slightly let down. It seemed their consent came with a high price. Still, she remembered Daed's ashen face earlier and her concerns for his health, and she thought perhaps the price was not too high after all.

8

"This is a dream come true," Bekka said after Katrina told her the news later that day. They were in Bekka's cramped office, and Bekka was busily working the keyboard. "We need to get you preregistered first."

"Preregistered?" Katrina was confused.

"Yes. I was reading about it a few days ago. You have to go online and fill out a preregistration form."

"I don't know how to do that."

"Of course you don't." Bekka beamed at her. "That's why you have me. I've already started it for you."

They spent about a half hour answering lots of questions, but Bekka finally proclaimed it done. "I'm going to hit Send."

Katrina held her breath as Bekka clicked something.

"Now we wait."

Katrina exhaled. "How long do we wait?"

Bekka shrugged.

"Well, I don't have time to wait here," Katrina told her. "I told Mamm I'd be back within the hour."

"I'll let you know as soon as I hear back," Bekka promised. "In the meantime, I hope you're practicing."

"Practicing?" Katrina frowned.

"You know, singing."

"Oh . . . *ja* . . . of course."

But as Katrina hurried home, she didn't even feel like singing. She just felt nervous. After all that had been said and done amongst her family, what if the *American Star* people rejected her preregistration form? Would her family be pleased or disappointed?

That night as she was getting ready for bed, she felt Sadie watching her—even more than usual. "Are you really going to do it?" Sadie asked.

"The show?"

"*Ja*. Are you really going through with it?"

Katrina sighed as she hung up her dress. "Bekka sent my preregistration form in. I suppose *American Star* could refuse me. I don't know if they have rules against Amish participants."

"But if they do accept you, you will truly go and do this?" Sadie was looking at her with what seemed a mixture of fear and admiration.

"What do you think I should do?" Katrina asked gently.

Sadie's eyes lit up. "I think you should do it."

"Truly?"

"*Ja*. I would do it . . . if I had a singing voice like yours."

"You don't think it's vainglory?"

Sadie giggled. "*Ja*, it probably is vainglory. But won't it be fun?"

Katrina couldn't help but laugh.

"I saw that dress in your drawer. And those strange shoes."

"You did?" Katrina was surprised. "You never said anything about it."

"I was waiting."

"Waiting for what?"

"To see what you were going to do with them."

"You didn't tell your friends about them?"

"Not yet." Sadie smirked. "I only found them a few days ago. What are they for?"

Katrina explained that they had belonged to Mammi.

"You can't be serious."

"*Ja.* Aunt Alma gave them to me. They were from when Mammi was young, before she married Daadi." Suddenly Katrina remembered the seven hundred dollars. She wondered if it was still safe in the bean jar. Perhaps some of it would be helpful in getting her to Cleveland. Bekka had said she would need to take a bus to get there.

"Was Mammi English?"

"No. She left her settlement for a while, but then she came back." Katrina was tempted to tell Sadie the full story, except that she knew Daadi did not want it told. And she wasn't sure she could trust Sadie to keep it to herself. After all, it was a fairly exciting story.

"I wish I could go with you to Cleveland," Sadie said wistfully.

"You have school," Katrina reminded her.

"*Ja, ja* . . . I can't wait until I'm old enough for *rumspringa.*"

Katrina laughed. "Don't worry, it will come soon enough. And then you might not be so glad about it." She slipped her nightgown over her head. "It comes with responsibilities, Sadie. Some very big decisions. Free will has a price."

"You sound like Mamm."

"Thank you," Katrina told her before she blew out the lamp and hopped into bed next to her sister.

"I'll miss you," Sadie said quietly.

"I'll only be gone two or three days," Katrina told her.

"*Ja,* well, even so I will miss you."

On Friday morning, just when Katrina was about to give up on ever being accepted by the show, Bekka rushed over to Katrina as she was repairing a hole in the chicken coop fence where a critter or neighbor's dog had broken in.

"You're in," Bekka gasped breathlessly. She waved a piece of paper in her hand. "This is your acceptance letter from *American Star*."

Katrina set down the hammer and took the letter, staring at it in disbelief. "Really, they want me to come?"

"*Ja*. Look, there is your name right on it. Down at the bottom here it has all the directions for where to go and what to do when you get to Cleveland," she explained happily. "You are on your way to becoming an American Star!"

"This is really happening." Katrina read through the letter, then tucked it into the band of her apron. "I can't believe it."

"Oh, I almost forgot. Peter said he will drive the buggy to group singing again tomorrow night if you and Cal want to ride with us."

"*Ja*. Thank you!" Katrina hugged her.

For the rest of the day, Katrina happily sang along with the golden oldies. By now she had learned the words to at least a dozen or more songs. She hoped that one of those songs would be just right for her audition—she knew that was what they called it because Bekka had shown her some of the auditions from the last season, and she knew that "last season" meant the previous group of shows, not winter or spring. She'd been encouraged to see others auditioning, because Bekka was right—most of them did not sing very well. Katrina felt she might truly have a chance to win that prize money for Daed.

On Saturday night, all her friends were excited to hear the news. Some of them even seemed to know what *American Star* was, but most of them were simply happy to hear that she might win some money to help her father get the surgery he needed to get well. At the end of the meeting, they even took time to pray for her to succeed at winning the prize. Katrina was touched.

On the way home, Cal suggested that Bekka should accompany Katrina to Cleveland next Friday. "Since Bekka was just there with her family, she probably knows how to ride the bus and find her way. And she'll be good company for you."

"*Ja!*" Bekka exclaimed. "That's a great idea." Her eyes sparkled as she smiled at Cal. Katrina could see she was thrilled that Cal had thought of her for this.

"I wish I could go with you," Cal said, "but you know I can't miss that much work . . . not with Daed laid up."

"I know." Katrina patted his back. "But you're right. Bekka will know what to do, won't you, Bekka?"

"*Ja.* I will take care of everything for you."

"I would drive you to Millersburg," Cal told Katrina, "except we're cutting hay next week. It'll be busy."

"I can't take them," Peter said from up front where he was driving the horses. "Especially not if Bekka is gone—and that is *if* our parents agree, Bekka. We have too many orders to fill for both of us to go."

"Our parents will agree," Bekka assured him. "I'll tell them this is my *rumspringa* too. And I'll work really hard all next week. I won't play a single computer game either."

They all laughed.

"I will drive the girls to Millersburg," Cooper offered in

a serious tone. "I'd been planning to go up there to visit my uncle anyway."

Katrina had noticed that Cooper seemed quieter than usual. She wasn't sure if it was related to her or something else. "You don't mind?"

"No." He turned away, looking out over the field that was washed in moonlight. She wished she knew what he was thinking. Was he upset that she was doing this? But hadn't he encouraged her too? Perhaps he was thinking about his apprenticeship. Had he already made up his mind to do it? If so, where did that leave her? And them—or was there even a them? It seemed lately she'd been too busy to fully consider this.

By Sunday afternoon, it was settled at the Lehmans'. Bekka was allowed to go, but only if she worked very hard to get every order filled. She told Katrina, "I'll give Cooper a message through Peter—letting him know when we need to be dropped off and picked up at the bus station."

"Thank you." Katrina sighed in relief. "I couldn't do this without you."

"Now we need to decide what you're going to wear," Bekka declared.

"Oh?" Katrina frowned. "You don't think I should wear my Sunday dress, do you? I thought I'd just wear my green dress. It's my favorite, and Mamm says it matches my eyes."

"What?" Bekka looked shocked.

Katrina was confused. "My blue dress then?"

"No, that's not what I mean."

"What do you mean?"

"I mean you can't dress like that." Bekka frowned. "You need to wear English clothes."

Katrina's hand flew up to her mouth. "English clothes?"

"*Ja*. You're competing with the English, Katrina. You do know this, don't you?"

"I might be competing"—Katrina didn't even like the sound of that word—"but that doesn't mean I have to look like them."

"It's all right," Bekka assured her. "It's your *rumspringa*, remember?"

Katrina stood up straight, looking Bekka right in the eyes. "*Ja*. It is my *rumspringa*. But that does not mean I will wear English clothes. Do you understand?"

Bekka looked worried. "*Ja*, I understand. But do you understand that might make you lose?"

"If I lose, I lose. I will wear my green dress."

"*Ja* . . ." Bekka sounded discouraged.

Katrina put a hand on her shoulder. "I know you mean well, Bekka. But if my voice isn't enough to win this thing, I don't want it. Do you understand?"

Bekka shrugged. Katrina knew that if Bekka were able to sing, she would have no problem making these compromises. In fact, life would be much easier if Bekka were the one to enter a singing contest. Except that she couldn't carry a tune in a bucket.

"I wonder how much money I should bring," Katrina mused. "I'll need to get some out of my bean jar."

"Your what?"

Katrina waved her hand. "No matter. And don't worry, I will pay for all we need—you and me both."

Bekka's eyes lit up. "Oh, I nearly forgot. You still have the money your grandmother left you."

"*Ja*. Maybe she knew I would have need of it."

On Thursday night, Katrina thought she would be too anxious to sleep, but it had been such a busy day that she was exhausted. "Are you afraid?" Sadie asked quietly in the darkness.

"Afraid?" Katrina considered the meaning of the word. "No, I don't think so. But I am nervous."

"Do you think you'll get homesick?"

"Homesick?"

"I've read about it in books. A girl goes away from home for the first time and she misses it so much she gets homesick. Do you think you'll get it too?"

Katrina chuckled. "I doubt it. I'll only be gone a few days."

"Did you decide what you're going to sing yet?"

"Not exactly. But I have narrowed it down to three songs." She didn't tell Sadie that one of the songs—the one she was leaning toward—was one that their very own mammi had written and performed nearly fifty years ago. Bekka had made the discovery on her computer, learning that "After the Storm," a moving song about the destructiveness of war, had been written by Starla Knight.

"I hope you sing the tin soldier song," Sadie said wistfully.

"It's one that I'm considering."

"I'll be praying for you, Katrina."

"Thank you." Katrina reached over, hugging her little sister in the darkness. To her surprise, she felt tears in her eyes. "I'll be praying for you too."

Sadie laughed. "Praying that I don't let your tomatoes dry up, I'll bet."

The next morning, Katrina got up before the sun, which was quite early in June. She had already packed her bag for the trip, and the blue dress she planned to wear for traveling hung on a peg, ready to go. In the darkness she pulled on her black stockings and then the dress, pinned her apron into place, pinned on her shoulder shawl, and slipped her feet into her good black leather shoes. Tucking her nightgown into the bag, she looked around the room, which was so dark she could barely see. Without making a sound, she slipped out and down the hallway and was just going to the kitchen when she noticed a golden glow in there.

"Mamm?" she said in surprise. "You didn't need to get up this early."

Mamm, still in her long white nightgown, turned toward Katrina. "I couldn't let you go without saying a proper good-bye." She handed Katrina a paper bag. "I know you already packed some food for your trip, but I made some moon pies last night."

Katrina hugged her. "Thank you, Mamm."

"I will be praying for you," she said solemnly.

"I know you will."

Mamm looked out the window to where a buggy, with its lanterns glowing, was just pulling up in their driveway. "Don't keep them waiting."

With her arms loaded with the bags—and tears in her eyes—Katrina told Mamm goodbye, then hurried out into the darkness. She hoped this wasn't a mistake.

"Morning," Cooper said as he helped her into the buggy.

"Good morning," she said brightly.

"Morning?" Bekka grumbled. "This is the middle of the night."

"You can tell Bekka's not a farm girl," Cooper teased. "Katrina and I are used to getting up with the chickens."

"The chickens aren't even up yet," Bekka pointed out.

"Why don't you curl up here and take a nap," Katrina suggested. "I'll ride in front with Cooper."

Bekka didn't argue, and Katrina, relieved at the idea of having Cooper to herself for a while, happily sat beside him. "Thank you so much for taking us," she said quietly.

"I was going that way anyway."

"*Ja* . . ."

"I'm sorry," he said more gently. "I don't know why I'm acting so grumpy lately."

"I've wondered if something was wrong."

He let out a long sigh. "There's a lot to think about."

"I know . . ."

"Decisions to make."

She just nodded.

"Life decisions . . . you know?" His voice sounded husky. Maybe it was just the cool night air.

"I do know."

He glanced at her and the buggy lanterns illuminated his face, but she couldn't really see what was in his eyes as he pushed his straw hat more firmly on his brow.

"I feel confused a lot," she admitted. "I never really intended to do this . . . I mean, to go and sing and try to win a prize. Sometimes I feel like I grabbed ahold of the bull's tail, you know, and he's pulling me around the pasture, jerking me around, but I'm too scared to let go because he'll kick the stuffing out of me."

Cooper chuckled. "You have a way with words, Katrina."

"Can I tell you a secret?"

"A secret?" His voice lilted ever so slightly. "*Ja*, sure."

As they drove into the gray dawn, she told him the whole story of her grandmother. At least as much as she knew.

"I knew there was some mystery there," he admitted. "Now it makes more sense."

"So . . . maybe I feel like Mammi is directing this whole thing. Is that silly?"

"Not at all."

"I wish I knew the rest of her story," Katrina said. "That might help me."

"Well, I can ask Aunt Martha to tell me what she knows."

"Will you?" Katrina looked at him.

"Sure."

She continued looking at him, admiring his strong profile in the light of the golden sunrays that were just coming over the eastern horizon, loving his straight nose, how his hair curled around his ears, and the way his lower lip jutted out ever so slightly as he clutched the reins in both hands. Suddenly everything inside of her seemed to want to grab on to him, to hold on to him, to kiss him . . . and to never let go. She'd never known such a strong yearning in her life. Truly, she wanted to hold on to this boy more than anything. Even more than she wanted to sing. And that shocked her.

"Good morning!" Bekka called cheerfully. "It looks as if the sun finally decided to get up after all."

The three of them conversed back and forth and ate their bagged breakfasts as the buggy rumbled along the road. They were all excited, happily looking forward to whatever it was that lay before them today. But Katrina knew that if Cooper simply asked her, she would change her plans and give it all up for him. She truly believed that.

When they reached the bus station, though, he simply wished her good luck and told her he'd pick them up here at midday on Monday. Then he drove away.

9

Katrina didn't know what she would have done without Bekka. Everything seemed so busy and crowded and confusing. Yet Bekka managed to get them bus tickets, and after a couple hours of waiting in the station, where they ate their lunch and used the restroom and endured the curious looks of numerous English travelers, they were finally on the bus to Cleveland. Katrina sighed. She had never seen so many strangers before, never been out in the English world like this, not without her parents anyway. It was overwhelming.

"It's about eighty miles," Bekka told her, "but we'll be there in less than two hours."

Katrina had never traveled so fast in her life. Just looking out the window made her feel dizzy—everything whizzed by in a blur. But when she didn't look out, her stomach began to feel queasy. "I'll be glad when we get there."

When they got there, though, she discovered that Cleveland was even bigger and busier than Millersburg. "This doesn't even look like a place where people can live," she whispered to Bekka as they went out onto the street, where they saw nothing but cars and trucks and many enormous buildings.

She clutched her bag to her chest, smelling the fumes from the traffic. "How can they breathe? How do they find their way? And where do they live?"

Bekka wasn't listening. Instead she was waving to a car and yelling, "Taxi!" as if she knew what she was doing. Maybe she did—maybe she'd seen that on her computer too. Because just like that a yellow-and-black car pulled up, and the driver got out and opened the rear door with a curious grin. "Where you ladies headed?"

They got in, and Bekka told him the name of the hotel at the bottom of Katrina's letter. Katrina was almost afraid to breathe as he pulled his car right out into the other fast-moving cars. If she thought the bus ride was scary, this was way worse. *God, help us*, she silently prayed again and again. This time she kept her eyes firmly shut.

"Here you go, ladies," he said when the car came to what was thankfully its final stop. "That'll be sixteen dollars."

Katrina looked at Bekka. "Is that right?"

"*Ja*. Just pay him."

Katrina opened her bag and fingered through the change left over from their bus tickets, counting it out exactly as she handed it to him. He looked at her as if that wasn't enough.

"Sixteen dollars?" she repeated. "Isn't that right?"

He said a word she didn't understand, then waved at her as if to say, "Get out of my car." Katrina and Bekka had barely closed the door when he took off. "Did I do something wrong?" she asked Bekka as they looked up at a big, glossy-looking building.

"I don't know." Bekka smiled at her. "Here we are."

"What do we do now?" Suddenly Katrina was tired—the end of the day kind of tired—but it wasn't even suppertime yet.

"Let's go inside and find out."

Katrina could feel people looking at them as they went into the fancy hotel, where there were indoor fountains and huge potted plants and high, high ceilings and all sorts of strange sights. While Bekka went up to a counter, Katrina couldn't help but gape and stare at everything. Somehow she felt that wasn't as rude as when people gaped and stared at her. Oh, she knew she should be used to it by now. It happened whenever they went to town. Sometimes tourists came by the busloads just to look at them and to take pictures, which was the worst. It was as if the English thought Amish folks had no feelings and didn't notice the curious onlookers. To be fair, sometimes Katrina stared back, because some of the clothes that the English wore—well, even if she went around in her underclothes, she would be more covered than they were!

Bekka returned now. "They said to go over there." She pointed to where some young people were waiting in line. Katrina followed her, and they waited too.

When they finally got up to a counter, a pretty blonde woman in a white shirt asked if she could help them. "We're here for the *American Star* TV show," Bekka explained. "My friend Katrina here is going to audition tomorrow or the next day."

The woman peered curiously at Katrina. "Yes, well, I work for the hotel. Not the TV show. Do you girls have a reservation?"

Bekka glanced at Katrina, but Katrina just shrugged.

"What's a reservation?" Bekka asked the woman.

"A reservation is how you get a room. Do you girls have a room?"

"You mean to sleep in?" Bekka asked in a nervous tone.

"Yes. Do you have a place to stay while your friend does her audition for the show?"

Bekka shook her head. "I thought the show took care of that."

"No. The show uses our hotel to film in, but the contestants are responsible for their own lodging."

Bekka tossed Katrina a nervous look, so Katrina stepped up. "Do you have sleeping rooms here?" she asked politely.

The woman gave her a grim look. "I'm sorry, but we're booked."

Katrina bit her lip. "What should we do?"

The woman was punching her fingers on a keyboard now, similar to what Bekka did in her office. It seemed that their problems were of no concern to her.

"I'm sorry," Katrina told her. "We didn't mean to trouble you, but—"

The woman looked up. "Do you girls have money? Enough for a room here? I think I found a cancellation."

Katrina nodded. "We have money. How much does a room cost?"

"We have a special rate for the show—ninety-nine dollars a night. Can you afford that for three nights?"

"Three hundred dollars for three nights?" Katrina asked Bekka.

"Do you want the room or not?" the woman asked.

"Yes," Bekka said. "We'll take it."

"But—"

"If you win the prize money, it will seem like nothing," Bekka whispered.

Katrina's hands were shaking as she pulled out three hundred-dollar bills and handed them over to the woman in complete disbelief.

"I'll need more than that," the woman told her.

"But you said—"

"Yes, I'm sorry if I was unclear. There are also taxes, and since you have no credit card, you'll need to leave a deposit as well."

Katrina knew what taxes were. "Deposit?" she asked meekly.

"In case you use the minibar." She chuckled. "Or other services."

"What?"

The woman explained that some things cost extra. "If you don't use anything out of the cabinet that says minibar, and if you don't order up movies or room service, you should be fine. Normally we'd need a much bigger deposit"—she smiled—"but I think I can trust you girls. An extra hundred dollars should cover it."

"Another—"

"You'll get it back," the woman assured her. "I promise. Unless you steal the towels or—"

"We would never steal anything."

"Yes, I believe you." She explained that the hundred dollars would be refunded when they left.

Katrina handed over the money, realizing she only had one hundred-dollar bill and some smaller ones left. Fortunately, they had their return bus tickets already, as well as the food they'd both brought from home. She hoped that would be enough.

The woman took down their names and addresses and did some more clicking on her computer, then handed Katrina a piece of paper as well as a tiny envelope with some pieces of plastic in it. "Those are your keys."

Katrina stared at the strange things. "Keys?"

"I'm going to get a bellhop for you."

"Bellhop?" Katrina gave Bekka a quizzical look, but she seemed as confused as Katrina.

The woman was already on the phone. After she hung up, she pointed to a gigantic potted plant. "You go wait right there, and Vinnie will show you to your room." She smiled again. "Good luck, Katrina."

"Thank you." Katrina smiled nervously, and they went over to wait by the plant. The pot was as tall as Bekka.

"I'm sorry," Bekka said humbly. "I've never done anything like this before. Mamm and Daed got us a room at a guesthouse. Maybe I should've checked—"

"Never mind. We're here now. Let's just hope we have enough money to stay here."

An older dark-skinned man in a red jacket with brass buttons came over. The nametag on his pocket said "Vinnie." He smiled politely. "Afternoon, young ladies. Miss Campton asked me to see you to your room. Can I carry your bags?"

Katrina looked at Bekka.

"All right," Bekka said, handing him her shopping bag of food. "But I'll carry my clothing."

Katrina gave him her food bag too.

With their bags in hand, Vinnie began to walk. "Right this way, please."

"Thank you for helping us," Katrina told him as she hurried to keep up.

"This your first time in the city?" he asked.

"*Ja,*" Katrina said.

"She's going to audition for *American Star*," Bekka announced loudly enough for anyone within shouting distance to hear.

"You're a singer?" he asked Katrina.

"She's an amazing singer," Bekka told him as he led them down a corridor to where people were waiting in clumps in front of a bunch of steel doors.

He pushed a button on the wall. "These are the elevators. You ladies ever been in one before?"

They both shook their heads and he chuckled. "Well, it's gonna take us up. Way up." He pointed to the button he'd just pushed. "See how that says 'Up'? You push it when you want to go up. And you push 'Down' when you want to go down. Easy breezy."

Katrina could see other people were looking at them, but suddenly the doors opened and everyone was going inside what looked like a fancy box stall. "Go on in," Vinnie said. Then he stepped in beside them. "Your room's on floor number 32." He reached for the wall that was covered with buttons and numbers. "So you just push this one here." He pushed 32 and it lit up. "See?" Now he pointed above the door. "When that number 32 lights up, it's time to get out."

They waited, and when 32 turned bright green, they got out. "It's this way to your room," he said as he walked down a long hallway. "You're in Room 3242. Right here. Get out your key and I'll show you how that works."

Katrina pulled out a plastic card. "This does not look like a key."

"I know. I remember when hotels had real brass keys. Those were the days." He showed them how to slide the plastic key into the slot, how to wait until a tiny light turned green, and how to open the door. "You gotta do it quick," he said. Then he took them into a room much bigger than a bedroom. In fact, it had two big beds as well as two chairs and a table where Vinnie set their food bags.

"Is this all for us?" Katrina asked in wonder.

"Yep. All yours." He showed them how everything worked. He told them what the hotel would charge for and what was free. "See this cabinet?" He somberly pointed to a door with the word *minibar* on it. "Do not touch it—or it will cost you a lot more than it's worth."

They both nodded.

"And behind this door"—he opened a wooden cupboard—"is your fridge."

A refrigerator in a bedroom? Katrina thought she'd seen it all now.

He showed them a spacious closet with lots of pretty hangers and its own ironing board and iron. "This here is to the bathroom." He pushed open a door to a brightly lit room with an enormous mirror. It was the third mirror Katrina had seen. Why did anyone need so many mirrors? "You can use anything you want in here," he told them. "It's all free." He pulled something off the wall and pushed a button so that hot air blew out. "Hairdryer," he said.

"You're sure these soaps and shampoos and things are free?" Bekka looked doubtful as she held up a basket filled with pretty little bottles.

"Yep. Use 'em up, and you can have more if you need them."

"And the toilet paper is free?" Katrina asked.

He laughed. "Yep. And the tissues too. You even get free coffee and tea." He showed them an area for making it, giving them a quick lesson on the coffeepot. But he shook his finger at a couple of bottles of what looked like water. "Don't drink these," he said.

"Why not?" Bekka asked. "Isn't it just water?"

"Yep. But those are not free."

"You charge money for water?" Katrina asked.

"Just the water in *those* bottles." He pointed to the glasses and coffee mugs. "All the water in the tap is free."

"Oh . . ." Katrina shook her head. Water cost money, but soap was free. And why put a water bottle in the room when there was water in the tap? So many things about the English made no sense.

It seemed Vinnie's tour was finished as he showed them how to lock and bolt the door. "If you have any trouble, you just call downstairs and ask for Vinnie."

They both thanked him, and he shook their hands and wished Katrina good luck with her audition, but before he left, he reminded them to secure the door. As soon as he was gone, they both burst into giggles and then thoroughly explored every little detail of this strange and luxurious room. They unpacked their bags and put everything away in the drawers by the bed and the hangers in the big closet.

"Do the English really live like this?" Katrina picked up the phone receiver in the bathroom and laughed. Their room had three phones! And the bedding and pillows—each bed had half a dozen pillows on it! Why would anyone need all those pillows? But she was relieved that everything looked clean and smelled nice.

Bekka was busy with the TV now, trying to figure out how to make it do something. Katrina went over to the window and pulled back the long, filmy curtains. She peered out and nearly fell over when she saw how far from the ground they were. "Come and look at this!" she yelled. "We're clear up in the sky!"

Bekka came over and gasped. "Look how small those cars seem from up here."

"The people look like bugs."

"It's making me dizzy." Bekka stepped back, holding on to a chair. "And hungry." They opened their bags, pulled out the assortment of food they'd both brought from home, and fixed themselves an early supper of peanut butter and jam sandwiches and applesauce, which they ate at the little table. Then they cleaned everything up and put the rest of their food in the little refrigerator.

"A person could live in here." Bekka flopped happily on the bed.

But who would want to? Katrina wondered as she sat down on the other bed. She looked across the room, studying a painting of a faded red barn, a golden meadow, and an old oak tree. Why would anyone settle for a room like this when they could have what was in that painting—only for real? Nothing about this strange room, or this fancy hotel, or this big city . . . none of it felt very real to her. She remembered what Sadie had said last night. Katrina wasn't sure, but she thought perhaps she was homesick. And she missed Cooper.

10

After they'd both had a short nap, they spent the rest of the evening "rehearsing." At least that's what Bekka had called it as she made Katrina sing song after song for her. By the time they went to bed—at nine o'clock—Katrina still hadn't decided which song she wanted to sing for her audition, but her green dress, apron, and shawl were all neatly pressed (thanks to Bekka and the hotel's nice iron and ironing board) and waiting for her.

To Katrina's surprise, it was nearly seven o'clock when she woke up the next morning. She realized the dark, heavy curtains they'd pulled over the flimsy ones had completely blocked out the light. Even in the daytime, it was as dark as night in the room, but the clock between their beds said 6:56.

"Bekka," she said as she jerked open the heavy curtains, "it's morning already!"

"Wh—what?" Bekka sat up, sleepily rubbing her eyes. Her red hair was sticking out all over.

"Look at the clock," Katrina told her. "My audition!"

"Oh . . . *ja*." Bekka climbed out of bed, yawning. "We need to go see when you'll sing."

They quickly dressed, and without even eating breakfast,

they went out in search of where and when the audition would be. It took them a while to figure out the elevators again, but thanks to a hotel worker carrying some towels, they made it all the way down to what she called the lobby.

"The *American Star* auditions are down by the Erie Room." The woman pointed toward a hallway. "Go that way and you'll see the signs."

The hotel was much quieter than it had been yesterday. Before long they saw signs that said *American Star* in glitzy gold letters. Eventually they found a room where hundreds of chairs were set up and ready.

"Will those chairs be filled?" Katrina asked nervously. "Will I have to sing in front of that many people?"

"No," Bekka assured her. "Those are for contestants."

"What?" Katrina stared at the rows and rows of chairs. "All those chairs will be singers?"

"Lots of people want to win this," Bekka explained. "But most of them can't sing. Remember the auditions I showed you on my computer?"

Katrina just nodded. She hoped Bekka was right.

"Can I help you girls?" a pretty woman with pale blonde hair asked. She had on tight blue jeans, tall sandals, and a pale yellow shirt with the words *American Star* embroidered near the collar.

"We're here for your show," Bekka said politely. "I'm Bekka Lehman and this is my friend Katrina Yoder."

"I'm Brandy." She was flipping through papers on a clipboard as if she was quite busy.

"Katrina is going to audition for your show. We preregistered her on my computer." Bekka held up the paperwork. "We came to see—"

"The auditions won't begin for a few hours. The judges are supposed to be down at ten, although the contestants will start trickling in anytime now—not that it will get them on any sooner." She reached for the paper in Bekka's hand. "See this number here?" she pointed her pen to 1377.

"*Ja,*" they said in unison.

"That means you're one of the last ones to audition. And that means you won't need to be here until tomorrow afternoon. Probably not until after three or even later."

"What?" Katrina frowned at the number. Was that how many people were auditioning?

"You must've been one of the last contestants to sign up. Some kids signed up six months ago."

"*Ja.*" Bekka nodded sadly. "We had to talk Katrina into doing this. She was being quite mulish."

Brandy made a tolerant smile. "Well, you girls should just enjoy yourselves in the meantime. See the lovely sights of Cleveland." She laughed like that was funny.

"Not until tomorrow?" Katrina said meekly. "After three, you say?"

"Well, you never know. Sometimes we get a bunch of no-shows and everything goes more quickly than planned. Just check in tomorrow—say, noonish—and you should be okay." She peered curiously at Katrina now. "Can you really sing?"

"She can sing," Bekka declared. "You want to hear?"

Brandy tipped her head to one side with a curious expression. "Sure, why not? The day is young."

"Sing for her, Katrina." Bekka nodded.

"Right here?"

"Come on," Brandy urged. "If you compete on this show

you'll have to be able to sing at the drop of a hat—nobody waits for anyone around here."

Katrina took a deep breath, then began singing "Puff, the Magic Dragon." She'd only sung one verse and was just getting warmed up when the woman held her hand up to stop her. She snatched the paper from Bekka, pulled out a black pen, and crossed out the number and wrote "LAST" instead. Then she put her initials next to it.

"What is this?" Katrina frowned. "Did I do something wrong?"

Brandy smiled coyly. "Not at all. I just changed your number, Katrina."

"Does this mean I'm last to audition?" Katrina was confused.

"Yes. But make sure you're here *today*."

"Today?" She felt even more confused. "I thought you said—"

"For some camera time."

"Camera time?" Katrina winced at the idea of cameras.

"You girls are so cute in your Amish dresses and bonnets. We need to get that on camera." She peered curiously at Katrina. "You really are Amish, aren't you? This isn't some kind of publicity stunt?"

"What?" Katrina looked at Bekka.

"People do all kinds of things to get on our show," Brandy said, then frowned. "But if you really are Amish, why are you willing to be filmed? I thought the Amish had strict rules about not being photographed. Don't they believe it steals their souls or something?"

"We are on *rumspringa*," Bekka said as if that explained everything. "We can be photographed if we want to."

Brandy laughed.

"The reason Amish do not like being photographed is because we believe it's vainglory to have your picture taken. Not because it steals our souls," Katrina clarified. "Only the devil can steal a soul. And only if you let him."

Brandy grinned. "Okay, I'll keep that in mind. Now, don't forget. I need you girls down here today as well as tomorrow. Not the whole day, but for an hour or two. You got that?"

They both nodded.

"Let's go eat breakfast," Katrina said as they walked away.

"Or go back to bed," Bekka said sleepily. "I felt like I was awake half the night. Did you hear all the noises?"

"*Ja*. Doors opening and closing. Sirens down below. I did not sleep much either."

They went back up to their room and had some breakfast and a short nap. Then, since it was only ten o'clock and seemed too soon to go back down, Bekka insisted Katrina should practice singing again.

"Why do you think Brandy changed me to last?" Katrina asked as she pinned her apron back into place. "Is it because I'm not good enough?"

"Maybe it's like the Bible says." Bekka helped Katrina straighten her *kapp*, pinning it snugly down. "The first will be last and the last will be first."

"What does that mean?"

"I don't know, but my mamm says it all the time."

With everything put away, and feeling more confident about using the elevators and finding their way around the massive hotel, they went back downstairs. When they reached the Erie Room, they were both stunned to see it was packed. Not only was it packed, but it was noisy and crazy, and Katrina felt more out of place than ever.

"Is it only young people who audition?" she asked Bekka as the two of them stood off to the side, feeling safer next to a large column.

"Contestants must be between the ages of seventeen and thirty," Bekka informed her. "But I do agree. They all seem very young to me."

"And their clothing . . . is very unusual." Katrina tried not to stare at a skinny girl with hair that resembled a skunk except that the white stripe was as pink as Mamm's favorite rosebush.

"Maybe this is their *rumspringa* too," Bekka whispered.

Katrina pointed to three very large and prominently displayed photos. "Are those some of the contestants?" she asked with concern, wondering why some contestants would get such attention. One of them looked older than thirty.

"No, those are the judges." Bekka's hand flew to her mouth. "I should've told you all about them by now."

Katrina was reading the names below the photos. "Ricky Rodriguez."

"Ricky was a pop singer in the eighties," Bekka explained.

"Pop?"

Bekka shrugged. "I think it's for popular. Anyway, Ricky is always making jokes. He's the easiest judge." She pointed at the photo of a very pretty blonde woman. "That's Celeste Dior. She's a really good singer, but a really hard judge." Next she pointed to the photo of an unsmiling man with shaggy gray hair and a fuzzy beard. "That's Jack Smack."

"Jack Smack?"

"*Ja*. It's a funny name. I think he made it up."

"I recognize the name. I've heard his songs on the golden oldies station."

Bekka nodded. "*Ja*. He was a singer a long time ago. I don't think he sings anymore. He's the harshest of the judges. He even makes contestants cry sometimes."

"Oh . . ."

"I thought that was how he got his name," Bekka admitted. "Smack." She giggled. "Because he likes to smack singers down."

"There they are!" Suddenly Brandy and two men with what appeared to be television cameras were right next to them. "My Amish girls."

"Which is the contestant?" the cameraman with no hair asked.

"That one." Brandy pointed at Katrina. "I want you to get some shots of her coming into the hotel." She looked at them. "Can you run upstairs and get your bags so you look like you just arrived?"

"What?" Katrina frowned. "But we're unpacked."

"You don't have to pack them," Brandy explained. "Just get your bags and meet Mike and Lou outside so they can get some footage of you." She turned to the cameramen. "Get Bruce to go out there with you—ask Katrina some questions. Got it?"

"We're on it," the one with no hair told her. He turned to Katrina. "I'm Mike and that's Lou. We'll meet you out in front with Bruce."

She just nodded, looking at Bekka for support. Bekka grabbed Katrina's arm, dragging her back toward the elevators. "I think this is a good sign," she said as they practically ran down the hall. "On the show, you always see certain people telling about themselves—early on—and sometimes those are the people who win."

Feeling somewhat encouraged but very confused, Katrina hurried with Bekka to get their bags, which looked flat without clothes in them. "Here." Bekka took one of the smaller pillows from the bed. "Let's put these in them. To look better."

Feeling silly about carrying pillows in their cloth bags, the two girls went outside into the bright sunlight to see that Mike and Lou were already there with another man. This man had dark, curly hair and a big smile. "Hello," he called out to them. "Just go on over there by the taxis. Maybe get in one and then get out again. I'll ask you some questions and you try to look natural. Like you just arrived here. Okay?"

"Okay!" Bekka yelled back at him, and grabbing Katrina's hand, she dragged her over to a taxi.

"Where you wanna go?" the driver asked.

"We just need to get in and get out," Bekka explained.

He frowned but opened the door for them to get in.

"That's Bruce Betner," Bekka said. "He's the host of the show. Isn't he handsome?"

The door opened again. "Okay, kiddies, come on out," the driver said with a smirk. "I'll bet I don't even get a tip."

"Hello," Bruce said again as he held out what looked like a silver stick toward them. "Welcome to Cleveland."

"Thank you," Katrina muttered, nearly tripping over the curb.

"Where are you girls from?" Bruce asked pleasantly.

While Bekka answered, Katrina stuffed her pillow back into her bag. "This is Katrina Yoder," Bekka said as if she did this sort of thing all the time. "She's a really good singer, and I think she's going to win *American Star* this year."

Bruce chuckled. "You do?"

"Yes. Everyone at home—I mean, the young people, think so too. You should hear her."

"I hope to hear her." He frowned slightly. "Are you girls really Amish, or did you just dress up like this to get our camera guys out here?"

"We are truly Amish," Katrina said, "although we haven't been baptized into the church yet."

His eyes lit up. "So is this your *rumspringa*?"

Katrina nodded. "This is part of it."

"Will you be smoking and drinking and—"

"No!" Katrina scowled. "Why would we do those things?"

"I thought that was what Amish kids do for *rumspringa*. Haven't you seen the reality show?"

"The what?"

He laughed. "So if that's not what *rumspringa* is—smoking and drinking and going wild—what is it really? Explain *rumspringa* to our viewers."

"*Rumspringa* means running around, and it is a time of freedom. But it's also a time for young people to decide which way they will go," Katrina somberly told him. "We are born into our family and community, but we must choose whether or not we will stay. It's a very serious decision, you know. Not something to be taken lightly." She knew she sounded like Daed, but she couldn't help it.

Bruce's brow creased. "I see." His face lit up into a big smile. "I hear you can sing, Katrina."

She nodded. "I love to sing."

"But is singing allowed in the Amish community? I heard that even in church it's not real singing but more like chanting."

She considered her answer. "Our singing is different than

English singing. It's from our European roots. But sometimes
. . . some people . . . they sing."

He laughed. "Well, obviously you do, or you wouldn't be
here. Right?"

"*Ja.* I sing."

"Will you be singing an Amish song for your audition?"

She shook her head. "No. It will be an English song."

"Are you going to give us a hint about which song it will
be?"

"No. I have not decided yet."

He laughed again. For some reason he thought a lot of
things were terribly funny. "One more thing, Katrina. I heard
that you're the last audition in Cleveland—not until tomorrow. What do you think of that?"

She frowned. "I was afraid that I did something wrong."

Now he laughed really loudly. "No, no, you didn't do anything wrong." He turned back to the men with cameras and
continued chatting at them, almost as if he was really speaking
to a whole bunch of people. Then he waved at them. "That's
a wrap," he told Mike, then thanked Bekka and Katrina. "I'll
see you girls tomorrow. Feel free to come early enough to
watch some of the fun. Maybe we'll get some more footage
of your reactions to it."

And just like that—as a crowd of onlookers was beginning to gather—Bruce Betner and the cameramen, trailed
by some other men wearing uniforms, hurried back into the
hotel. Katrina looked down at the pillow sticking out of her
bag and shook her head. What was next?

11

By Sunday morning, Katrina felt utterly confused. She had so many questions about *American Star* that she didn't even know where to begin. To make matters worse, Bekka seemed to get more aggravated every time Katrina questioned something. As a result, Katrina was not saying much . . . but watching everything. They'd been in the Erie Room for several hours, and the crowd of contestants was slowly dwindling. Katrina would watch contestants full of excitement—some danced around, some even did cartwheels—waiting for their turn to audition. Then they would come out of the audition room with tears running down their cheeks. Or they would tear up their paper and use foul words. One guy even slugged one of the cameramen.

By Sunday afternoon, three things seemed clear to Katrina. One, everyone auditioning really wanted to win. Two, everyone seemed to believe they were the best singer of all. And three, only a few were getting chosen—and those chosen few were called the "finalists."

"How many finalists are there?" Katrina asked Bekka.

"A lot."

"Will they all compete again later on tonight?" Katrina asked. "So the judges can decide?"

"I don't know." Bekka put her nose back into the book she was reading.

Katrina frowned. How was it that Bekka had watched this show for three seasons—or so she claimed—and she did not know these answers?

Finally, it was almost Katrina's turn. A man from the show told her to wait by the door, and she made Bekka come with her.

"Don't worry," Bekka assured her. "It will be over before you know it. You only sing a verse. Sometimes just a few lines."

"How can they decide so quickly?"

Bekka shrugged. "They do this a lot."

Bruce came over, trailed by the same two cameramen, and began to ask her some more questions. "Did you decide on your song?" he asked.

She nodded. "Yes, I did."

"But you're not going to tell me?"

She shook her head.

"Are you nervous?"

She bit her lip. Just hearing him ask that made her feel like she could lose her lunch. She looked at Bekka hopefully. "Can my friend go in there with me?" she asked Bruce.

He shrugged. "Sure, if you like."

Katrina nodded eagerly, grabbing hold of Bekka's arm. "I do."

Just then a girl with short-cropped hair came stomping out. "Those judges need to get their heads out of—"

"Easy does it," Bruce said. "We have ladies in the house."

The girl glared at them. "Good luck! Those judges are the worst. They should've thrown them all off last season. Jack Smack oughta get smacked down by—"

"Thank you for your opinion," Bruce said cheerfully. "Now if you'll excuse us." One of the uniformed men (Katrina now knew they were security guards) came over to escort the unhappy girl away.

Bruce beamed at Katrina. "Are you ready?"

She nodded, and suddenly the mysterious door was open and she and Bekka were led inside by a petite woman in black, who took them past a curtain and into a well-lit area. There were even more cameras in here, and Brandy was sitting in a chair off to one side. She smiled and waved. "Come on in," she called. "Go ahead and take the stage."

Katrina couldn't let go of Bekka's hand, so both of them went up onto the platform that faced a long table where three people—the ones from the posters—were seated. They seemed preoccupied with papers in front of them, and they all looked slightly bored, or maybe just tired. Although her knees were shaking, Katrina actually remembered their names: Ricky, Jack, and Celeste.

"This is Katrina Yoder," Brandy said loudly. "The final contestant."

"Is this a joke?" Ricky said.

"What?" Celeste frowned up at them. "Is this a duet?"

"Her friend is for moral support," Brandy told them. "Katrina is the one on the right—the brunette."

"Seriously?" Ricky frowned. "Are you punking us?"

"Well, get on with it then." Jack scowled at Katrina. "I'm already way better acquainted with this chair than I want to be."

Bekka elbowed her. "Go ahead. Introduce your song."

"*Ja.*" Katrina nodded. "My song is called 'After the Storm.'" Without looking directly into the judges' eyes, she began to sing the antiwar song. She could tell her beginning was a little weak, but she hoped she made up for it as she continued. She kept expecting them to make her stop, but no one did. She sang the whole song, and when she quit, the room was quiet. The judges all had a slightly astonished look on their faces, and then they began talking quietly amongst themselves.

"You did just fine," Brandy said as she joined them on the stage. "I've never heard that song before, but it was a good one. Especially for your voice . . . and your, uh, well, your Amishness."

"Come over here," Jack belted out to her. "I want a better look at you."

Still clinging to Bekka's hand, Katrina cautiously approached the table.

"Well, Katrina," Celeste began slowly. "You have the voice of an angel. Not disputing that. But I don't think so, honey."

"What?" Jack asked Celeste.

"I'm saying no," Celeste told him. "This poor girl would be eaten alive by our show and you know it."

"Don't be so quick," Ricky said. "We've had innocents before. It gets interesting. Remember Molly McGee?"

"Yes, but it's cruel to take someone like"—Celeste looked down at a paper—"Katrina here. It's cruel to expose her to—"

"Where'd you learn that song?" Jack asked her with narrowed eyes.

"Her mammi wrote it," Bekka declared.

"Bekka!" Katrina flashed a warning glance her way, but Bekka wasn't looking.

120

"Her name was Starla Knight," Bekka continued. "She was in a group called Willow Tree."

"Is that true?" Jack demanded.

Katrina just looked down at her shoes.

"What is Willow Tree?" Ricky asked.

"A folk group from the sixties," Jack said. "Starla was their lead singer." He got up and walked over to stand in front of Katrina. "Look at me, girl."

She looked up.

"Is that true? Is Starla Knight really your grandma?"

"She was." Katrina explained that she had died recently. "I never knew she was a singer. No one did. I only just found out. My grandfather doesn't want people to know. I wanted to keep it a secret."

"Too late for that," Jack told her.

She bit her lip and twisted the corners of her shawl.

"Do your people watch TV?" he asked.

"No," Katrina said.

Bekka chuckled. "A few like me do, but they don't tell anyone about it."

"So your secret about Starla will be safe." Jack turned back to the other judges. "I'm voting yes on this girl, and if you guys are smart, you'll vote yes too."

"Katrina," Celeste said gently. "Tell me why you're here, honey."

Katrina went over to her. "I do love to sing," she said. "But I'm really here for the money."

Suddenly everyone was laughing, and Katrina felt her cheeks flushing hot.

"It's for her daed," Bekka said defensively. "He needs surgery. He's in so much pain. He can't even work anymore.

121

The only reason we talked her into this was so she could win enough money for his operation."

The judges got very quiet. Jack went back over to the table and bent down to talk quietly to the others. Finally he turned around. "It's unanimous. Katrina Yoder, you are a finalist for *American Star*."

Bekka jumped up and down and hugged her. "I knew you could do it," she said happily. "I knew it!"

Katrina felt tears coming. "Thank you," she told them all. "You don't know what this will mean—for my daed—for my family. Thank you."

"Well, this is only the beginning," Celeste told her. "You still have a long journey ahead of you."

"What?"

"Come on." The woman who had brought them in was now escorting them out. "We need to let the judges go home."

Suddenly Katrina was out the door and Bruce had his microphone in her face. "How'd it go in there?"

"She won," Bekka exclaimed. "Well, she's a finalist anyway."

"Congratulations." Bruce turned to the cameras. "So you'll be seeing our little Amish girl in Hollywood next week when she competes against all two hundred of our other finalists to see which of them are good enough to become an American Star. Goodnight!" He waved his hand.

"That's a wrap," someone said.

"Hollywood?" Katrina was very confused now. "Where is that?"

"California," Bekka told her.

"I'm supposed to go there next week?" Katrina looked at Bruce and the others, but they seemed to be packing things up, getting ready to go. "How can I possibly do that? I'm nearly out of money."

Brandy had joined them. "Your expenses are covered by the show from here on out," she explained. "Didn't you know that?"

"I don't understand."

"We will fly you out and pay for your room and board and everything for as long as you're on the show. Hopefully it'll be a long time."

"A long time?" Katrina looked from Brandy to Bekka. "In Hollywood?"

"The show goes for a whole season," Bekka said meekly.

"All the contestants stay in Hollywood," Brandy told her. "I thought you knew that. Do you want to change your mind now?"

Katrina didn't know what to do. She looked in Brandy's eyes. For some reason she trusted this woman. "Do you really think I have a chance—not to get first place, but do you honestly think I could win enough money to cover my daed's surgery?"

"That's up to you—and I can't promise you anything—but I've been doing this for a while and I think you have enough natural talent to make it to the top eight. If you really want it. You have to really want it, Katrina."

"I do want it—for my daed—I want it."

"Then you should come to Hollywood."

"*Ja,*" Bekka said happily. "You should."

"Next week?" Katrina frowned.

"No, not next week. Bruce only said that for the airdates to match up. We have one more audition in Seattle. You don't need to be in Hollywood until mid July. We'll send a crew out to your town in a week or so."

"A crew?"

"To get footage of you at home, with your family, in your community. It gives the show a personal touch that viewers love. It will be especially important in your situation, Katrina. Is that going to be okay? Will your family object to being photographed?"

Katrina looked nervously at Bekka, so Bekka explained that it could be a problem. "But maybe you could come to group singing," she said. "And some of us—like me—we'll let you take our pictures." She giggled nervously. "It's my *rumspringa* too. And my parents will have to forgive me."

Brandy laughed. "We'll be in touch."

"How?" Katrina asked.

"I have your information in my file. Your phone and email."

"I don't have a phone or—"

"It's mine," Bekka told her. "I'll let Katrina know what's going on," she assured Brandy.

"You're her manager?"

Bekka giggled. "*Ja*. I guess I am."

Brandy lowered her voice now. "I probably shouldn't tell you this, but all the judges loved you. And Jack Smack fought hard for you. I've only seen him do that a time or two. It's not something we take lightly."

"Oh?"

"You could have a strong ally in that man, Katrina. That alone should motivate you to come and do your best."

Katrina nodded. "Thank you for telling me."

As they walked back to the elevators, Katrina had a wild mix of feelings rushing through her—almost like a bunch of puppy dogs all pulling on the same sock. She was pleased to be a finalist but dismayed to learn that it was not over. It was far from over. And although she enjoyed knowing that Jack Smack knew who her grandmother was, she was worried that Daadi might be upset with her for letting this information out. Of course, Jack was right. Daadi—and the rest of them—didn't watch TV. So how would they know? Finally, she was excited about the idea of getting to sing more, but at the same time she just wanted to go home . . . to walk in her garden and check on her cucumbers and tomatoes and peppers.

12

By Monday morning, Katrina was having serious second thoughts. Why had she agreed to go to Hollywood? And a film crew visiting their settlement? That was a disaster just waiting to happen.

"Are you all right?" Bekka asked with concern as they rode down in the elevator, thankfully for the last time. "You seem awfully quiet this morning."

"I think I made a mistake," she mumbled as they exited the elevator.

"Did you forget something?"

"Just that I'm Amish." Katrina looked over to the desk where she'd paid for their room three days ago. "I need to go see if I can have my hundred dollars back."

"*Ja.* I nearly forgot about that." She took Katrina's bag. "I'll hold this for you."

Katrina went over to where only one man was waiting in line, perhaps because it was early. It seemed city people didn't get up early. Certainly that would be difficult considering how late they seemed to stay up. She'd heard people cavorting up and down the hallway until after two in the morning.

"May I help you?"

Katrina went to the desk, where a man in a white shirt and a tie was waiting to help her. She pulled out the papers the other woman had given her, telling him her name and room number. "The woman who took my money promised I could have one hundred dollars back when we left. We didn't open the minibar and we didn't take anything. I promise you."

The man chuckled. "Well, if you did, we'd know it."

"Oh . . ."

She waited as he clicked on his keyboard. Then he handed her back a paper and counted out five twenties for her. She almost asked where her one-hundred-dollar bill had gone but stopped herself.

"Wait," he said. "I see a note here that you have something else."

"Something else?"

"Yes. We left a message on your phone, but you must not have seen the light flashing."

"Oh, the red light going off and on. We saw it."

He grinned. "That was your message to pick something up down here. I'll see if I can find it."

A minute or two later he returned with an envelope and handed it to her. She looked at the outside, which had the hotel's name on it. "From the hotel?" she said.

"I heard that it was from Jack Smack," he said quietly. "From *American Star*."

She blinked. "Jack Smack."

He looked eagerly at her, as if he wanted her to open it and read it to him. "Thank you," she said. Then she hurried back to Bekka, waving the envelope. "Jack Smack wrote me a letter."

"Really?" Bekka peered at it. "Well, maybe you should read it in the taxi. We need to hurry if we want to catch the 8:40 bus."

Once in the taxi, Katrina opened the envelope and pulled out the note.

Dear Katrina,

I should have said something to you after your audition, but I was pretty blown away when I heard about your grandma. Anyway, this really good buddy of mine, Larry Zimmerman, was part of Willow Tree with your grandma. He lives out in LA. I'd like to invite him to meet up with you when you're in Hollywood. I know it would mean a lot to him.

Hang in there, kiddo,

Jack Smack

"Katrina!" Bekka exclaimed. "Can you believe that?"

Katrina read the letter again. "That's amazing."

"It almost seems like it's your destiny to do this," Bekka said in a serious tone.

"What does that mean?"

"I heard that line in a movie on the computer once. Like maybe this is something your mammi wanted you to do. Don't you think so too?"

"It is strange." Katrina watched out the window as cars and buildings and people flashed by. Such a big, busy place. She would not miss it. But would Hollywood be any different? Was she really going there?

"Will you be able to come to Hollywood with me, do you think? In July?"

"Oh, Katrina, you know I wish I could. But I doubt Mamm and Daed will let me. Just getting away for these three days was hard enough. You'll be out in Hollywood for weeks."

"For weeks?"

"*Ja.*" She sighed. "I should've told you."

"*Ja*, you should've."

"I think I was just caught up in all the excitement. I knew it was possible you could win a ticket to Hollywood, but the truth is, I didn't really believe it would happen."

"You didn't believe it, yet you encouraged me to do this?"

She nodded sheepishly. "I'm sorry. Was that terribly selfish?"

Katrina pressed her hands to her cheeks and sighed. "I guess I wouldn't have gone if I hadn't wanted to. I can't blame you for the mess I've gotten myself into."

"It's not a mess," Bekka said. "You saw how much the judges like you. And Jack Smack, he doesn't like anyone. Now he's planning a meeting for you in Hollywood."

Hollywood . . . How would she explain that to Mamm and Daed? The only thing she felt truly happy about as they fished out their tickets and got onto the bus was that in a couple of hours she would see Cooper again. They would have a nice long buggy ride to catch up on things. It seemed as if it had been years since she'd last seen him. So many things she'd wanted to say, so many things they had almost said, so many things still left to say. Hopefully Bekka would want to take a nap while they talked.

Katrina spotted the dark gray buggy as they climbed out of the bus. But instead of Cooper's head popping out, it was Peter's. "Why is Peter here?" she asked as they hurried over to join him.

"Cooper called from his uncle's cabinet shop yesterday,"

Peter explained after Bekka told him the good news about Katrina being a finalist. "He's decided to stay on there. Seems his uncle has something wrong with his elbow and really needs Cooper's help just now. So he's already started his apprenticeship."

Katrina didn't know what to say. She was disappointed clear down to her toes. Not just because Cooper wasn't driving them home, but because this meant she wouldn't see him again . . . for how long? Only God knew. Instead of Bekka sleeping on the way home, Katrina curled up on the rear seat, listening as Bekka told her brother the whole story of their "amazingly exciting" visit to Cleveland. To hear Bekka tell it, one would think they really did have fun. Katrina wondered if it was possible for two people to be in the same place at the same time and have entirely different experiences.

Katrina tried to downplay being a finalist on *American Star*, but both Sadie and Cal seemed determined to keep talking about it, asking her questions about Cleveland and what was to happen next. She told them someone from the show might be coming to visit and that she would have to go on to Hollywood to participate in the final competition for the cash prizes. That didn't seem to concern either of them, and fortunately they both had the good sense not to discuss these topics much around their parents or Drew.

"You seem unhappy," Aunt Alma told Katrina as they sat on Daadi's porch sipping iced tea together. It was the first time Katrina had seen her aunt since going to Cleveland. "Is something worrying you?"

"It's just the same old things," Katrina admitted. "And then some."

"I know you're worried about singing in that show, and I don't want to influence you one way or the other, but I believe if you're doing it for your daed, it is a good thing. You should not feel guilty for helping your family. Besides, what about getting to meet Larry—Mammi's singing partner—wouldn't that alone be good reason to go to Hollywood?"

"But I looked on a map, and Hollywood is so far away. It's scary to think of going there all by myself. Bekka says I'll have another contestant for a roommate when I get there. An English girl. But I know I will feel lost . . . and alone."

"I wish I could go with you."

Katrina chuckled to imagine Aunt Alma at such an event, but the idea of it warmed her heart. "I wish you could go too."

"You do?"

"*Ja*. That would be great."

"Then I shall do it."

"Do what?"

"Go to Hollywood with you."

"Really?" Katrina was worried now. "But how will you afford it? I know my way is paid, but that's all. And believe me, after three days in Cleveland, I know it will be expensive."

"I have money." Aunt Alma patted her chest. "I've been saving my quilt money for years and years. I can afford to go if I want to go. Besides, if you have a place to stay, why can't I just sleep on the floor next to you? I will buy my own food, of course, but if your room is as big as what you told me about in Cleveland, you should have plenty of room for an old woman like me."

"If it's like the room in Cleveland, you can share the big bed with me. Did I tell you there were two great big beds? Bigger than the one Mamm and Daed share—one for Bekka and one for me. And each bed had six pillows on it. Can you imagine?"

"Six pillows? That seems extravagant. Even for the English."

"Will Aunt Fannie let you go?" Katrina asked quietly.

"She cannot stop me." Aunt Alma stood now. "I will ask Daed. If he says to go with you, I will."

"But what will you tell him? He doesn't know about the TV show, does he?"

"No. But I will tell him I'm going to be your guardian while you are on *rumspringa*. If he doesn't agree to that, I will tell him that I'm going on *rumspringa* myself. And if he doesn't like that, I will tell him what I know about Mamm. That will keep him quiet enough."

Katrina was stunned. She'd never seen Aunt Alma like this before. "You'd really do that for me?"

"For you." She nodded firmly. "And for me."

Katrina told Aunt Alma about how a camera crew would be coming soon. "Probably in the next week or so," she explained. "I don't want you to feel you need to let them take your picture. I just wanted to warn you. Mamm and Daed don't know yet. I think I'll wait and tell them right before the crew comes."

"Oh, my." Aunt Alma's eyes twinkled. "You are shaking our settlement up."

"I hope they'll let me back in when it's over and done."

"Of course they will. If you confess and repent, they have to forgive you."

"*Ja* . . . so I've heard."

"Just remember your mammi. She left—and stayed away for years—and she still came back."

"That's true. But not to her own family."

"*Ja*. But we became her own family."

Katrina was tempted to tell Aunt Alma about Cooper and how he was apprenticing with his uncle, but she figured if Aunt Alma went to Hollywood with her, they would have time to talk about that later. It was reassuring to think of her aunt traveling with her, staying in the hotel with her, being there for her. And it seemed Aunt Alma wanted to go with her. Katrina hoped and prayed that nothing would stop Aunt Alma from coming.

The film crew came in late June—Bekka had warned a week earlier that she'd received an email announcing they were coming, so for the next few days, Katrina tried to be prepared for them. They didn't show up right away, so she decided to just forget about it. When the big white van finally pulled into their driveway—straight out of the blue—she wasn't sure what to do. Wearing her working dress with a dirty garden apron since she'd been working in the garden, she had bare feet and no *kapp* on her head. She apologized and offered to go inside and clean up, but they would not let her.

"We just want you to be yourself," Brandy assured her. "Just go about your regular day."

Feeling nervous and worried about what her family would think, she led them to the garden where she'd been pulling weeds, trimming the raspberry bushes, and staking cucumbers, tomatoes, and peppers. While she continued to work, they followed with their equipment, and Brandy asked her questions, trying to get Katrina to open up. But Katrina was too self-conscious, not to mention afraid that Mamm would soon show up and demand to know what was going on, so her answers stayed short and crisp. Brandy was not pleased.

After a while, Katrina decided that Mamm and Sadie were too busy doing laundry to notice anything amiss. She began to relax, and after she made the crew sample some strawberries and cherry tomatoes that had come on early, she forgot all about the cameras and began to talk to Brandy like she was just a friend.

"The garden is my favorite place," Katrina said as she picked the tiny tomatoes, gently setting them in her basket. "I think it's because God is here in the garden with me. I've heard that you can't be closer to God than when you're working the soil." She held up an oversized cherry tomato. "It's so satisfying to grow this from a tiny seed that I started last winter in our greenhouse. Now it's ready to eat." She bit into it and it squirted juice and seeds down her chin, which made everyone laugh.

Then she got more serious. "I don't understand how you city people can live the way you do, with your cement everywhere and tall glass buildings and all those noisy cars and trucks and exhaust fumes. I could not live like that. I do understand how you might lose sight of God, living in the city like that. But out here"—she waved her hands—"with my fingers in the soil and a song in my heart and all these beautiful fruits and vegetables growing—well, God is all around me. Can't you feel him too?" She smiled at them, hoping they understood.

"That's a wrap," one of the guys said.

Relieved to be done, Katrina walked them back to their van.

"We still need to get some B roll," Brandy said.

"What's that?" Katrina frowned. "Food?"

Brandy laughed. "No, just some film of where you live." She explained that they planned to drive around the settlement and get some more shots of the landscape and barns and cows. "Is that okay?"

Katrina shrugged. "It's a free world. Just don't expect anyone to let you take their picture up close. It's just not done here, and it's rude to try."

They promised to respect that, and after thanking her for cooperating, they went on their way. She glanced at the house, thankful that Mamm hadn't seen them here—at least Katrina didn't think she had since Mamm hadn't made an appearance. In all likelihood, she and Sadie were still up to their elbows in laundry. Although Sadie would be disappointed to have missed the film crew, it was probably for the best.

It wasn't until the following Sunday, after church, that Katrina found out that the film crew had stirred up some trouble by trying to get a little too close to some children playing outside of the school where Hannah taught. Naturally, it was tracked back to Katrina and her family, resulting in a meeting with Bishop Hershberger. Because Daed was still laid up in bed, it was Mamm, Drew, and Katrina who went.

It didn't make things a bit easier that Bishop Hershberger was Hannah Hershberger's father. And Hannah was Drew's intended . . . or nearly. Still, there wasn't much to be done about it except to go and listen to the bishop's lecture about the Ordnung's position on photography and vainglory and singing, as well as the importance of taking her *rumspringa* time seriously. "This is meant to be a time for you to plan for your future, not to destroy your future before you get there," Bishop Hershberger told Katrina.

"I am sorry that the photographers were not more considerate," she told him.

"I am sorry you felt that it was acceptable to invite such people into our settlement."

She wanted to point out that she hadn't invited them but knew it was futile. He continued to talk at length about how he had raised his daughter to be humble and gentle and kind, "to serve others before thinking of herself." He glanced at Drew.

"Hannah is a fine girl indeed," Mamm conceded. "Katrina would do well to imitate her."

"We apologize for Katrina's thoughtlessness," Drew said curtly. "If I were her father, I would be most disappointed in her behavior. You can be sure that my children, if God blesses me to have any, will be much more obedient than her. If my father hadn't been injured and laid up, I'm sure none of this would have happened."

Bishop Hershberger pointed a finger at Katrina. "Your freedom is not meant to be a stumbling block for you or others. It is meant to show you the value of serving God."

"I understand that." She looked down at her lap, biting her lip.

"Our community is not for everyone. The road to righteousness is narrow, and few can travel it. It is up to you to decide which way you will go."

"I'm certain Katrina will make the right choice," Mamm said firmly. "I've been assured that she and her brother Cal plan to follow Drew's fine example and begin to train for baptism very soon. Isn't that right, Katrina?"

She forced herself to look at the bishop. "I—uh—I think so."

"But your decision isn't firm yet, is it?" Bishop Hershberger peered curiously at her.

"I love God with my whole heart," she said.

"Do you love the Lord enough to put all folly behind you,

to obey all his commands, and to live as a humble servant without seeking out any form of vainglory?"

Katrina looked back down at her lap. She knew he was referring to singing.

"Yes, I was afraid of that." He sighed heavily. He lectured a while longer before, finally satisfied that he had made himself clear, he allowed them to leave.

Drew didn't say anything as they got into their buggy, but it was clear he was angry. She didn't even blame him.

"I'm sorry, Drew. I didn't know—"

"That's just it," he snapped. "You don't *know* anything. You go around acting like you are the center of the world, like no one matters but you, like you are English! I don't know why you even came back from Cleveland. You obviously don't belong here. You don't want to be here. Why don't you just go to Hollywood and stay there? At least stay there until you're certain that you want to be part of this community."

"*Drew.*" Mamm's voice was stern. "That is a harsh way to speak to your sister."

"My sister?" Drew turned with a red face. "She has just humiliated me in front of Hannah's father. You know that I want to marry Hannah. You know I took classes—I went through baptism—even though I was so busy working the farm ever since Daed got hurt. I knew it was important. Part of growing up! And while I'm over there breaking my back for Uncle Willis, knowing full well that he and Aunt Fannie might take over the farm completely when Daadi dies, and I might be left with nothing and Hannah will never marry me, my little sister is out gallivanting around, competing in *English singing contests*, and making our family look like a bunch of shallow fools who get called in by the bishop!"

Katrina was crying now. She had never been spoken to like that by Drew—or anyone. His words stung worse than a beating. And she knew what he said was true. She deserved his wrath . . . and more.

No one said anything the rest of the way home, but as soon as the buggy stopped, Katrina jumped down and ran straight over to Daadi's house—not to see Daadi but to speak to Aunt Alma. Finding her in the garden, she told her the whole story.

"Oh, poor dear." Aunt Alma hugged her. "Well, I'm not surprised that Drew was upset. I know how much he cares for Hannah Hershberger. But it seems unfair to blame you for what those silly camera folks did. They're English. How can they know better?"

"Maybe we shouldn't go to Hollywood," Katrina told her. "Maybe it's a big mistake."

Aunt Alma looked truly disappointed now. "Well, dear, that's your decision to make. But I was looking forward to it. I have my airline ticket. Bekka helped me to get it a few days ago. It's not on the same airplane as you, but I will get there first and wait for you to arrive."

Katrina wiped her damp cheeks. "Yes, I suppose we should just go ahead with it. Daed's back has been worse than ever this week. And now Drew wants me gone anyway. He hopes I never come back."

"I'm sure that's not what he meant."

Katrina was not so sure, but as she walked back home, her resolve grew stronger. She would go, and she would do everything possible to win some money for Daed, and then if she was no longer welcome at home, she would find a life somewhere else. After all, hadn't Mammi done just that?

13

The following week made it easy for Katrina to say farewells to her family. Although it was not said, she felt as if her family was shunning her. They seemed to avoid her, saying no more than necessary, or if they saw her coming they would distract themselves with a chore. Of course, she knew that Cal and Sadie still stood behind her—when no one else was around to hear or see. Katrina understood this. She knew that Cal had to work with Drew every day, and if he showed his sympathy toward Katrina, it would drive a bitter wedge between the two brothers. And if Sadie revealed her true feelings about Katrina going to Hollywood, it would earn her many a stern lecture from Mamm. Because they had to stay and live in this house with this family, they needed to distance themselves from her. They needed to keep peace.

Katrina knew it would be easier for everyone after she was gone. Even Aunt Alma was suffering over at Daadi's house. Aunt Fannie was determined to make Aunt Alma's life even more miserable than it had been before. She'd even told Aunt Alma that if she left, she'd better not plan on coming back. Yet Aunt Alma remained determined.

Meanwhile, Daed gave no resistance whatsoever, but that was only because he was getting worse. Katrina knew he was worse because now he was taking his pills daily. The same pills he had detested before. As a result, he stayed in a permanent fog, so much so that he had barely understood Katrina when she told him goodbye.

"You are getting married?" he'd said with confusion in his eyes.

"No, Daed, I'm going on a trip."

"With your husband?"

"No, Daed. With Aunt Alma."

He'd barely nodded. "*Ja, ja.* You go with Aunt Alma. It's good."

"We're going to get you the money you need to get your back fixed, Daed."

His eyes had barely flickered with what she imagined was hope. "*Ja, ja.* That's a good girl, Katrina. God bless you, and Aunt Alma too."

At least she had Daed's blessing when they left the following morning, even if it was a somewhat drug-induced sort of blessing. Hadn't she heard that God worked in mysterious ways?

Because the Lehmans had a large order of soap and candles needed immediately in a shop in Millersburg, Bekka had talked her parents into letting Peter drive the buggy. Since she'd gotten all her work done ahead of time, Bekka was allowed to go too. Katrina suspected that Bekka had something to do with the fact that the Millersburg order hadn't been shipped last week, but she didn't mention this. Mostly she was grateful.

"Are you sad to be leaving?" Bekka asked as Peter drove them through the settlement in the gray dawn light.

"*Ja* . . . I would be lying if I said I wasn't," Katrina confessed.

"I'm glad to be going," Aunt Alma said. "I think we're having an adventure."

"*Ja*, I hope so." Katrina smiled to cover up the pain that was inside of her. Mamm had not gotten up this morning to say goodbye. She had not even said goodbye the night before. Nor had Drew. It helped some to know that Cal and Sadie still loved her. But at the same time, she couldn't help but think that she had divided their home.

"We missed you at the group singing last night," Bekka told her.

"I missed it too." Katrina had purposely stayed home in the hopes that she would have an evening with her family, but Cal and Drew had gone out and Mamm went to bed early. She did have a nice evening with Sadie, though. They made four dozen sugar cookies to take on the trip.

"We had something for you last night." Bekka giggled. "Should I give it to her now?" she called up to Peter.

"*Ja*. Why not?"

Bekka pulled out a box wrapped in brown paper. "Everyone— well, not everyone, but a lot of your friends contributed money so I could buy you this." She handed it to Katrina.

Katrina slowly unwrapped the small parcel. To her surprise, it was a cellular phone. "What?" She looked at Bekka.

"It's so you can stay in touch. You can call my office phone and let me know how you're doing. Then I'll pass the news on to the others."

"But I don't know how to use this."

"All the instructions are in the box," she said excitedly. "I ordered it online right after Cleveland, but I spoke to a man on the phone, and he said there's some kind of smart thing inside, and when you get to Hollywood, you take it to one of their places and they'll get you all set up."

Katrina didn't know what to say—or what she would do with a cell phone. She hugged Bekka. "Thank you. I hope I can figure it out."

As the sun was coming up, they all urged Katrina to sing. "It will be good practice for you," Bekka persuaded her. So for the next hour or so, Katrina sang. She had to admit, she did feel better when she sang. It seemed to smooth out all the rough spots in her life. She'd also brought Mammi's radio and a good supply of batteries.

Once again, the buggy stopped at the Millersburg bus station. Goodbyes were said, and Katrina led Aunt Alma inside and up to the ticket counter, where they purchased tickets to Cleveland. "When do you want to come back?" the man asked.

"I don't know for sure," Katrina admitted.

He peered curiously at her. "Well, let's just leave them open-ended."

"Open-ended?"

"So you can return whenever you like."

She nodded. "*Ja* . . . whenever we like." The man did not know that she and Aunt Alma might not be welcome to return whenever they liked.

As they rode the bus, Aunt Alma was excited to see everything and asked lots of questions, but after an hour she fell asleep. Katrina tried to listen to her radio, but for some reason it wasn't working right. Lots of scratchy noises interrupted some of her favorite songs. She finally turned it off and instead looked out the window to where the farmland had disappeared and in its place were houses, then bigger buildings, and eventually the city. She nudged her aunt. "We're almost there."

Aunt Alma opened her eyes and blinked. "Oh, my. What big houses the English have."

Thanks to Bekka, they were met at the bus station by an Amish couple named Mr. and Mrs. Zook. The Zooks belonged to a district where they were allowed to drive cars as well as have electricity in their homes. Bekka had explained that the Zooks ran an Amish guesthouse where even the English were welcome. It was where Bekka's family had stayed last spring.

"Thank you for fetching us," Katrina told them as she and Aunt Alma got into the back of the car.

"I never knew there were Amish who drove cars," Aunt Alma said in wonder. "Not where we live."

"Our district interprets the Ordnung differently," Mr. Zook said as he drove. "Instead of worrying so much about outward things—like should our pants have pockets or not, or should our suspenders have two straps or one—we try to be mindful of our hearts."

"*Ja,*" Aunt Alma said happily. "I like that."

"But you dress Amish," Katrina pointed out.

"We do," Mrs. Zook said, "because we are used to it and it is comfortable to us. But if we wanted, we could wear different clothes. Oh, not too different. But I can wear a cardigan sweater if I wish."

"We believe that Jesus isn't as concerned about what you wear as he is concerned about what you think . . . and do."

"*Ja,*" Aunt Alma agreed. "I think so too."

The guesthouse was, for the most part, simple and plain like Katrina's house, except that it had electric lights and the kitchen had an electric stove as well as a small television set, which remained off while they were there. Other than that, there seemed to be little difference. The Zooks made her and Aunt Alma feel at home. The conversation was interesting—and spiritually stimulating. Aunt Alma continued to talk of the Zooks and their liberal Ordnung as she and Katrina rode a shuttle bus to the airport. "If Aunt Fannie refuses to let me come home after Hollywood, I will go live in the Zooks' settlement," she declared.

Katrina forced a laugh. "Then so will I."

The airport was a big, busy place, but thanks to Mr. Zook's advice, they got there with plenty of time to ask questions and figure things out. And although Aunt Alma's ticket was for an earlier flight, the woman at the counter fixed it so she could fly with Katrina instead.

"Everyone is so helpful and kind," Katrina said after they finished going through what was called "security," taking off their shawls and shoes and putting everything through a funny little tunnel. After that it seemed like they walked a long way. "Maybe we are walking to Hollywood?" Aunt Alma said after a while. Eventually, they found their "gate," which was not really a gate but a place to sit and wait.

"Are you scared?" Katrina asked Aunt Alma as they sat looking out the windows at the giant planes that were coming and going.

"*Ja.*" She nodded grimly. "Being up in the sky . . . I hope we don't fall."

"*Ja.*" Katrina twisted the handle of her bag in her hands. "Me too."

"I know what we'll do," Aunt Alma said suddenly. "We will pray."

"*Ja*, that's a good plan."

Sitting there at the gate that was not really a gate, they bowed their heads and prayed silently, as they always did. But then Aunt Alma did what Mr. Zook had done last night before supper—she prayed out loud. "Dear God, you are our Father. We are your children. I know you do not want us to fall out of the sky. I ask that you keep your big strong hands beneath the belly of the airplane, and you keep us safe up there until it is time to come down again. Amen."

"Amen," Katrina whispered. She smiled at her aunt. "Thank you."

"*Ja*. I think it was all right to pray like that . . . this time."

Aunt Alma's prayer worked, and their plane did not fall out of the sky. It landed on time in Hollywood, and to Katrina's surprise, Brandy and a cameraman were waiting for them when they went to pick up their baggage—which wasn't really baggage but a big box that Aunt Alma had packed full of food from home. They hadn't known it would be an extra twenty dollars to bring it, but what could they do—leave the food behind?

"Welcome to California," Brandy said as they started walking toward the exit. "Did you have a good trip?"

"*Ja*, it was good," Aunt Alma told her. "We did not fall from the sky."

Brandy laughed, and Katrina introduced her to her aunt. "I hope it's all right she came with me."

Brandy frowned. "You already have a roommate, Katrina."

"I can sleep on the floor," Aunt Alma said quickly.

"Or in the bed with me," Katrina said, "if it's big enough."

"I can sleep on the floor," Aunt Alma said again.

"No, no, we won't make you sleep on the floor," Brandy assured her. "We can get you a rollaway if necessary."

"Roll away?" Aunt Alma frowned.

"Never mind." Brandy nodded to the cameraman. "You are getting this, aren't you?"

"We're hot," he called back.

"Hot?" Aunt Alma looked around. "It feels comfortable to me."

"So, Katrina, have you been practicing your songs?" Brandy asked.

"*Ja*. I sing to the radio whenever I can. Except that now it's not working." She shook her head as she dug in her bag for the radio. "I changed the battery, but all I hear is scratchy noises and screeches. No music. I hope it's not broken. It belonged to my grandmother."

"Did you adjust the dial?"

Katrina pulled out the radio.

"Wow, that's a real oldie." Brandy examined the radio. "It's probably a collectable." She tried to turn one of the dials. "It's stuck," she said.

"*Ja*, I know."

"It looks like someone glued it stuck." Brandy handed it back to her.

"My grandmother, maybe." Katrina slipped it back into her bag.

"Speaking of your grandmother, Jack tells us that he's set up a meeting with a good friend of your grandmother's. Is that right?"

"*Ja*, that's right," Aunt Alma declared.

Katrina tried to shoot her a warning look, but it was too late. Aunt Alma was telling Brandy—and the cameraman—

about how they wanted to find out all they could about Starla Knight. "We didn't know her name was Knight—that was before she married Daed and became Mrs. Yoder—but she was Mamm to me."

"So Starla Knight was your stepmother?"

"*Ja.* But I called her Mamm," Aunt Alma told her.

"Mamm means mother?" Brandy asked.

"*Ja.* She was my mother."

"Did she sing a lot when you were a child?"

"No." Aunt Alma firmly shook her head. "Hardly ever. She kept that part of her life hidden away. It was only when she passed—last spring—that Katrina and I began to figure out her story. But Katrina, she has her mammi's gift of song."

"You think of it as a gift?"

"Oh, *ja*, it is a gift. A good gift."

Brandy looked at Katrina now. "Your aunt is a talkative one."

"*Ja.*"

"Tell us how it feels to be here."

Katrina looked out to where cars and buses and taxis were coming and going, and she sighed. "Hollywood looks a lot like Cleveland."

Brandy laughed. "Well, this isn't Hollywood. This is LAX. But I think you'll discover that California is a beautiful place. And Hollywood—well, you'll see." She pointed to a long, black car pulling up in front of them. "Your limousine."

"Such a big car just for us?" Katrina was puzzled.

"Make sure you get some good shots of her going in," Brandy called. So Katrina had to take her time and say some things before they got inside the roomy vehicle. "This is like a small hotel room," Katrina said as she looked around to see a mini refrigerator and television. "I think a person could live in here."

It wasn't long before Katrina could see that California was different from Cleveland. For one thing, it had lots of tall, odd-looking trees. Each one had a long trunk going all the way up with a head like a flower on top. They called them palm trees. Maybe it was because the foliage on top fanned out like fingers splayed from a palm. She wasn't sure. But there certainly were a lot of them growing on both sides of the streets. There were also more flowers and green plants here than she'd noticed in Cleveland. It wasn't anything like home, but it seemed like someone was trying.

Still, this city seemed mostly a mishmash of vehicles and cement—and how anyone knew how to get from one place to another was lost on her. Thankfully, she would never have to drive a car and figure these things out for herself. At least she hoped not!

14

As they drove, Brandy continued to ask Katrina questions. It was obvious she wanted to get reactions from her as they saw different things, and Katrina did not hold back. "The English world is such a different world," she said. "It's hard to even describe how different it is."

"So, tell me, what does it mean to be Amish?" Brandy asked. "Can you explain the difference between Amish and English? In a way our viewers can understand?"

Katrina thought hard. "A few years ago, I was shopping in town with my mother, and one of those big buses—the ones that bring English tourists who come to look at us—was parked there. I decided to watch the group of English people as they stood outside of a store. One English woman asked the man who was leading the group that same question: 'What is the difference between the Amish and the English?' The man said to the group, 'How many of you have a computer in your house?' and they all raised their hands. Then he said, 'How many of you feel your home might be better off if you *didn't* have a computer in your house?' He encouraged them to be honest, and again, they all raised their hands. He said,

'So how many of you will go home and get rid of your computers?' and no one raised a hand. Then he said, 'That is the difference between English and Amish. The Amish choose to do without the things that they believe are harmful. The English do not.'"

Brandy nodded as if she understood. "Very interesting." She glanced at the cameraman. "You got that, right?"

"Yep."

"Here we are," Brandy proclaimed as the big car pulled up into what appeared to be the entrance of a fancy hotel. "Home sweet home."

Feeling a combination of exhaustion and curiosity, Katrina reached for her bag.

"Breezy Vicks is your roommate. I chose her because she claims to be a good Christian girl. But I'll let the desk know that your aunt will be staying with you too." She handed Katrina a packet of papers. "These are your keys and your schedule and whatnot. For the first few days, the competition will be held right here in this hotel—on the main floor in the Monterrey Ballroom. It's all there in your packet. The fun starts tomorrow at nine o'clock sharp. I'm sure you won't be late."

"No, I promise I will be early." Katrina looked back at the shiny black car.

"Do you have to pick up all the contestants?" Aunt Alma asked.

Brandy laughed. "All two hundred of them? No way. For the most part, they're on their own when it comes to transportation."

Katrina was puzzled.

Brandy patted her shoulder. "You, my dear, are special."

"Oh." Katrina thanked her again. But she wasn't sure she wanted to be special—not like that, anyway. Still, what could she say without sounding ungrateful?

"Just go straight on up to your room. It's on the twenty-second floor," Brandy said. "You're all checked in. Your room number's on the key envelope."

When they got up to room 2278, Katrina was unsure. "Should I knock on the door or just go in?"

"Knock," Aunt Alma suggested.

But when she knocked, no one answered. Katrina explained to Aunt Alma how to slide the card in, just like in Cleveland, and when the light turned green, they opened the door. Just as they were going in, carrying all their things, a girl dressed in very little and with purple goop all over her face let out a scream. "What is it?" she demanded. "I didn't call for a maid."

"We're not maids." Katrina explained who she was and introduced her aunt. "You must be Breezy Vicks."

"Yeah, I'm Breezy." She reached for a white robe, tugging it on. "Don't you believe in knocking first?"

"I did knock. No one answered."

"That's because I was washing my hair and I couldn't hear ya." She ran her hand over her shoulder-length hair. It was pale yellow like dried wheat and appeared to have the texture of straw. "I need to go condition it before it dries."

"Yes, don't let us keep you," Aunt Alma said politely.

"I flew in last night from Dallas, Texas," Breezy called from the bathroom, "so I just made myself at home. I took the bed by the window. Hope y'all don't mind."

"That's all right." Katrina looked at the beds, then at Aunt Alma. Both beds were heaped with clothes and shoes and things. It looked like enough clothes to outfit a small town.

Breezy emerged from the bathroom, rubbing something into her hair. "I just started unpacking all over the place, but you can just toss those things on my bed if ya like." She smiled. "Hey, I bet y'all won't need much room in the closet. That's good news for me."

"I brought three dresses," Katrina told her.

"*Ja*, so did I," Aunt Alma said.

"You're staying in this room too?" Breezy frowned.

"She will sleep with me," Katrina said. "Brandy told me it was all right."

"You already saw Brandy?"

"*Ja*, she picked us up in her big black car," Aunt Alma said. "So big, it could hold a dozen people in it."

"Brandy picked you up in a limo?" Breezy seemed displeased. "I had to take a taxi."

"She said she cannot pick up all contestants," Aunt Alma told her. "But she said Katrina is special."

Breezy's eyes narrowed slightly.

"Brandy was probably worried that we'd get lost," Katrina said. "We're not used to cities and getting around."

Breezy's brow softened. "Yeah, that's probably true. You'll have to excuse me. Some people say we Texans act like we own the world." She laughed. "Brandy is sweet, though, isn't she?" Without waiting for a response, she went back to the bathroom and closed the door with a bang. Katrina and Aunt Alma began to move Breezy's clothes from their bed.

"Should we hang them on hangers?" Aunt Alma asked.

"*Ja*, maybe so."

Some of the slippery clothes and tops without much to hold them together didn't seem to want to stay on the hangers, so they decided to carefully fold those pieces, placing them into the drawers on Breezy's side of the room. When those got full, they used some of the drawers on the other side since they knew they wouldn't need them all.

"I don't know how she possibly walks in these shoes," Aunt Alma declared as they paired up Breezy's shoes, lining them up two rows deep on the floor of the closet.

"There are enough here for a centipede," Katrina said quietly.

Finally, all Breezy's clothes were put away. They started to unpack their own things, but as they were hanging up their dresses, Katrina was surprised to see Aunt Alma unfolding a colorful dress—the dress that had belonged to Mammi when she was young.

"What is that doing here?" Katrina asked.

Aunt Alma gave her a sheepish smile. "Sadie brought it over to the house the other day." She held up the pair of boots. "She thought you might have use for them here."

Katrina frowned. "I don't think so."

"Well, just in case." Aunt Alma studied the patchwork dress. "I wonder if Mamm made this herself. She was always good at sewing."

"*Ja*, I'll bet she did." Katrina ran her hand over the fabric.

"I brought sewing too," Aunt Alma said as she began to open up the food box. "I used my quilting fabrics to pack these jars." She took out jars of pickles, tomatoes, applesauce, and beets, lining them up in a pretty row on the counter by the coffeemaker. Then she put the perishable foods in the little refrigerator.

With their things put away, Katrina and Aunt Alma decided to tidy up the room a bit. As they made Breezy's bed, attempting to make it look just like the other one, which was a challenge, Katrina tried not to feel envious that it was near the window. Finally, with the room put back together, they sat down in the two chairs.

"Do you think Breezy is all right?" Aunt Alma asked quietly. "She's been in the bathroom an awfully long time. Do you suppose she's sick?"

"I don't know. I hope not."

Aunt Alma looked around the room. "A hotel room is like a small house," she observed. "I expected a simple bedroom like we had at the Zooks' last night. But this is better, I think."

"All three of us in a room like last night"—Katrina lowered her voice—"with all Breezy's clothes . . . would've been crowded."

"*Ja*. For sure."

Breezy came out of the bathroom again. The purple goop was gone from her face, and her hair now gleamed like a freshly groomed horse on Sunday.

"Oh, you cleaned the room." She laughed. "I guess you really are maids." She went over to peek in the closet, then looked at her bed. "Nice work. But you didn't need to do that. The hotel maids will take care of it." She looked at the clock. "Or maybe it's too late. But in the future, you don't need to make the beds."

"We always make the beds," Aunt Alma said.

"But this is a hotel. The maids are supposed to do that."

"No, no," Aunt Alma assured her. "We are supposed to do that. Idle hands are the devil's tools."

Breezy laughed, then pointed her finger at Katrina. "Do you really sing, or is this just some kind of publicity stunt for the show? I heard their ratings are way down. I hope this isn't just a scam. It's not, is it?"

156

"Katrina truly sings," Aunt Alma told her. "Go ahead, Katrina. Sing for her."

Katrina didn't feel like singing.

"Come on," Breezy begged. "I've never heard a Quaker sing before."

"We are Amish," Katrina said.

"Okay then, I've never heard an Amish girl sing before."

Katrina considered giving her a halfhearted rendition of "Puff" but then realized she could not sing unless her heart was in it. So she sang it with her usual energy, but only a few verses this time, not the whole song.

"Wow, you really can sing." Breezy sat down on the edge of her bed with an astonished expression.

"Now you sing," Aunt Alma commanded.

Breezy looked reluctant.

"Come on." Katrina imitated her. "I've never heard a Texan sing."

Breezy sang, and although her voice was loud and interesting, something about it didn't feel quite right to Katrina, although not really knowing music, she couldn't begin to explain it. Instead, she clapped her hands and thanked Breezy.

"A bunch of us are getting together downstairs for drinks," Breezy told her. "Y'all are welcome to join us if you like."

"No, thank you," Aunt Alma said. "We have water up here to drink and our food too if we are hungry. We are fine, thank you."

"You sure?" Breezy looked at Katrina.

"*Ja*, I'm sure." However, as she watched Breezy leaving later—after she'd changed her clothes several times—Katrina was not completely sure. Mostly she was curious. She wanted to see what it was the young people spoke of and did down there together. She wasn't even sure why she cared or was interested, but she was.

Even though the clock said seven thirty, Katrina and Aunt Alma both decided they were tired enough to go to bed. "It's later at home," Katrina reminded her aunt as they pulled on their nightgowns. "Everyone there will be asleep by now."

Worried that Breezy might stumble in the darkness, Katrina turned on the bathroom light and left the door partly open. But when Breezy arrived, she entered the room singing loudly and turned on all the lights.

Katrina and Aunt Alma sat up in bed, blinking into the light. When Breezy saw them, she seemed shocked, and then she began to laugh hysterically—as if they were the funniest thing she'd ever seen. She was laughing so hard that she was snorting as loud as a hungry hog.

"Are you all right?" Katrina asked as she got out of bed, peering closely at Breezy as she staggered around in her high-heeled shoes, still laughing. When Katrina got close to her she caught a whiff of something—something that reminded her of a time when Drew had come home smelling like that and acting funny, long before he got baptized and got serious about Hannah and before Daed got hurt. Daed had gotten angry and said that Drew was drunk!

"Are you drunk?" Katrina demanded.

"Nah, I'm not drunk," Breezy told her, waving a finger in her face. "Are you drunk?"

"No, of course not!" She sniffed Breezy again. "You've been drinking, though. I can smell it."

"Well, duh, I tol' ya I went down for drinks." She kicked off a shoe and nearly fell over. "Tha's drinking, isn't it?" She kicked off the other, and this time she did fall down.

"Let me help you." Katrina pulled her back up.

"I don' need no help. And I'm not gonna be a member of the goody-two-shoes club no more . . . no more, no more." She started singing again. "Hit the road, Jack."

"Come on." Katrina guided her to the bed. "You should get some sleep."

"Yep. Tha's jus' what I plan on doing." She flopped back onto her bed and with her clothes still on, fell asleep. Katrina went to the closet to retrieve a white cotton blanket she'd seen earlier. She laid it over Breezy, then went to get a drink of water. On her way back to bed, she was surprised to see that it was 2:13 a.m. Seemed awful late to be going to bed.

"Do you really think she was drunk?" Aunt Alma whispered as Katrina crawled back into bed.

"*Ja*, I think so."

"Oh, my." She sighed. "We will have to pray for her."

Before she went to sleep again, Katrina did pray for Breezy. She figured Aunt Alma was doing the same. But it was odd praying for an English girl. What did one ask God to do? Finally Katrina decided to simply ask God to bless Breezy. How could she go wrong with that? After all, the Bible said to bless your enemies. Not that Breezy was an enemy. But what could it hurt to ask God to bless her? And if Breezy was going to feel anything like Drew had felt the day after he'd gotten drunk, the poor girl would need it.

15

The next morning, Katrina and Aunt Alma both woke up a little after six. "It might be too soon to wake up Breezy," Katrina said quietly. "The English don't get up as early as we do. And she got to bed awfully late."

They tiptoed about with only the light from the bathroom, whispering as they got dressed and braided their hair and even had their breakfast. Finally it was eight o'clock, and Katrina was ready to go downstairs. "Let's open the heavy curtains and let the light in," she said. "Maybe that will help to wake her up."

Even with the light pouring in, Breezy continued to sleep. Katrina decided to nudge her. "Breezy," she said quietly. "You might want to get up now."

"Leave me alone," Breezy said with a growl. "I wanna sleep in."

"All right." Katrina stood. "But *American Star* will begin in—"

"American Star!" Breezy threw off the blanket and jumped out of bed. "What time is it?" She gaped at the clock, then shrieked. "Why didn't y'all wake me up?"

"We tried—"

"Never mind," she yelled as she tore off to the bathroom.

Katrina and Aunt Alma just exchanged looks and quietly slipped out. "I hope she's not late," Katrina said as they went down on the elevator. She had her packet of information in her arms and knew that a contestant could be "sent home" for being late. That's what they called it—*sending someone home* when they were no longer in the competition. Katrina had read it all carefully several times yesterday. Still, she wasn't so sure that even *American Star* could send her home—not if her family refused to accept her back.

Before long, they were standing in line with the other contestants. Katrina tried to ignore all the curious looks, the whispered questions, and the blatant stares they were getting. She was used to English rudeness, but she did wonder how they would feel if it were reversed. What if everyone stared at them? Some of them seemed to invite staring. She'd never seen such strange haircuts and hair colors, and it seemed that many of these people had pictures printed right on their skin. She overheard a girl complimenting another girl, pointing to her drawing of a horse with a horn and saying "Nice tattoo," so she assumed that's what the body art was called. There was also some very odd jewelry. At least she thought that was what it was, although jewelry wasn't allowed in their Ordnung. Here she saw gold and silver sticking out of noses, eyebrows, and even lips! And the clothing—or sometimes the lack of clothing—it all made Katrina want to stare too. But she controlled herself.

"Are you really going to compete?" a young man asked her. "Or are you just here to watch?"

She studied him. He was nice looking for an English

young man. His sandy brown hair was neatly cut, his face was shaven, and his brown eyes looked sincere. He was even dressed in a light blue shirt and tan pants that looked as if they'd been recently pressed. In fact, she decided, he stood out from the others for looking tidy and clean.

"*Ja.*" She nodded. "I'm here to compete."

"So you're not just a stunt like some of them are saying?"

"I don't know what they're saying."

"Some of them saw you arrive in a stretch limo yesterday. With Brandy and some cameramen. They think you're a setup. Probably to improve ratings."

She frowned. "I'm not really sure what you mean. But I assure you, I am here to sing."

He grinned. "Sorry, I didn't mean to offend you. My name's Tyler Jones. I'm here to sing too."

"I'm sorry," she told him. "I didn't mean to be rude. My name is Katrina Yoder."

"I know. Everyone knows who you are."

She blinked, trying not to show her surprise. "This is my aunt, Alma Yoder."

He shook both their hands. "Nice to meet you. Where are you from?"

"Holmes County, Ohio," Aunt Alma proudly proclaimed.

"I'm from Indiana. That makes us kinda like neighbors."

"*Ja* . . . I suppose that's true."

"You're Amish, right?"

"That's right."

"We drove through an Amish community once," he said with enthusiasm. "I thought it was so cool. I told my parents that when I grew up I was going to become Amish too."

Katrina couldn't help but laugh.

"I meant it. I like all that old-fashioned stuff. I think I could do it."

"It's not just about living the old ways," Katrina told him. "It's about serving God too. And serving others."

"But they let you come do this?" He waved his hand.

Katrina let out a sigh, but before she had to answer, someone was up on the stage in front, trying to get everyone's attention. "It's time to take your seats," the man said. "You can sit wherever you like this time. But only contestants, please."

Katrina looked at her aunt. "I think that means you have to go now."

"I will wait out there." She pointed out the door.

"You have your key," Katrina reminded her, "if you need to go to the room for anything. Or just to put your feet up."

Aunt Alma laughed. "Put my feet up at this time of day?"

Katrina just waved, and then, with Tyler trailing her, she found a seat and he sat right next to her. Suddenly Bruce Betner was on the stage, talking into the microphone. "Welcome, everyone," he told them. He took a few minutes to introduce the panel of judges, who were sitting down in front of the stage. It sounded as if they were all very experienced in the music business.

"Well, here we are," Bruce said cheerfully. "The fun is about to begin. As you can see in your packets, you've been given a number for this morning. That number is for the elimination round. There are ten contestants in each group. When your number is called, you will come up to the stage and have a sing-off with the others in your group. You only get one minute to sing, so have your song ready to go. And there are no do-overs. If you blow it, you blow it, and it'll be adios, amigo."

Katrina frowned, trying to make sense of what he'd just said.

"That means goodbye, you're going home," Tyler whispered.

She nodded.

"Okay, it's time for all you lucky number ones to get on up here. There will be no mikes. Just you and your pipes and the judges. Come on up, group number one. You're on."

As ten contestants from different parts of the room hurried up to the stage, Bruce continued to talk. "Those of you in group number two can come up here to the holding area. You'll be on deck and ready to go. Group three follows, and you get the picture. Remember, if you're late or a no-show, that's it. No second chances at this stage of the game. Today is all about eliminations. We are thinning the herd." He laughed, then looked over his shoulder. "Great, it looks like all ten of group number one made it. Good job, guys and gals. Now who's the lucky person with number 1-A for this morning? As you probably guessed, that means you go first."

A petite, dark-haired girl raised her hand.

"Tell us your name and where you're from and the title of your song, and go."

"I'm Lulu Bannister from Atlanta, Georgia, and I'm singing 'Rolling in the Deep.'" The room was quiet as she sang a song that Katrina had never heard. But she seemed to have a good voice, and when she finished—after Bruce waved his hands for her to stop—everyone clapped with enthusiasm, including Katrina. On they went until all ten had their one minute of singing. Some, like Lulu, were good and everyone clapped. Others struggled, like a boy named Brandon who was so nervous his voice cracked. Katrina felt sorry for him.

Then the judges talked amongst themselves, and after a bit they told some singers to step forward and some to step back and some to step to the left and then the right. Finally only Lulu Bannister stood in the middle of the stage.

"Congratulations, Lulu," Celeste called out from where the judges were seated. "You have made it to the next level."

Katrina was shocked that only one had been chosen. Some of the contestants were actually crying, and one girl was begging for a second chance—to sing again.

"Are the other nine really going home?" she whispered to Tyler. "Already?"

He nodded glumly. "This is how it works." Yet based on the comments she was hearing, it seemed that almost everyone was as shocked as Katrina. Would they all be sent home?

"I wonder if the judges are in a bad mood," Tyler said quietly as the second bunch of singers assembled themselves on the stage. They looked even more nervous than the first group. "What group are you in?" he asked her.

"Group six," she told him.

"I'm in group four."

Katrina was relieved to see that four people from this group made it to the next level. As group three went onstage, Tyler went down to the holding area. Katrina watched as they took turns singing, including Breezy. Apparently she had made it downstairs in time after all, but would she be able to sing? To Katrina's relief, not only did Breezy sing, but she seemed to do a good job, and everyone clapped with enthusiasm. When it was time to "send people home," Breezy remained.

Next Tyler's group was going up. It looked like Tyler would be the third one to sing. Katrina wondered if his voice was any good. The first two singers didn't seem very special, but when Tyler sang what sounded like a ballad (which she now knew was what story songs were called), his voice was clear and strong and interesting. She thought he might have a real chance of staying. She hoped he would make it.

She held her breath as the judges rearranged his group, having them move forward and back. Finally Tyler and three others were told that they'd made the cut.

As the next group went to the stage, she knew it was time for her to go to the holding area. Her knees were shaking so badly, it felt strange to walk. As she walked, she silently prayed—begging God to help her to do this or send her home, assuming her family would take her. She straightened the strings on her white *kapp*, then smoothed her freshly pressed apron with trembling hands. Although she'd worn her favorite green dress and clean black stockings and had even polished her Sunday-best black shoes, she knew she looked very different from everyone here. She knew that her clothing was causing people to look curiously and to whisper amongst themselves. She told herself there was nothing she could do about this, but it made her even more nervous.

Katrina was so filled with anxiety, she couldn't really listen as the next group sang. It was as if her ears were stuffed with cotton. When the judges began to speak, she tried to pay attention. She felt even worse when she realized that only two girls had escaped being sent home. It seemed the judges were being very picky.

"Okay, group six, come on up," Bruce said merrily, as if he was inviting them in for cookies and milk and not elimination.

Katrina knew she would be the third one to sing. She knew what song she planned to sing. According to Bekka, it had been described on the computer as Willow Tree's biggest hit.

The song was called "Windy Grove," and Katrina loved singing it. She knew that Mammi had cowritten it with her friend Willy Brown. Whether it was because of the lilting music or the sweet words, singing it always made Katrina happy.

When her turn came, she gave them her information. Then, pushing out all thoughts of everything except the song, she took a deep breath and sang with abandon, putting her whole heart into it. When Bruce waved his hands for her to stop—after her minute was up—someone in the audience yelled out, "Let her keep singing." Several others called out too.

"Hopefully we'll get to hear more from her later," Bruce told them, "but for now it's just one minute for everyone."

Everyone was clapping and cheering and whistling, and Katrina felt tears coming. Even if she did get sent home like so many of them, this was a truly wonderful moment. They liked her—she knew it in her soul. She couldn't wait to tell Aunt Alma how well these English kids had responded to her.

After hearing the last one in the group—a girl who partly yelled and partly sang—the judges began telling the singers to move back and forth and left and right. Katrina obeyed their instructions but was starting to feel confused and flustered because it seemed she'd been all over the stage. Would they ever decide? Finally she was the only one standing out in front.

Ricky Rodriguez waved his hand toward the stage. "Everyone behind Katrina Yoder, we thank you for your time, but you can go home now."

She felt her heart pounding. Was she the only one in her group who had made it? Just like the first group? It seemed impossible.

"You're safe, Katrina," Celeste assured her. "You're not going home."

"Thank you!" Katrina said as she began to exit the stage. As relieved as she felt, she couldn't help but feel sorry for the others as they slunk away, some of them crying openly. With a pounding heart, she hurried down the steps, watching each one lest she fall on her face, because she knew it could happen—in fact, it probably would happen. Before this was all over, before they sent her home, she would probably fall on her face. Somehow she just knew it.

16

Breezy grabbed Katrina by the arm before she found her way back to her seat. "Come with me," Breezy said urgently, guiding her to one of the exit doors.

"Is something wrong?"

"No. I just want to talk to you. But not in here," she whispered.

"Don't we have to stay here?"

"No, it's okay."

Breezy led Katrina out into the big hallway where a number of contestants were milling around, some in tears because they were going home and some dancing around joyfully. It was a strange mix. Just as Katrina spotted Aunt Alma sitting on a bench, working on some quilting, Tyler hurried over to join them.

"You were great, Katrina." He grinned. "Really super. I never would've guessed you could sing like that. I was totally blown away."

"Thank you . . . I think. Why were you blowing away?"

"Don't worry, it's a good thing," Breezy told her. Then she turned to Tyler with a frown. "So who are you?"

171

Katrina introduced them.

"And you're still in it?" Breezy asked him.

"Yeah. I made the first cut."

"Tyler sang beautifully," Katrina told her.

"I guess I missed it. I barely made it here in time for my own group, and then I went, uh, to the restroom afterward."

"You sang really well too," Tyler told her. "I heard you."

"We need a coalition," Breezy told Katrina.

"A what?"

"We need to join forces," Breezy said. "The next competition will probably be groups of four or five. We need to start forming our group."

"That's true," Tyler confirmed. "That's usually how it goes."

"Will we each sing for a minute again? Or more?"

"No, it's not like that." Breezy quickly explained that they would all sing a song together. "And we'll need choreography too."

"What?" Katrina was lost.

"Don't worry, we'll help you," Tyler said.

"So are we three together?" Breezy asked hopefully.

"*Ja.*" Katrina nodded. "Sure, I think so."

"We'll still need one or two more," Breezy said. "I'll go back in and watch and see who the best candidates might be." She reached out and shook hands with each of them. "So we have a deal then? The three of us and one or two more?"

They both agreed.

"Because everyone is going to want to sing with Katrina," she told Tyler. "She's like the hottest commodity here."

"What?" Katrina was even more confused. Sometimes it seemed like the English spoke a completely different language.

Breezy pointed at a cameraman coming their way. "See, that's what I'm talking about, Katrina. The cameras love you. The closer the other contestants can get to you, the better their chances of getting more camera time. We gotta protect you."

"Hey, Katrina," a young woman walking with the cameraman said, "you were great out there. Tell us how you're feeling right now."

"Very confused," she admitted.

They laughed. "That's understandable," the woman told her. "I'm guessing you didn't grow up watching *American Star* like some kids."

Katrina just shook her head. "No, not at all."

"I grew up watching *American Star*," Tyler said quietly. "My mom . . . before she died . . . absolutely loved this show. Even when she was in the hospital, she and I would lie there in her bed watching it."

The cameraman pointed his camera at Tyler, and the woman held her mike in front of him. "You're Tyler Jones from Indiana, aren't you? Nice job out there today. I'm sorry about your mother. Go ahead and repeat what you just said, this time so the viewers can hear you."

Tyler's brown eyes glistened as he explained how his mom had gone through several years of cancer treatments. "It's because of her that I'm here doing this."

"Tell us what you think she'd be feeling right now, Tyler."

"She would be real proud. Mom always loved hearing me sing. She said it made the pain go away. She used to tell me that I'd be on this show someday."

"How long ago did she pass away?"

"A little more than a year ago."

"So you and Katrina have something in common. Her

grandmother died recently too. Right, Katy?" The woman smiled. "Is it okay to call you Katy?"

Katrina shrugged. "I don't mind. I went by Katrina because there were three other Katys at my school."

The woman laughed. "Okay then, maybe I should call you Katrina. Anyway, your grandmother was your inspiration for competing in *American Star*, right?"

Katrina considered this. "My grandmother was a singer. But I am competing here because I want to pay for my father's surgery. It's very expensive, and my friend thought I might have a chance to win some money." She felt her cheeks warming, wishing she hadn't said that. It sounded as if she thought she was going to win. "But I didn't know there were so many contestants or that the show would take so many days. Now I'm not so sure . . . about anything."

"I'll bet you're feeling pretty overwhelmed."

Katrina just nodded. Then, noticing that Breezy looked a little left out, she pointed at her. "But my roommate, Breezy, is helpful. And she sang very well this morning. She isn't going home yet either."

"Breezy"—the woman held the mike in front of her—"how is it having an Amish girl for a roommate?"

"Well, she doesn't use much closet space," Breezy told her. "And she and her aunt keep cleaning our room. I told them there are hotel maids to do that, but they don't seem to care. You should've seen how neatly they made their bed this morning."

"Maybe we'll send a camera crew to your room," the woman said, "to give an inside peek. I'm sure our viewers would love that."

She asked them all a few more questions, then finally moved

on to some other contestants—both the ones being sent home and the ones staying.

"That's nice they take time to speak to the ones not winning too," Katrina said to Tyler as Breezy hurried back into the ballroom.

"It's because it makes for good TV," he told her. "Viewers like seeing the winners and the losers."

"Oh." Katrina again noticed her aunt, sitting with her head bowed down as she sewed. "Do you want to meet my aunt?" Tyler seemed eager to meet Aunt Alma, and after telling her that they'd both made it through the first round and eating some of the food that Aunt Alma had brought along with her, they decided to go back inside to hear the others singing. By the end of the day, the group of two hundred had been cut down to seventy-five. Just as Breezy had predicted, it was announced that the next round of the competition would be with groups of five singers.

"We're going to have a blast from the past. Everyone will be singing songs from the sixties," Bruce told them all. "Beatles, Stones, Turtles, Supremes, Jefferson Airplane, Iron Butterfly." He laughed. "You get the picture. Since none of you were exactly around way back then, we've got lists of suggestions in the back. You'll have the rest of today and all of tomorrow to work on your act. Competition will start first thing on Wednesday morning." He grinned. "Congratulations to today's winners. Enjoy it while you can, because after the next elimination almost half of you will be heading home."

"He can be such a buzz kill sometimes," Tyler said.

"Buzz kill?"

Tyler laughed. "Always reminding us that we can be history."

"Hey." Breezy grabbed Katrina by the elbow. "You gotta

meet these two." She tipped her head to a guy wearing a big black hat and the petite, dark-haired girl who had been the only person in group one not sent home. "Cowboy and Lulu."

The guy in the hat shook their hands. "My real name is Tommy, but everyone here is calling me Cowboy."

Lulu smiled at Katrina. "You were really good. I had no idea Amish could sing."

"We need to get busy," Breezy told them. "Let's go out in the hallway where we can talk privately. I've got my iPad so we can start pulling up tunes." She snatched one of the papers listing the song suggestions.

"I listen to songs from the sixties," Katrina told them as Breezy ushered them down a hallway. "I really like Peter, Paul and Mary."

"No, not them," Breezy said. "Too tame."

Suddenly they were all talking, going over the list and arguing about what group was the best and what song to sing. Katrina finally got tired of the bickering. "Excuse me," she told them. "I need to go check on my aunt." Relieved to escape the noise, she hurried over to where Aunt Alma was still working on the quilt. "How are you doing?" she asked.

Aunt Alma looked up and smiled. "I am not used to sitting so much." She stood and rubbed her back. "Are we done now?"

Katrina explained about the new group of five and how they were supposed to choose a song and practice it a little. "Why don't you go back to our room? It's after seven o'clock."

Aunt Alma seemed reluctant, but Katrina insisted. "I'll be with Breezy," she assured her. "We'll come up together when we're done."

Aunt Alma frowned. "Breezy might want to go drinking again."

"I don't think so." Katrina explained that she'd read in the *American Star* rules that any contestants caught in underage drinking would be automatically eliminated, and she knew that Breezy was only nineteen. "I plan to warn her of this."

Aunt Alma nodded. "Good for you. I hope she listens. But remember, you can preach a better sermon with your life than with your lips."

"*Ja*. That's true."

Aunt Alma handed Katrina some of the leftover food from lunch, including a slightly smashed peanut butter and marshmallow spread sandwich. "You must eat," she insisted. "Keep up your strength."

Katrina thanked her, pausing to give thanks before she hungrily devoured the food. "You go and eat your supper too," she told her aunt. Feeling somewhat fortified, Katrina returned to her new friends and was informed that they'd chosen the song "Aquarius" for their performance.

"It was originally recorded by the Fifth Dimension," Tyler explained. "Their voices might be similar to ours."

"Cowboy already went to register us," Breezy said, "so no one else can take that song."

"Aquarius?" Katrina tried to remember. "Yes, I think I've heard that on the radio."

"I just loaded it on my iPod," Breezy said. "And Tyler's got it on his iPad."

"I what?" Katrina frowned.

"Never mind." Breezy held up a sheet of paper. "We already wrote out the lyrics. Fortunately, it's a pretty simple song. But it's got all kinds of possibilities for harmony and solos and rearranging."

Katrina felt lost again. But she studied the words on the

paper, and then someone started playing the music from a flat plastic thing. She couldn't believe all the things that could play music. Before long the five of them were singing it together. It was amazing how their voices, though all very different, actually sounded nice when combined. It reminded Katrina of how very different tasting ingredients, like salt, vanilla, baking soda, sugar, eggs, and flour, could be mixed together to make a delicious cake.

Breezy seemed to enjoy telling everyone what to do. Sometimes Cowboy and Lulu argued with her, but eventually they agreed. After they'd sung the song so many times that they all knew the words by heart, Breezy and Cowboy began directing the singers to move around as if they were on a stage.

"I'm not good at this," Katrina admitted after bumping into someone for about the tenth time. "Maybe I should just sit and watch."

"Your voice is so good that you make up for not dancing," Lulu told her. "But how about if we simplify the choreography. Let's put Katrina in the center, and the four of us will dance around her. She can move forward and back, and hopefully no one will notice that she's not really dancing."

Eventually, they worked out a routine that everyone seemed to like—and Katrina was able to do. But Katrina was so tired that her head was beginning to throb. She knew it was past eleven o'clock and long past her usual bedtime. "I'm sorry," she finally told them, "but I need to get some sleep."

"Katrina's right," Tyler said. "We all need to get some sleep. We have all of tomorrow to get it really finessed."

"But the night is still young," Breezy insisted. "Y'all are a bunch of party poopers."

"What did you have in mind?" Cowboy asked her.

"Let's all go get something to drink," Breezy said. "Anyone else? I mean, besides Katrina."

Katrina cleared her throat. "I read in the *American Star* rules," she began carefully, "that underage alcohol drinking is not allowed. You could be sent home."

"I'm twenty-one," Cowboy told them. "I can have a beer if I want."

"Breezy is only nineteen," Katrina told him. "She's not old enough."

"No one pays attention to those rules," Breezy said.

"Listen to Katrina," Tyler told her. "I say that anyone in our group who doesn't comply with the rules should be kicked out of our group. And I know there are plenty of other contestants who would be glad to take your place, Breezy. I just noticed a group down the hall that is having some serious issues. Maybe you want to trade with—"

"No thanks." Breezy frowned.

"He's right," Lulu agreed.

"Come on." Katrina hooked her arm in Breezy's. "You were up late last night. You need a good night's sleep more than any of us." Although it was a reluctant Breezy walking toward the elevators with them, Katrina was relieved that her roommate had given in.

"We're all investing ourselves in this competition," Lulu told Breezy. "Why take the chance of blowing it all by partying?"

Breezy shrugged. "I guess I wasn't thinking of it like that. I just wanted to have fun."

"Well, you better ask yourself if you just wanna have fun or if you wanna try to win this thing," Cowboy told her as the elevator carried them up. "If all you want is fun, you might as well go home now."

A Simple Song

As Katrina and Breezy got off on their floor, Breezy paused to remove her high-heeled shoes. "My feet are killing me," she said.

"Why do you wear shoes that hurt your feet?"

Breezy laughed as she twirled a bright pink shoe around on her finger. "Because they're hot and make me look sexy."

Katrina sighed, wondering if she would ever understand the English way of thinking. If something hurt them—like wearing painful shoes or drinking too much alcohol—why would they keep on doing it?

17

It wasn't until the following evening, after they'd done their stage rehearsal with instrumental musicians and lights and all sorts of technical things Katrina didn't understand, that Breezy began to pressure her about clothing. Aunt Alma had just delivered them a bunch of food orders—after they'd all gotten hungry at seeing what she'd brought earlier for Katrina. Now everyone was sitting on the floor in the hallway having an indoor picnic.

"It's fine for you to wear your little Amish dress if you're competing solo," Breezy told Katrina, "but when you're part of our group, it's only fair that you should dress like the rest of us. Otherwise you're putting us all at risk of getting kicked out." She peered at Katrina. "Would you really want to see us sent home just because you refused to dress appropriately?"

"Appropriately?" Katrina looked at Breezy's sleeveless shirt—if one could call it a shirt. One whole shoulder was missing. Katrina's camisole was more modest.

"We're dressing like the sixties," Breezy explained, "to go with the song."

"Yeah, I've got these funky plaid bell-bottoms," Tyler said.

"And I've got a retro minidress and white knee-high boots," Lulu told her.

"I've got these awesome paisley bell-bottoms," Breezy explained, "with a macramé halter top."

"I've got a leather vest with long fringe," Cowboy added.

"Katrina," Aunt Alma said, "you could wear Mamm's dress and boots."

"What's that?" Breezy asked.

"Something of her grandmother's," Aunt Alma explained.

"But I don't want—"

"Katrina," Breezy interrupted. "You have to cooperate with us. It's no different than me agreeing to not drink alcohol. If I give up something, you give up something."

"But her grandma's dress?" Lulu looked skeptical. "That's probably not going to work."

Suddenly they were arguing again, and Katrina's head was starting to hurt again. "Excuse me," she said as she stood up. "I need to use the restroom." The sounds of their voices followed her down the hallway, as did the sounds of the voices of other groups. Sometimes it seemed there was no place to go to escape the constant noise. Even at night she could hear the sounds of sirens and things on the street. How did English people stand it, day after day, for their entire lives?

After using the toilet, Katrina stood in front of a mirror as she washed her hands. She had never seen so many mirrors. Every bathroom had them. And not little ones, either—most of them had great big mirrors that took up entire walls. Just now it was reassuring to see her reflection. With her white *kapp* and her shawl and apron still neatly pinned in their places over her plain blue dress, she felt as if there was still a smidgeon of order left in the world. As she adjusted her *kapp* strings, she tried not to feel pride as she compared her sensible clothing to what her new friends wore. Katrina had no concerns about anything slipping off or revealing too much. Not that Breezy or Lulu, or any of the girls, for that matter, seemed particularly concerned about modesty. Even some of the boys didn't seem to mind that their undershorts showed when they bent over. Had they not heard of suspenders?

Katrina disliked feeling so judgmental and knew it was wrong to feel pride. But so many things about these young people confused her—their dress, their talk, their love of attention, their eagerness to argue—and yet she liked them. Despite all their differences, they had qualities about them that reminded her of friends at home. Breezy's bossiness and enthusiasm reminded her of Bekka. Tyler's gentle concern for her welfare reminded her of Cooper. In some ways they were worlds apart, and in some ways they were not so different.

"Are you all right?" Aunt Alma asked as she joined Katrina in the restroom.

"*Ja*. I am fine. Just tired, I think."

"Your friends are concerned that they offended you."

Katrina sighed. "No . . . I'm just confused. What do you think I should do? Would it be wrong to dress in English clothes?"

"You are in the English world . . . competing in an English contest," Aunt Alma pointed out.

"You think it's all right?"

Aunt Alma shrugged. "Only you can make that decision, Katrina."

"*Ja*. I know."

"Your friends want to practice the song some more." Aunt Alma patted Katrina on the back. "I am going to the room. Unless you need me."

"No. You go on up." She could tell Aunt Alma was weary. Katrina understood this kind of weariness—it was a tiredness that seeped into the soul. It was easier to cook and clean and garden from dawn until dusk than to live here in this English hotel with all the noise and activity. The English world was not only confusing, it was exhausting. Even the singing had lost its joy. Rehearsing the same song again and again—until she almost felt she hated it. Truly, the only thing keeping her going was the hope that she might be able to win enough money to get Daed his surgery.

Breezy and Lulu helped Katrina to dress for their performance on Wednesday. Because they weren't scheduled to compete until seven o'clock, Katrina had simply dressed in her usual clothes that morning. Naturally, this had gotten the producers' attention, and she'd been interviewed twice as to her wardrobe choices. At her group's suggestion, she'd told everyone they would have to wait and see.

"Your hair is perfect," Breezy said as she brushed out Katrina's waist-length brown hair.

"And this dress and these boots," said Lulu, "are awesome. Seriously, you could sell these on eBay for a small fortune."

"I'd buy them from you," Breezy told her. "And since we're about the same size, they'd probably fit me too."

"I can't sell them," Katrina said.

"Now for some makeup." Breezy pulled out a small tube.

"No," Katrina told her. She'd watched these girls painting their faces. She was not going to let them do it to her.

"You need just a little," Breezy said. "So you don't look shiny in the camera. You heard what Brandy said earlier."

Katrina sighed. "All right. But just enough for the camera."

"Don't worry. We're trying to look like the sixties," Breezy said. "They liked a natural look. Close your eyes and trust us."

A few minutes later, they pushed Katrina in front of the closet mirror to look at herself. But she didn't recognize the girl in front of her. "I'm not me."

"Yes, you are," Breezy said. "Just a different kind of you."

"You look really pretty," Lulu told her.

Just then Aunt Alma came in, and when she saw Katrina, she put her hand over her mouth and began giggling. "Oh, my."

"Is this a mistake?"

"No, no." Aunt Alma set a bag on the counter. She had found a nearby grocery store and visited it to replenish their supplies.

"Time to go," Breezy said. "We'll be on deck in twenty minutes."

"I wish I could watch," Aunt Alma said.

"After today—if I'm not sent home—we'll be recording at the *American Star* studio instead of the hotel, and I'll be given tickets," Katrina told her. "And you can come."

"Yeah," Lulu said. "*After* the next cuts."

"Let's go, girls." Breezy was pushing them toward the door. "Tell us to break a leg," she called to Aunt Alma.

"Oh, no, please, don't break any bones," Aunt Alma called back. Breezy and Lulu just laughed, but Katrina wondered if wearing these strange tall shoes, including Mammi's old boots, which made walking a challenge, might not be inviting a broken leg.

Tyler and Cowboy were already waiting on deck when the girls returned to the ballroom. Their group was the last one to perform, and since the eliminations would begin after the final performances, all the contestants had remained in the audience. Katrina could feel the anxiety in the air. No one wanted to be sent home. Except maybe her, although that was the selfish part of her—the other part of her wanted to win the money for Daed. This was what she kept in mind when Bruce announced that it was their turn to take the stage.

In her center position, where she knew she was supposed to take five steps forward when she did her solo and five steps back for the others to do theirs and finally move forward again for the end of the song, she took in a deep breath and waited for the music to begin. She felt like someone else as she sang the strange lyrics—words she still hadn't figured out—but wearing Mammi's old dress, she imagined she was Mammi all those many years ago. Everyone in her group did their best performance ever, and when the song ended, she knew that no one could feel sorry or guilty.

The audience seemed to agree as they erupted in applause, and the judges, clapping with equal enthusiasm, stood as if to show their approval. "We got a standing ovation," Tyler whispered to her as the crowd settled down.

"That was beautiful," Jack Smack said loudly. "Truly beautiful. I feel like you kids got it. You took us right back to the sixties, and then you did it even better. The Fifth Dimension would be proud."

"I agree," Ricky said. "Every one of you pulled your weight tonight. You kids were spot on. Good job!"

"Really, really nice," Celeste said. "Not just the arrangement, which was brilliant, but your voices and how they blended." She laughed. "Even your wardrobe is perfect." She pointed at Katrina. "And I am so proud of you, honey. I was so worried that you were going to come out in your little Amish dress. I'm sorry, but that would not have worked. If you want to compete—if you want to win *American Star*—you have to be willing to take some risks. And you did that tonight, Katrina. Good for you!"

As they exited the stage, the judges were conversing and looking at the papers in front of them, and Katrina knew they were deciding who would go and who would stay. Despite all her earlier reservations and tiredness, she did not want to be sent home. Being on the stage just now, singing together in front of everyone, was exciting and exhilarating. She felt strangely energized.

The judges brought the groups back one by one and gave them some more comments and critiques. They slowly divided people into groups, sending some to one side of the ballroom and the rest to the other. Sometimes they would send a whole group to one side, but usually they split the groups up. Finally it was Katrina's group's turn, and after some discussion, the judges sent the whole group to the left side of the room.

"Now it's time for the big moment," Bruce said from up front. "Time to find out who stays and who goes. I know you're all nervous. I can see it on your faces. And I could keep talking and making you feel even more nervous . . . but instead, I will put you out of your misery." He pointed to the right side of the room. "All you guys here—you can put your minds at ease and you can pack your bags—because you are all going home." He made an apologetic smile. "Sorry about that." Now he pointed to the left side. "And you guys—all forty of you are going to the next level. As you know, the rest of the show will be filmed at our studio."

Bruce waited for the contestants who were going home to cry and complain and hug each other until eventually they left. After that he explained what the next challenge would be for those who remained. "You need to reorganize yourselves into groups of four," he told them. "This time you'll be doing a song from the seventies. Groups of four doing the seventies. Tomorrow will be another practice day, and Friday you will perform. Good luck and goodnight."

As everyone began scrambling to find groups of four, Breezy, Lulu, Cowboy, Tyler, and Katrina clustered together in a corner. Of course, a cameraman was filming the whole thing. "One of us has gotta go," Breezy said quickly. "And the sooner we decide, the better chance that person will have of getting in a good group. Now, I think it makes sense for a girl to go. That way we'll have two girls and two guys."

Everyone nodded, but no one said anything.

Katrina bit her lip. As much as she didn't want to go out and find a new group, she knew that she should offer to leave. "I'll go," she told them.

"No, wait," Tyler said. "If you go, I'm going too."

"Don't do that." Breezy held up her hands. "Let's vote. If y'all agree one girl should go, let's just vote." She held up her forefinger. "One stands for me." Now she held up two fingers. "Two for Katrina. And three is for Lulu. Hands behind your backs." When the vote was counted, even though Katrina voted for herself to go, Lulu was the one who got voted out.

"I'm sorry," Katrina told her. "I hope you find a good group."

Lulu looked partly sad and partly mad as she hurried away.

Once again, they began to discuss and argue over songs. Breezy wanted to do "Hotel California," but Tyler wanted "Stairway to Heaven" and Cowboy wanted to sing "American

Pie." Finally they put it to a vote, which essentially meant it was up to Katrina to choose since she was the only one who hadn't suggested a song. Truthfully, she wasn't that familiar with these songs, although she'd heard "Stairway to Heaven" before, and even though she didn't know the lyrics, she had been intrigued by it. So it was decided they would do the Led Zeppelin song, and while Cowboy ran over to tell the producers they were taking this song, the others began to copy down the words from Tyler's iPad.

"That's a lot of words," Katrina said.

"We'll break it into parts," Breezy suggested, "so no one has to memorize the whole thing." Suddenly she was assigning sections and working on an arrangement. How she knew how to do this was a mystery to Katrina, but she didn't argue with her. When Cowboy returned, they started to practice, singing along with the iPad until they mostly had their words and their parts down. It was getting very late, and Katrina knew she needed to go to bed.

"I think it's quitting time," Tyler said.

As usual, Breezy resisted, but eventually the other three convinced her that they'd be fresher and more clear-headed in the morning, and they called it a night.

"I almost forgot you were Amish," Breezy told Katrina as they were walking to their room. "You seemed like just a normal girl tonight."

Katrina looked down at the strange and colorful dress, wondering how a garment could make a person seem like someone else. The truth was, she hadn't felt Amish tonight. Not that she'd exactly felt English either. Maybe she was just caught between the two worlds . . . slowly slipping between the cracks.

18

The next morning, Katrina felt more like herself as she and Aunt Alma ate breakfast in the dimly lit room. This had become their routine: rising early and quietly dressing, tiptoeing around as Breezy slept, eating breakfast, cleaning up. At seven thirty they would open the heavy drapes, letting the light shine in, and Katrina would nudge Breezy and tell her it was time to get up.

"Are you sure you don't want some breakfast?" Aunt Alma asked, just like she always did. "We have plenty of food to share."

"No way." Breezy yawned. "I don't know how y'all eat breakfast every morning like you do."

"I don't know how you can keep on going eating as little as you do." Aunt Alma shook her head.

"Trust me, I would be fat as a pig if I ate as much as Katrina," Breezy said as she went into the bathroom.

Katrina and Aunt Alma made Breezy's bed and tidied up a bit more before they headed downstairs to take a little walk around the hotel. As they walked, Katrina told her aunt of her new resolve. "I'm going to compete as myself from now on," she said. "I'm going to wear my own clothes, and I refuse to compromise."

Aunt Alma just nodded.

"If I can't win just being myself, I don't deserve to win." They had finished the whole big loop and were back near the elevators. By now Katrina had convinced her aunt that she didn't need to act like Katrina's personal security guard, especially now that they'd be riding the shuttle bus to the *American Star* studio, so when they saw Breezy emerge from the elevator, Aunt Alma said she was going to the little grocery store. But as she left, Katrina noticed a sad and slightly lost expression in her aunt's eyes. Kind of how Katrina felt most of the time.

"Ready to rock and roll?" Breezy said as she joined Katrina.

"Rock and roll?"

"Never mind." Breezy laughed as they walked out to where the bus was waiting to take them to the studio.

As they sat down on the bus, Breezy began to chatter at her. "I dreamed about the lady who is buying the stairway to heaven last night. Can you believe it? In my dream this rich woman who looked just like Carrie Underwood had a giant handbag, and she was shopping for stars in heaven. I tried to sell her some plastic stars, but she didn't want what I was peddling—so I started singing to her. That's when I woke up with a whole new song going through my head. Too bad I didn't have time to write it down. It was actually pretty good."

"Are you a songwriter?"

"Yeah. I've got a whole notebook full of songs that I hope to record someday." She frowned. "Man, I wish I'd brought my guitar on the plane. I really miss it."

"Why didn't you bring it?"

"Because I had so much clothes and stuff I wanted to get out here. So I had my mom ship my guitar to me. It should be here by now. Remind me to check for it at the desk later."

Before long they were at the studio, which was massive but plain-looking—until they got inside, where there was a huge stage with rows and rows of seats encircling it. Cameras and lights were everywhere, and crews of people were scrambling about. Before long their group found a quiet corner backstage where they could practice. Later the groups would take turns rehearsing on the stage, where they'd also talk to the crews about their upcoming performance, picking out backgrounds and lights and props. Fortunately, Breezy was happy to take charge for their group. Although Cowboy and Tyler had opinions, they usually went with Breezy's plans since she always seemed to know what was best. Katrina simply watched and listened. It was like learning a new language.

After a midday restroom break, Katrina and Breezy were stopped by Brandy and a cameraman. "Hey, girls," Brandy said. "Really nice job last night. So, tell me, are you both feeling jazzed and upbeat now?"

"Yeah." Breezy nodded eagerly. "We've picked a great song, and we're really getting it down today."

"We heard you pushed Lulu off to another group. Do you think that was the right decision?"

"I was sad to see her go," Katrina admitted.

"Our quartet is strong," Breezy assured her. "I think the judges will be pleased when they hear us tomorrow."

"Katrina." Brandy pointed the mike at her. "I see you're wearing your Amish clothes again. Mind if I ask—what's up with that?"

Katrina was unsure. "I, uh, these are my clothes. What else would I wear?"

"Well, I suppose our viewers will be wondering . . . I mean, last night you didn't look Amish . . . today you do. What's it going to be?"

"I don't understand."

"I mean, what do you plan to wear when you perform tomorrow?"

"I, uh, I don't know." Katrina glanced at Breezy, but she just shrugged. "I thought my green dress perhaps."

"Do you realize that people—including our esteemed judges—are saying you have a chance to win this thing, Katrina? Your voice is that good. The show has barely started to air, and already the buzz is beginning."

"Buzz?" She imagined the bees around her family's honey hives.

"The entertainment shows on TV. Haven't you heard the rumble?"

"What?"

"You know, 'the Amish girl with the voice of an angel,'" Brandy declared. "Don't you even turn on the TV in your room?"

Breezy laughed. "No way. Even when I get a chance to turn on the TV, Katrina and her aunt always insist I angle it toward my bed and keep the volume down low."

"We're curious, Katrina," Brandy persisted. "How badly do you want this thing? What does it mean to you?"

"You mean to win?" Katrina asked meekly.

"Yeah. What are you willing to sacrifice to become the next American Star?"

Katrina felt the cameraman moving in closer. "I don't know for sure."

"Because to win *American Star*, you can't just sing like a star, you've got to look and act like a star too." Brandy's brow creased. "Are you willing to do that? Can you take it to the next level? Our viewers are going to want to know."

Katrina bit her lip. "I'm not sure what that really means. But I do want to win . . . at least enough to get my daed his surgery."

"But you understand that after tomorrow night, the viewers will be voting, don't you?"

"Voting?"

"They call or email," Breezy explained, "and they vote for different contestants."

"People usually look forward to some support from their hometown crowd." Brandy chuckled. "Do you think we can expect the *Amish vote*?"

"No, no . . . I don't think so." Katrina shook her head. "The Amish don't watch TV. No one from home will vote for me." She almost added that Bekka might vote but that she'd be the only one. However, she knew that one vote would make little difference.

"You do realize that you'll have to appeal to the other voters out there, don't you? You've got to make those viewers love you and want for you to win. That's no easy task."

Katrina suddenly remembered the time Cal had told her to jump into Daadi's grain silo. It only had a few feet of grain in it at the time, and the cool feeling of sinking into the silky wheat grains had felt wonderful at first. But when she'd realized she could barely move her arms and legs—and that she couldn't get out—she'd started to panic. Feeling as if she were being swallowed by the grain, she'd pleaded with Cal to pull her out. That was how she felt right now—like *American Star* was pulling her down, and she couldn't get out.

"Don't worry." Breezy smiled into the camera. "I'll ask the people in my town to vote for both of us. You hear that, Dallas, Texas? I hope you'll vote for this little girl too. She's got one terrific voice."

"That's generous," Brandy told her.

Breezy smiled brightly as she wrapped an arm around Katrina's shoulders. "We're friends. Why wouldn't I want to help her?"

"Well, I can't wait to see your performance tomorrow," Brandy told them. "And now I'll let you get on with your rehearsing. Good luck!"

After a long day of practicing their song, rehearsing on-stage, and working with all the sound guys, light technicians, and musicians, Breezy declared it was time for a meeting.

"A meeting?" Cowboy questioned. "About what?"

"A wardrobe planning meeting," she explained. "As y'all know—well, except maybe Katrina here since she's never actually watched the show—after we make it into the top twenty, which I expect we will—"

"That's pretty optimistic," Tyler said.

She grinned. "Have you heard any of the other groups? I'd say our chances of winning are superb."

"Don't count your eggs before they're laid," Katrina said.

"I thought it was hatched," Tyler said.

"No, I believe it's laid," Katrina told him.

"Anyway, back to this meeting," Breezy said sharply. "As I was saying, after we make it into the top twenty, which I optimistically believe will happen, we will have stylists to help us with wardrobe and hair and everything. But as you know, we're still on our own for tomorrow's performance.

Even so, we need to look hot. I mean really hot. So let's coordinate our wardrobe now." She began to describe what she planned to wear—a heavy dress that Katrina had hung up the other day after she'd held it in the sunlight, where it sparkled like polished brass. "Because I sing the opening verse about the lady who thinks all that glitters is gold, I think my gold sequined gown is perfect." She pointed at Katrina. "You can wear my dark green satin dress. It'll look great on you."

"But I—"

"No arguments. The dress really works with your lyrics—remember the tree by the brook? That's like the green gown and—"

"But I already have a green dress," Katrina told her. "Why can't I just—"

"We're part of a group, Katrina. If you don't look like you're part of our group, you will bring us all down. You heard what Brandy said earlier. If you want to be a star, you have to *look* like a star." She pointed to Katrina's simple blue dress. "And I'm sorry, sweetheart, but that is just not star material." She looked at the guys. "Am I right or am I right?"

They both just nodded. Breezy went over what the guys would wear, and after one more run-through of the song, it was time to get back onto the shuttle bus and return to the hotel. Katrina rode back in silence. She felt defeated. As badly as she wanted to stand her ground and insist on dressing in her Amish clothing, she had given in. She folded her arms across her front, staring out at the dusky sky and city lights. She used to think of herself as a strong person, but more and more she saw herself as a pushover. She almost hoped that she would get sent home tomorrow.

Back in their hotel room, Katrina saw that her aunt had finished piecing together her quilt top and had spread it across their bed in a pretty pattern of blues and purples and black squares.

"It looks very nice," Katrina told Aunt Alma.

"*Ja*. It makes me feel at home." Aunt Alma smiled sadly.

"Are you homesick?" Katrina asked.

"Homesick?"

Katrina explained what Sadie had told her.

"*Ja*, I suppose I am homesick."

Katrina nodded. "*Ja* . . . me too."

They weren't scheduled to go to the studio until four o'clock the next day. As a result, Breezy insisted on sleeping in until nearly noon. Katrina and Aunt Alma couldn't imagine how it was even possible for someone to sleep so long. They walked around the hotel lobby and went to the grocery store, and just as they were heading for the elevators, they were met by Brandy and a cameraman.

"Just the ones I'm looking for," Brandy said. "I'd hoped you'd let us come visit your room."

"Our room?" Katrina glanced at her aunt. "But Breezy is probably still sleeping."

"That's okay." Brandy grinned. "This is, after all, a reality show. Mind if we follow you up?"

"All right," Katrina agreed halfheartedly. "If you think Breezy won't mind."

Breezy was just getting up when they came into the room. "What're y'all doing here?" she asked, ducking into the bathroom. "I haven't even done my face yet."

"It's okay," Brandy called out. "We just want to see how

the Amish live." She pointed to the quilt on the bed. "Now will you look at that. Very pretty."

"Aunt Alma just made that," Katrina explained. "She's one of the best quilt makers in our settlement."

"No, no, that's not true. Many women are much better sewers than me."

"And look at this." Brandy moved over to where the colorful jars of preserved foods still lined the counter. There was also a small bouquet of daisies that Aunt Alma had gotten for Katrina—to make her feel more at home. "Isn't this quaint?"

"Aunt Alma canned those foods," Katrina told them. "Her pickled beets are the best."

Aunt Alma opened the little fridge. "And you see, we have cheeses and sausages and lots of good things to eat."

"You're making me hungry," Brandy told her.

"We can fix you some lunch, if you like," Aunt Alma said.

"No, but thanks anyway. So would you say that this is like how you live at home?" Brandy asked Katrina. "With your quilts and foods around you?"

Katrina shook her head. "This is nothing like home."

"What do you miss most about home?"

Katrina sighed. "I miss the grass and the trees . . . and my garden. I really miss my garden." She felt tears in her eyes. "And my family . . . I really miss my family. And my friends."

"But you mentioned the grass and trees and your garden first," Brandy said quickly. "I'm curious. Do you miss those more than the people?"

"I miss the green growing things because I don't see much of that here. But there are lots of people here. And I've made some new friends. Breezy and Tyler and Cowboy. And Lulu. And you. And of course, I have my aunt. But it's true I do miss the trees and grass." She sighed. "And the simplicity. I miss the simplicity."

Brandy seemed to be thinking about this. "Hearing you speaking of it like that . . . and having been to visit your farm . . . well, I almost miss it too." Brandy looked into the camera. "Who knows? By the time *American Star* ends, we might all want to become Amish." She laughed, then turned back to Katrina. "By the way, Jack Smack is setting up a meeting for you with Larry Zimmerman from the old sixties group Willow Tree. Are you looking forward to that?"

She nodded eagerly. "Yes. I have so many questions about Mammi."

Brandy explained to the camera that Katrina's grandmother had sung with Willow Tree. "Some of our viewers aren't familiar with Starla Knight, but she was one of the great folksingers of the sixties. After a short but illustrious career, she disappeared so completely that most people assumed she had died. But now we know that she simply became Amish." She peered curiously at Katrina. "Do you know why she ended her career so abruptly?"

Katrina slowly shook her head. "I don't know. But I hope that her friend Larry Zimmerman will have some answers to my questions."

Brandy smiled. "I hope so too."

Breezy emerged from the bathroom with her face made up and every hair in place. But it seemed clear that Brandy didn't want to spend much time with her. "See you girls later. Good luck tonight."

Breezy seemed a little let down when they left. "It's like I said, Katrina—the cameras love you. You're the big story. 'The Amish girl with the voice of an angel.' It's all over the airwaves." But the way Breezy was saying all this sounded unconvincing. Or maybe it was just insincere. Katrina wasn't sure she really understood Breezy. Sometimes she seemed sweet and kind and reminded her of Bekka. Other times she reminded Katrina of Aunt Fannie.

There wasn't time to think about such things now, though, since they had to pack up everything they would need for this evening's performance. Fortunately, Breezy took charge. Katrina simply followed her directions. When it was time to go, Katrina and Aunt Alma offered to carry the two bags filled with dresses, shoes, makeup, and hair things . . . and Breezy let them.

As they rode to the studio, Katrina wondered if this might be her last night to compete and how she would feel if it were. The truth was, she didn't really care if they sent her home tomorrow. She was more than just tired of the show—she was fed up. But then she remembered how she'd felt just the same way before the last competition, and yet when it had all been said and done, after the crowd had clapped and cheered, she'd been elated. And she'd been even more elated when she didn't get sent home. Perhaps she no longer knew herself so well . . . or perhaps she'd simply lost sight of what really mattered.

19

Once again, Breezy took charge of getting Katrina ready for the stage, but only after Breezy was completely dressed with her makeup and hair done to perfection—or at least to Breezy's idea of perfection. "It's a good thing you don't much care how you look," Breezy told Katrina as she smeared some pinkish lip color onto Katrina's mouth. "It does make this go faster." She pushed Katrina in front of the mirror now. "There, how does that look?"

"Like someone else," Katrina confessed.

"Good. That's what we're going for. Especially since we've already been labeled the goody-two-shoes group."

"You said that before." Katrina remembered the night Breezy came back to the room drunk. "What does that mean?"

"It means we've got a reputation for being polite, rule-abiding, sweet Christian kids." She wrinkled her nose.

"But that's a good thing."

Breezy's mouth twisted to one side as she brushed something onto Katrina's cheeks. "Maybe . . . but not if we get pigeonholed as boring and stodgy and dull."

Other girls were crowding in to use the dressing room

mirror, so, relieved to be done, Katrina moved out of their way to make more room. Out on the stage, they moved into the holding area where Tyler and Cowboy were waiting. Both guys looked neatly groomed with dark suits and dark ties. Together, the four of them watched from behind the scenes while the group on stage finished their performance.

As usual, the judges made comments about the performance, giving advice or suggestions along with a few compliments to the competitors. Katrina tried to wiggle her toes in the shoes Breezy had insisted she wear, but her toes were wedged in so tightly that they felt slightly numb. The shiny black shoes had tall heels that made walking tricky. She hoped she wouldn't fall down. Fortunately, they weren't doing much more than walking and singing tonight. Katrina ran the choreography through her mind as the judges continued to banter with the contestants. Mostly she just needed to remember to walk in a Z design forward, then sing her verse, then walk in a backward Z while the others sang, then straight forward when they sang together. Really, it wasn't that complicated.

Bruce Betner was announcing them, and as the crowd clapped, they went out onto the stage and took their places in the semidarkness. The music began, slowly and quietly, and the lights came on. Breezy started out the song, moving around in her sparkling golden dress, smiling with confidence, and singing the lyrics perfectly.

They all took their turns with their solo verses—Katrina put her whole heart into hers—and they sang the choruses together like Breezy had arranged. With no mistakes or glitches, Katrina felt they'd done a good job as they ended the song. Based on the loud cheering and clapping, the crowd agreed.

"Nicely done," Ricky told them. "Very, very nice. And a great choice of song for your mix of voices. I know it's not Cowboy's favorite sort of song." He grinned at him. "But don't worry, man, you'll get to do your country music before this is over. Tyler, you sounded great as always. I could tell you were really singing from your soul. Now Breezy . . ." He paused as if considering his words. "You were technically perfect, but I don't know . . . it might just be me, but it seemed like something was missing." He pointed at Katrina now. "And you—well, I don't know what to say. Every time I hear your voice it's just like the tabloids are saying—the Amish girl with the voice of an angel. It's truly a gift." He nodded. "By the way, you look great tonight."

"You do look great." Celeste jumped in. "And you sound great too, Katrina. You're making us proud, girl. Our little Amish angel is doing good. Keep it up." Celeste echoed what Ricky had said about the others, even the part about Breezy and that something seemed to be missing.

"I agree," Jack said. "Breezy's singing is spot-on technically." He shook his finger at her. "But for some reason you're not connecting with me. Maybe you need to forget about singing so perfectly and think about the meaning behind the song. I'm not really sure. But I do know I didn't enjoy it. And that's not good." He went on to offer the guys a few pointers, then looked back at Katrina. "I can tell just by looking at you right now that you're not comfortable in that dress. You'd probably be more comfortable with your little Amish bonnet and apron. Am I right?"

She just nodded.

"Well, that's what being a performer is about sometimes, Katrina. You have to do what it takes to please the crowds.

That's what you get paid for as an entertainer. Maybe someday, after you've really arrived, you can dress or act any way you like. But that's an earned privilege. And as beautiful as your voice is and as much as we love you, you haven't earned that privilege yet." He smiled. "But hang in there. Do your best and pay your dues. Maybe it'll come to you . . . in time."

They went down to sit with the audience now, watching as the other groups performed. Katrina was surprised at how good some of them were. It seemed that everyone was improving. She was also surprised at how harsh the judges could be sometimes, pointing out things she had missed or didn't even understand. It made her wonder if they hadn't been a little soft on her group, although she didn't know why they would be treated any differently.

At the end Bruce invited all the competitors onto the stage, this time telling the viewers which numbers to call to place their votes for everyone. As Katrina stood there, looking out into the blindingly bright lights, she wondered who would possibly vote for her. Really, it seemed useless to keep trying if it would take voters to win this. Other than Bekka, who would call or email?

"All right then," Bruce said cheerfully. "That wraps it up for tonight. The final forty all did a fabulous job, but as we all know, half of you are going home. The next time we meet, we will cut the competition down to the final twenty. The *final twenty*, ladies and gentlemen—that is getting down there. So place your votes now and make sure to tune in tomorrow for the results."

As the house lights came on, Katrina searched the crowd for her aunt. Finally she spotted her waving near the front. Katrina hurried down to join her.

"You sang beautifully," Aunt Alma said. "And you look pretty too."

Katrina shrugged. "Well, that was Breezy's doing."

As they rode the shuttle bus back to the hotel, Breezy seemed much quieter than usual. Katrina wondered if she'd said something to offend her. "Thank you for all your help," she told Breezy as they rode up in the elevator together. "I never could've done it without you."

"You're welcome," Breezy told her quietly.

"Are you feeling all right?" Aunt Alma asked her with concern.

Breezy frowned. "I guess so."

"You can sleep in again tomorrow," Katrina said.

"Did you get what the judges were saying about me?" Breezy said suddenly.

"What?" Katrina tried to remember.

"About me singing technically right, but that something was missing," Breezy said in a discouraged voice. "Do you get that?"

Katrina considered this as they exited the elevator. "I don't know."

"What is it?" Breezy continued. "What am I missing?"

"Jack said you need to sing about the meaning of the song," Katrina told her as they went down the hall.

"I *was* singing about the meaning of the song," Breezy argued. "I thought about it a lot. I even had a dream about it. Why do they think I don't understand that? It's not like I'm stupid."

As she slid her key into the slot, Katrina tried to remember her first reaction to Breezy's voice. Hadn't she felt like something was missing too? Yet Breezy was so knowledgeable about music. Katrina knew that she'd been studying music for years. And Breezy usually had so much confidence—more than most of them. Why was she struggling like this now?

"What is it?" Breezy demanded as they went into the room. "What is wrong with me?"

Katrina set a bag on the bed, trying to think of a gentle answer. "I think it's kind of like Jack said . . ."

"What?"

"When you sing," Katrina began slowly, "sometimes it doesn't feel like you mean it."

"Of course I mean it."

"When I sing," Katrina continued, "I try to feel like the song is part of me. Like it's singing inside of me. Like it's a story that I understand and care about. Like it's coming from within me. Does that make sense?"

Breezy flopped down on her bed. "Not really."

"I don't really know how to explain it, but somehow it works for me."

Breezy sat up with a scowl. "Yeah, but you have the advantage."

"The advantage?"

"The judges like you. They want to keep you on the show, Katrina. No matter what."

"No matter what?" Katrina was confused. Was Breezy saying that even if Katrina sang poorly, the judges would keep her on?

"Come on, surely you know that by now. You're the little Amish girl. You're different from the rest of us. That makes the show more interesting, and viewers like that, and ratings go up. They don't want you to go home. In fact, I'll bet that they plan to keep you on until the final six."

"How can the judges keep me on if the voters don't vote for me?"

"They can cheat."

Katrina frowned. "Cheat? You think they would cheat?"

"Sure. If it boosts ratings. Why wouldn't they? It's all about the bottom line."

"What is a bottom line?"

"Money." Breezy was going into the bathroom. "Just follow the money."

Katrina looked at Aunt Alma as the door to the bathroom shut loudly. But Aunt Alma merely shrugged as she began removing her clothing for bed.

The next evening, they gathered at the studio again. Tonight they had three previous winners of *American Star* performing, and Katrina didn't like to judge, but she felt that two of the singers weren't as good as some of the ones competing. Of course, she also knew that she was the last one to have such opinions. Compared to everyone else, what Katrina knew about music wouldn't even fill Aunt Alma's thimble.

"All right, it's the moment you've all been waiting for," Bruce was finally saying. "I want all forty contestants up here on the stage." He chatted with the audience as the contestants came onto the stage, lining up in the formation that they'd been told earlier to follow. Once again, the judges began to speak to each contestant, offering criticism and suggestions and a few random compliments. As they did this, they divided the singers into three groups: one on the left, one on the right, and one in the center. Katrina was in the right group tonight, along with Tyler. She wondered if that meant she was going home since the ones on the right had been sent home last time.

"You kids in the middle," Bruce said, "you are the judges' bottom five, and this could mean you're going home." He chuckled like he knew a secret. "Or not."

Katrina cringed to see that Breezy was in this group. Did this mean Breezy was going home? She hoped not.

"You contestants on the left," Bruce turned and gave them a sad expression. Katrina noticed Cowboy's white hat in the back row. "You got the least amount of votes yesterday. That means you're all at risk for going home." He looked at the ones on the right. "You guys got the most votes, which means you are staying." Everyone in this group began to hug and jump around happily. For their sakes, Katrina tried to act enthused.

"But as you can see, there are only sixteen in your group." Bruce turned back to the others now. "That means we have four more contestants who need to move to the right." He nodded to the judges. "That is up to you."

"That's right," Celeste said. "As you all know, we each have one vote, and I'm using my vote to pick Cowboy." She smiled at him. "I'm sorry you didn't get more votes, Cowboy, because I think you're doing a great job. But for some reason you're not getting the voters on board. So you'd better do something to get your fans excited enough to call in."

He thanked her, then came over to join Katrina's group.

Jack and Ricky took turns picking two more people from the other group on the left. According to Katrina's math, that meant there were still only nineteen, and this was supposed to be the top twenty.

"Now for the final contestant," Jack said. "There's one

contestant who is in the judges' bottom picks, but ironically it's someone who happened to get a whole lot of votes."

"According to my sources, this particular person got more votes than any of the other contestants," Bruce said. "Which does make me wonder how she got put in the bottom five. Kind of an anomaly."

"And that is precisely why this person is going to be rescued from the bottom tonight." Celeste cleared her throat. "Breezy Vicks, I'm talking about you. It seems that your voters have determined your fate this time, but if we judges had been choosing, you'd be going home, darlin'."

Breezy gave them a shaky looking smile. "Thank you," she mumbled as she came over to the edge of the group on the right, lingering on the fringe as if she felt she didn't really belong. Katrina moved over and reached out to grab Breezy's hand and hold it tightly.

"All of you top twenty have your work cut out for you," Bruce told them. "But you will also have some help from here on out. As you know, we've brought in the pros to help you with the rest of your performances." He introduced fashion designers, vocal coaches, hairstylists, makeup artists, and all kinds of people. Then he told everyone goodnight.

As soon as the stage lights went down, Breezy started to cry. Katrina put her arms around her, holding her as she sobbed. "It's all right," Katrina said softly. "They didn't send you home."

"But—but they wanted to." Breezy looked at Katrina with a tear-streaked face. "The judges hate me."

"They don't hate you." Katrina kept her arm around Breezy as they exited the stage. "They just want to see you do your best. Can't you do that?"

She sniffed. "I'm not sure I know how."

"At least you've got your guitar now," Katrina reminded her. "Maybe that'll help."

"I don't know . . . maybe it's hopeless."

"It's not hopeless. You're getting a second chance. Doesn't that mean something?"

"I guess so."

As they joined Aunt Alma and went outside to the shuttle bus, both Katrina and her aunt tried their best to encourage Breezy, but it was hard to tell if Breezy was really listening. It was as if she'd been flattened by the judges' harsh words. When they got back to their hotel room, Breezy silently climbed into her bed without even changing her clothes or washing her face.

"She feels really bad," Katrina whispered to Aunt Alma.

She nodded. "But she didn't get sent home."

To Katrina's relief, Breezy was in brighter spirits the next morning. As they went down to where they were supposed to meet in the ballroom, Breezy seemed almost like her old self. She hugged and greeted Tyler and Cowboy as if nothing had gone wrong last night. Then they sat down in a much less crowded room, waiting for Bruce and the cameramen to show up to give them their instructions for the day.

"We won't be going to the studio until tomorrow morning," Bruce explained following a quick congratulations for making the top twenty. "This morning you need to find a partner for the next competition. As you all know, from here on out, there will be two guys and two girls eliminated after each competition until we reach the final eight. After that, we'll eliminate a guy and a girl each time until we have the final pair who will each become the next *American Star* winners.

"Now, for this next competition, we want guys and girls partnered together. For this performance, you'll be singing love songs. So make sure you pick someone you get along with so you can sing a convincing love song." He chuckled. Then he explained about how they would need to schedule time with the professionals who were on hand to help them. "If you don't schedule your appointments, you will be left out. So don't forget."

Breezy, Katrina, Cowboy, and Tyler clustered together after Bruce finished his instructions. "There's no reason we have to keep working together," Breezy said to them, "but it seems like we've had some success. Maybe we should keep our coalition going."

Everyone agreed this was a good plan.

"I want to sing with Katrina in this competition," Tyler announced.

Katrina just nodded. Tyler would've been her first choice too.

"But what if *I* want to sing with Katrina?" Cowboy said.

"I asked first," Tyler told him.

"Maybe we should ask Katrina what she wants," Cowboy suggested.

Tyler nodded, turning back to Katrina, smiling hopefully. "Which of us do you want to sing with?"

Katrina was embarrassed at this attention, but she wanted to be fair. "Well, Tyler did ask first." She gave Cowboy an apologetic look.

"Doesn't matter who asked first," Cowboy told her. "You get to pick who you want, Katrina. I think you should pick me because I know we'll sound good together."

"We'd sound good together too," Tyler insisted. "And we'd look good together too. We have similar coloring."

Breezy's eyes narrowed as if she was mad or just feeling left out, but without saying a word, she simply watched as the three of them went round and round.

"I don't want to hurt anyone's feelings," Katrina told them. She was used to Breezy acting like their director and wished she'd make a suggestion.

"Tell us who it's going to be, Katrina," Cowboy said. "We're burning daylight here."

"Come on," Tyler urged, "I can tell you want to pick me."

Katrina turned to Cowboy. "I hate to hurt you, but I think it's best if I sing with Tyler. I think our voices seem good together. You and Breezy sound nice together, and you both like those country style songs, don't you?"

Cowboy folded his arms across his chest. "Maybe I don't want to sing with Breezy."

"Fine," Breezy snapped at him. "Maybe I don't want to sing with you either!" She stormed off.

Katrina didn't know what to do. "Maybe Tyler should sing with Breezy," she said uneasily. She didn't really want to sing with Cowboy, but she did want to make peace between everyone.

"But you said I can sing with you," Tyler reminded her.

"But Breezy is so sad." Katrina watched as Breezy headed into the restroom. "She needs someone to sing with."

"Breezy is way too bossy," Cowboy said.

"She is good at this," Katrina pointed out. "She's helped all of us."

"Don't forget she almost got kicked out," Cowboy reminded her.

"Yes, but I think it's because she needs to change some things. The judges want her to try harder." Katrina waved her hand toward where all the other contestants appeared to be paired off already. Some were even singing like they'd chosen their songs. "One of you guys is going to have to sing with Breezy." She made an exasperated sigh. "Figure it out and I'll go see if she's all right."

She found Breezy crying in the restroom. "This is too hard," she told Katrina. "I want to go home."

"You want to give up?"

"Uh-huh." Breezy pulled off a long section of toilet paper and loudly blew her nose.

"No one can stop you if you want to go home," Katrina said slowly, "but it seems a shame to quit before you've really given it your all."

"I have given it my all."

"You've given it a lot. But have you been singing from your heart?" Katrina peered at her. "Can you honestly say you've done that?"

Breezy pulled out another length of toilet paper, wadding it into a ball, and blotted her eyes.

"I told the guys to decide which one of them is going to partner with you. One of them *has* to sing with you."

"Oh, wow, did you hold a gun to their heads too?"

"What?"

She angrily threw the wad of paper into the wastebasket. "I'm not used to having to strong-arm guys, thank you very much!"

"I'm sorry." Katrina backed away. "Did I do something wrong?"

"No, not you. I did everything wrong. I never should've come here."

Katrina went closer to her now, looking into her eyes.

"Breezy, you are a really good singer. I think you are one of the very best here."

"Really?" She blinked. "Well, the judges don't seem to think so."

"That's not true. The judges all agree that your voice is—how did they say it—technically perfect?"

"That was supposed to be an insult."

"I don't know . . . I think they were trying to help you."

"You honestly think I'm one of the best singers?" Breezy looked doubtful. "Or are you just saying that to make me feel better?"

"I wouldn't lie to you. Your voice is truly amazing. But I agree with the judges. You sing the words and notes perfectly, but it feels like something is missing, like you hold something back. I don't know much about music, but I think people want to hear something warm and personal when they listen to a song—they want to feel a connection. I think you need to put your heart and your soul into your music. You need to believe in the words and sing them like you believe it . . . to make it feel real."

Breezy's brow creased in thought—as if she was seriously considering this. "Thank you," she finally told Katrina. "You might be right. Anyway, I'm going to take your advice." Then she linked her arm into Katrina's, and they left the restroom together and went off to find the guys.

Katrina thought about what she'd said to Breezy just now. It was an odd sort of moment, almost as if they'd switched places. In the past, Katrina had always needed Breezy's help, but today it seemed like Breezy needed Katrina. And that felt surprisingly good.

20

Cowboy had reluctantly agreed to sing with Breezy, but Katrina could tell that Breezy was hurt by his attitude.

"Don't forget," Katrina said to her quietly as the two couples prepared to part ways. "Sing from your heart. Think about that as you practice."

Breezy nodded. "I'll try."

"Do you have any songs in mind?" Tyler asked Katrina as they walked over to a quiet corner of the room.

"I only listened to the golden oldies station," she reminded him, "and I can't even remember a love song."

"I think we should sing 'When I Fall in Love.'"

"How does it go?"

Tyler started to sing a very sweet and simple song. It was about falling in love for the first time and how that love would last forever. "I really like that," Katrina said after he finished. "Is that all the lyrics?"

"Yeah, it's a relatively short song, but we can go through it a couple of times, maybe do some rearranging with the vocals." He pulled out his iPad. "You go tell the producers which song we're doing while I get the lyrics up for you to look at."

Fortunately, no one else had chosen that pretty song, and by the time she got back to Tyler, he had the song's lyrics ready for her to read through as well as a recording of the music to listen to. Before long they were singing it together. To her surprise, Tyler was as good at arranging the music as Breezy had been. His plan for when they'd do their solos and when they'd sing together sounded perfect. Once they tried it a few times and made a few changes here and there, she thought it was going well.

"We forgot to sign up with the professional consultants," Tyler said suddenly. "Remember, if we don't schedule our time, we'll miss out. And I really want some feedback on our arrangement."

They hurried over to where a woman was managing all the schedules, and although there weren't many slots left, they both got signed up with all of the experts.

"Meeting with all those guys is going to eat up some of our rehearsing time," Tyler said as they went back to their corner to work on their song. "So we should make the most of it now."

They practiced until Aunt Alma came down with a lunch for Katrina. "I was worried you would forget to eat," she told her.

"Is there enough for Tyler too?" Katrina asked.

Aunt Alma nodded. "*Ja*. I thought you would want to share."

As Katrina and Tyler began to eat, Aunt Alma held up the cell phone that Bekka had given Katrina. "I took it to the phone place this morning," she said proudly. "Then I plugged it into the cord in our room, like the man told me to do, and I think it should be working." She handed it to Katrina.

"Really?" Katrina studied the phone. "I don't know how to use it."

"I can show you," Tyler offered. "After we're done eating."

While they ate, Aunt Alma explained how she'd asked someone at the hotel where the phone place was and how she'd ridden in the taxi all by herself. She told them how the man at the store had put Bekka's phone number inside the phone for her. "The number Bekka wrote down inside of the box. He said that you just push some of the buttons to make it work." Aunt Alma frowned. "But now I can't remember which ones. Maybe Tyler knows."

"Yep." Tyler put his apple core in the bag for garbage, then took the phone, holding it up for Katrina to see as he pushed a button. "See, it says Bekka Lehman. Do you want to call her now?"

"*Ja*, I think so."

He looked at his watch. "It should be around four o'clock there." He showed her which buttons to push, then handed her the phone. She pressed the button and then held her breath as she put the phone next to her ear. Listening to the ringing sound made her giggle.

"Old Amish Soap and Candle Works," a female voice said.

"Bekka?"

"*Ja*. This is Bekka. Who is this?"

"Katrina!"

"Katrina?" Bekka let out a happy squeal. "It's about time you called me. I was beginning to get worried that you and Alma had been kidnapped or you'd lost your phone or something. But then the show started last week and I saw you were on it. I've been watching it on my computer ever since."

"It's been so busy," Katrina explained. "I forgot about the phone. Aunt Alma just got it running today."

"You're doing great on the show, Katrina. Really, really great. Congratulations for making it into the top twenty. I just saw that this morning. I knew you'd make it."

"Thanks. It's so good to hear your voice, Bekka. How are you doing? And everyone at home? And how is my family?"

Bekka told her bits and pieces of the local news, but it sounded like not much had changed there—and yet that in itself was very reassuring. Katrina longed to be there with Bekka right now.

"Is Cooper still doing his apprenticeship?" Katrina asked.

"*Ja*, I think so. He hasn't come home since the day he took you to Millersburg. Peter says he might never come back. He thinks the apprenticeship must be working out well for him."

"Oh . . . that's good. Good for Cooper." Katrina tried to sound happier than she felt.

"I cannot believe I'm really talking to you," Bekka said happily.

"*Ja*. Me too."

"What did you think about what happened with that Breezy girl?" Bekka asked suddenly. "I was so shocked. I thought for sure she was going home. I wish they'd gone ahead and just eliminated her."

"Breezy is my roommate."

"I know. Remember, I'm watching the show. And you're on it a lot, Katrina. More than anyone, it seems like. I get so excited every time they do interviews with you. You say some amusing things too. And that time they came to your room—that was so fun. But I was really hoping Breezy would get kicked off the show."

"Why?"

"Because I don't like her."

"Why not?"

"I don't know. She seems insincere or untrustworthy."

"Oh . . ."

"Do *you* like her?"

"*Ja*, I do."

"Really? You're not worried she's going to do something to ruin your chances of winning? That's the main reason I don't like her, Katrina. I think she's out to get you."

"No, no, I don't think so. You don't know her. And I don't think she's insincere. But I did tell her she needs to sing with her heart."

"That's good advice. And maybe I'm wrong about her. I hope so."

"*Ja*. Me too."

"So what's the plan for the next competition? And when are you going to do a solo?"

Katrina explained about singing as couples now and how she was partnered with Tyler. "We've been practicing all morning."

"Tyler Jones is so handsome," Bekka said. "I think he could win it for the guys."

"I will tell him you think so."

"And you will win it for the girls."

Katrina laughed. "Don't count your eggs before they're laid."

"Is he with you now?"

"*Ja*. Do you want to speak to him?"

"*Ja! Ja!* Please!"

Katrina handed the phone to Tyler. "My friend wants to talk with you."

She listened as Tyler chatted with Bekka. She could tell by the way he looked at her and laughed that Bekka must've been asking about Katrina. After a bit, Tyler looked at his watch. "Oh, Bekka, I'm sorry to cut you off, but I just noticed the time. Katrina and I have to get to an important appointment now. So I'll say goodbye and give you back to Katrina."

He handed Katrina the phone, and she told Bekka goodbye too.

"Promise you'll call me tomorrow," Bekka said.

"I will." Katrina handed Tyler the phone, and he showed her how to shut it off.

"We're scheduled to meet with Ronny Vanderzan in fifteen minutes," he said as he stood up.

"Who is he?" Katrina tried to remember.

"The clothing designer. Remember?" Tyler reached down to give her a hand, pulling her to her feet.

"*Ja.*" She handed her phone back to Aunt Alma. "Can you put this in the room for me?"

"Sure. Don't be late for your appointment."

As they walked through the hotel, Tyler asked Katrina how she felt about working with a stylist. "Will it be hard for you not to wear your Amish clothes?" he asked as they waited for the elevator.

"I cannot say that it won't."

"I wish there was a way you could compete without all this fuss over clothes," he said as the elevator doors opened and the people came out. "But you don't really have a choice—I mean, if you want to win."

"*Ja.*" She nodded as they went into the empty elevator.

"You know, I still remember when I first saw you. You were standing by yourself in your green dress with your white apron

222

and bonnet." He pushed a button and the doors closed. "You were like this wonderful spot of peace and purity right in the middle of all the crazy noise and shallowness." He chuckled. "Does that even make sense?"

She shrugged. "I think it was meant as a compliment. Thank you."

"I couldn't take my eyes off you," he continued as the elevator soared up. "I'd never seen anything like you before. Not really. And then when you sang, well, you totally blew me away."

She thanked him again as the doors opened on the top floor. Tyler figured out how to find the right door, which led into an enormous hotel room.

"It's called a suite," Tyler explained to her after a young woman invited them to sit and wait in the big, fancy room. Meanwhile, the woman went over to a desk where she was working on a laptop computer, clicking away on the keyboard with her back to them.

"Sweet?" Katrina wondered if they would be served dessert.

"Hello, hello," a short, bald man said as he emerged from another room. "Katrina and Tyler. I've been looking forward to meeting you two." He winked at them. "I'm Ronny Vander-zan, and I think both you kids have a very good chance of being the next American Stars, and I want to do all I can to help you get there." He called over his shoulder. "Ian? Are you coming or not?"

A tall man with black hair that stuck out like a scared rab-bit's joined them. Ronny introduced him as Ian the stylist. "I design the clothes, but it's Ian who really knows how to put them together and give them that pizzazz." Ronny was walking around Katrina now, rubbing his chin and examining her the same way Daed used to examine a cow at an auction. "Hard to tell what you've got under all those clothes, but I saw you in that green evening gown last night and it looked like you've got a good shape to you. Not too curvy, but not too skinny either."

She felt her cheeks growing warm.

He reached over and pinched her arm. "And it looked like you work out."

"Work out?"

"You're nice and fit."

"I do work out of doors a lot," she told him.

"What song are you kids singing?" Ian asked.

"'When I Fall in Love,'" Tyler said.

"Nat King Cole." Ronny nodded. "I like that."

"I'd like to see them in something classic and timeless," Ian suggested. "Tyler would look great in a sixties dinner jacket . . . narrow black tie, fitted trousers."

"I think a sleek little cocktail dress for Katrina," Ronny said. "With her dark hair I'd like to see her in a deep color . . . something sultry. Maybe that garnet sequined number. I think it's a size six. Should be about right."

Katrina felt lost again. What were they actually saying?

"And we need a little bling. Nothing too glitzy. I think the key is going to be classic and simple with this one." Ian turned her around. "I think she needs an updo. Something sleek and chic. Maybe a French twist."

"Are you getting this all down, Lisa?" Ronny asked the woman at the computer.

"I am," she called back.

Ian began measuring Tyler, and Katrina, not knowing what to do, went over to look out the window. They were very high up, but at least she could see the sky. It wasn't as blue as at home, though. It was kind of faded and worn looking. A bit like how she felt.

"Come with me," Lisa told Katrina. "We'll see how that cocktail dress fits."

Imagining a dress with a fluffy rooster's tail, Katrina was about to ask what a cocktail dress was, but she saw Lisa holding a deep red sparkly garment. It did not look like a dress. More like a shirt—or a pillowcase with straps.

"Go ahead and undress," Lisa told her. "Then put this on so we can see if it needs any alterations." She stood there watching and waiting while Katrina removed her shawl and apron and finally her dress.

"Well, you'll have to take those off too," Lisa pointed to Katrina's underclothes.

Katrina shook her head. "No, I'm not taking these off."

"No way can these spaghetti straps hide all that. Even if they could, the dress will be ruined with all those layers underneath." She frowned. "Don't you have any normal underwear?"

"This is normal . . . for me."

"What did you wear under your evening gown last night?"

Katrina frowned to think of the tiny garments Breezy had insisted she wear. "My roommate made me wear some of her under . . . things."

"Well, I'm sure we've got some shapewear around here somewhere. That should do the trick." Lisa was digging through a rack of clothes and then in some drawers, returning with a tan-colored tube-like garment. "Put this on."

Katrina just stood there, uncertain of what to say or do, but she knew this was going too far. She was not going to go on stage wearing clothing that revealed more of her skin than her underclothes covered.

"Look," Lisa said more gently. "I've heard you sing, Katrina. You are really good. Ronny thinks you have a chance to win *American Star*. Isn't that what you want?"

"I want to win enough money to help my father get the surgery he needs," she said quietly.

"Then you're going to have to trust us."

It took most of the hour before it was finally decided—after Katrina flatly refused to take a razor to her legs and underarms—that she would wear a dark blue full-length evening gown. This dress, like the short one, sparkled with sequins. But unlike the short one, it had long sleeves. The only flaw Katrina saw in this dress was that it was cut low in the back, but she figured her long hair would conceal it.

On performance night Katrina was disappointed that her stylist had insisted she wear her hair up, but as they waited in the wings for their turn to perform, Tyler assured her that she looked great and that no one would even notice the low back on her dress. "Compared to what the other girls are wearing tonight," he whispered, "you look like a real lady." He smiled at her. "A beautiful lady."

She watched as Lulu and Terrance finished their song, then waited to hear the judges' comments, which seemed a little harsh. Not only did they find fault with Lulu's singing, saying she was "pitchy," but they picked on her dress as well. Katrina blinked to realize that Lulu was wearing the short dress that Ronny had first wanted Katrina to wear.

"That dress is way too short," Celeste was telling her, "and way too sophisticated and mature for a seventeen-year-old girl."

Katrina and Tyler exchanged looks. That could've been her being criticized for her dress. But there was no time to think about that now because the stage manager was motioning for her and Tyler to take their places. Feeling unsteady in the high-heeled shoes, Katrina was grateful to hold Tyler's hand as they slipped out onto the darkened stage and waited for Bruce to announce them. As usual, to steady her nerves, Katrina remembered Daed and why she was doing this.

Bruce finished their introduction with "I give you Tyler Jones and Katrina Yoder singing 'When I Fall in Love.'" The spotlight came on and the music began, and it was Tyler's turn to sing, then Katrina's. She did it just like they'd practiced it—after their coach had given them some directions—looking intently into Tyler's eyes and singing the words as if they were meant just for him. But as she sang the song, she imagined she was singing it to Cooper, not Tyler. When they finished, the audience clapped and cheered, and for the first time that night, all the judges gave a standing ovation.

When the room quieted down, Ricky began to speak. "Well, you can see that we liked it. No, I take that back. We loved it. Not only did you kids pick the perfect song for your voices—which I have to say sound beautiful together—you look just great too."

"I agree one thousand percent," Celeste told them. "When the spotlight came on you two, I thought, 'Now, those guys really look like stars.' That dress is so classy, Katrina, and with your hair up and those gorgeous earrings, well, you remind me of Princess Kate. And Tyler, you look fantastic in that jacket. So stylish. Bravo!"

"I can tell you're both taking this competition seriously," Jack said. "Good for you. And I concur with the other judges.

You both look great, but more importantly, you both sounded great. I give you two thumbs up."

Katrina was relieved to go sit and watch the rest of the contestants, listening to the judges' comments and waiting anxiously for Breezy and Cowboy, who were the final performers tonight. Katrina had barely seen Breezy today, but the last thing she'd said to Breezy was that she'd be praying for her. "I'm praying that you'll sing with your whole heart," Katrina told her backstage. "That you'll sing it like you really mean it."

Katrina's prayer was answered as Breezy and Cowboy performed. For the first time, it seemed like Breezy was really singing from her heart. By the time they ended the song, if Katrina didn't know better, she would've believed that Breezy was actually in love with Cowboy.

Once again, the audience clapped and cheered heartily. However, the judges didn't stand up. Katrina hoped that wasn't a bad sign.

"All right," Ricky said finally. "That was pretty good. I was surprised, Breezy. I honestly didn't think you had it in you. Mind if I ask what's changed? Or are you really in love with Cowboy there? Because you sure had me believing."

Breezy laughed. "Oh, I like Cowboy just fine. But no, I'm not in love." She smiled sweetly at the judges. "What happened is that my roommate gave me some good advice . . . and I took it."

"Katrina told you her secrets?" Celeste asked.

"She told me to sing with my heart," Breezy told them, "and that's what I did."

"Well, you did it beautifully," Celeste told her. But she shook her finger at Cowboy. "You, however, were a bit disappointing tonight. That's a shame because I know you can do better."

"I have to agree with Celeste on that," Jack said. "It almost seemed like when Breezy found her heart, you lost yours, Cowboy. Any explanation for that?"

Cowboy shrugged. "I don't know. Just an off night I guess."

"Well, we'll have to wait and see what our voters think about it," Bruce said. He invited all twenty contestants back to the stage and talked about the importance of voting again. "Remember, if it hadn't been for Breezy's committed fans voting for her—I think most of Texas called in the other night—she wouldn't even be here tonight. And I'll bet all her fans are glad that she is, especially after that stellar performance tonight."

When the house lights came on, Katrina was about to go find Aunt Alma when Tyler stopped her. "Can I talk to you real quick?" he asked with a furrowed brow.

"*Ja.*" She nodded, concerned that something was troubling him.

"Come with me." He led her back up the side steps and into the shadowy sidelines of the stage area, safely away from where fans were starting to press toward the contestants, asking for autographs.

"Is something wrong?" she asked.

"No. Something is right." Even in the dim light, she could see the longing in his eyes. "Katrina, when we sang that song tonight, I felt like I was really singing it to you . . . and like you were really singing it back to me."

She made an uncomfortable smile. "We were supposed to sing it to each other like that . . . like we truly meant it."

"I know. But I actually did mean it. I really do mean it.

Katrina, I have fallen in love with you. Completely. It happened the moment I met you."

"Oh . . ." She looked away, wondering what to say.

"Please, tell me, do you feel that way too?" He chuckled. "I know, it sounds like I'm just repeating the lyrics to you again. But I mean this from my heart. I love you, Katrina. Do you love me?"

"I love you as my good friend," she told him.

"But as a boyfriend?"

"Tyler . . ." She took a deep breath. "Even if I did love you, it would be impossible. You know I am Amish. And even though I've left my community to do this show, I want to go back someday . . . if they will accept me . . . and that's something that I won't know until I return."

"I would become Amish," he said eagerly. "For you, I would."

"Really?" She studied him. "Do you have any idea what you are saying?"

"I'll admit I don't know that much about it. But like I told you before, I like old-fashioned things. And I love you. I would gladly become Amish to keep you."

"Katrina!" called a voice that sounded like Breezy. "You back here?"

"Over here," Katrina called back.

"Oh, there you both are. You guys were great tonight." Breezy smiled at them.

"So were you," Katrina told her. "Your best performance ever."

"I know." Breezy hugged her. "Thanks to you. Anyway, Alma is looking for you. She was worried that someone might've stolen you away."

"Someone was trying," Tyler said lightly, but Katrina could tell by the look in his eyes that he was hurt—and she knew that it was because of her. As they walked back to where the auditorium was slowly emptying, she wished there was something she could say to make Tyler feel better, but she had no idea what it would be.

As she sat on the shuttle bus next to her snoozing aunt, she felt the weight of guilt pressing down on her. This competition—this game she was playing where the stakes kept getting higher—could really hurt someone. It would be so wrong if someone as kind and sweet as Tyler got his heart broken due to her. All because she'd sung that love song like that. She knew she was to blame for looking into his eyes like that, singing to him as if she loved him. Tyler had gotten caught up in her folly and taken her words to heart. Now he was sitting by himself in the back of the bus, hurting. And why had she sung like that? *Vainglory.* Whether she meant to or not, she had wounded her good friend Tyler. All in a shallow attempt to win the approval of judges and voters . . . to win a foolish contest. She was so ashamed of herself.

21

The next morning Katrina went down to the lobby and called Bekka. "I'm going to quit the competition," she told her even before she said hello.

"Why?" Bekka demanded. "You're doing great. You and Tyler were amazing last night. And you looked so beautiful. You can't quit. Everyone on the internet is talking about you. You're like the biggest buzz—that means they like you and—"

"But it's all wrong and—"

"Wait, wait! There's something really important I need to tell you, Katrina. I was going to call you yesterday . . . but I didn't want to distract you from your performance."

Katrina could tell by Bekka's tone that something was wrong. "What is it?"

"It's your father."

"What? Is he all right?"

"He's in the hospital."

"Oh, no. I have to come home now. I have to—"

"No, Katrina, don't come home yet. You can win that money. I know you can. And if you do, your father can have surgery and—"

"But why is he in the hospital?" Katrina asked. She knew her family couldn't afford the expenses of a hospital. Daed would only be in the hospital if it was very serious—life or death serious.

"He had a heart attack yesterday. My mother said she heard it was because he stopped taking some medicine for his back and was in horrible pain, but I'm not really sure if that's it. Anyway, your uncle found him in bad shape yesterday, and he got him to the hospital in time."

"I have to come home," Katrina told her. "I need to see him."

"Katrina." Bekka's voice was firm. "God has given you this opportunity—you could win enough money to help your father get well. I know you could. But if you come home, what will you do? Just sit by his side and hold his hand and watch him slowly die?"

Katrina bit her lip.

"Greater love has no man than this," Bekka said somberly, "than to lay down his life for a friend."

Katrina felt a lump in her throat as she imagined Daed in a hospital. He would hate being there . . . feeling so helpless . . . so hopeless. He might even want to die.

"Jesus said those words," Bekka told her. "And you are doing that by competing on *American Star*. I know you, Katrina. You don't enjoy being in the spotlight. You're laying down your life for your daed."

Katrina looked around the hotel lobby. Everything in there seemed to glitter or sparkle or shimmer. Glass windows and fancy water fountains, glossy floors and shiny furnishings. It was like a modern-day palace—and she hated it.

"I've decided to get baptized," Bekka said quietly.

"Really?"

"*Ja*. I will tell you more about it when you come home. But something inside of my heart has changed. I know I'm ready for this commitment."

"I'm so happy for you." Tears were coming down her cheeks now.

"I know you have to decide what's best for you," Bekka said. "And I promise I'll keep praying for you. But I hope you stay long enough to win some of that money . . . for your daed."

Katrina sniffed. "Well, it might not be up to me, Bekka. I could be eliminated tonight."

"Don't count on it."

"Will you do something for me?"

"*Ja*. Of course. Anything."

"Go tell my mother that I am praying for Daed. Tell her that I will do whatever I can to win this money to help him. I don't want her to be worried about the cost of the hospital, Bekka." Katrina knew that Mamm would mostly be worried about losing Daed, but if Katrina could do anything to lighten her family's load, she would do it.

"*Ja*, I know she is worried. I will tell her. And you should know that Cal and Sadie have been sneaking over to the office here, Katrina, to watch you perform on *American Star*. They are so happy for you."

"Really?" Katrina's heart warmed to imagine her brother and sister crowding into Bekka's little office and seeing her on the computer screen. "Tell them I love them."

Katrina, Tyler, and Breezy all made it through the next cuts, but Cowboy and three other contestants were sent home.

Now instead of the final twenty, it was the final sixteen. For the next competition, everyone was supposed to sing a solo. Katrina was actually relieved at this news because it meant that she would have some control over what she sang as well as what she wore. As committed as she was to trying to win some money for Daed, she was determined not to compromise herself again. No more singing a love song to a boy as if she meant to marry him. No more baring of skin.

"The challenge for this solo is for each of you to sing a song that tells us about who you are and what you believe," Bruce Betner told the sixteen contestants. "We'll be rolling video as you perform, from those shoots we took in your hometowns. Keep that in mind for your song choice."

Thankful for some time alone, Katrina found a quiet spot outside of the hotel where she just sat in the sunshine, thinking and praying. Mostly she was praying for Daed. But she was also thinking about what she wanted to sing. Finally, she called Bekka, and after finding out that Daed was still in the hospital where they were running all kinds of tests, she asked for advice. "What should I sing?" She explained Bruce's directions for the next competition.

"The tin soldier song," Bekka exclaimed. "Everyone loves it when you sing that song. And it always feels like our Amish history. Sing that for them."

"All right." Katrina sighed. "That's what I'll do. Thank you."

Katrina didn't schedule an appointment with the stylist this time. She knew that people might think she was making a big mistake, but she had decided to take Bruce's challenge to heart. She would sing in a way that told everyone about who she was and what she believed. If it meant she was going home, well, maybe it was what God intended. Because now, more than ever, she was praying about everything. She was asking God to lead her each step of the way.

When it was her turn to rehearse with the musicians on the stage, she explained how she wanted the song done. "Plain and simple," she told them. "Like me." After some discussion and trying several combinations, they all decided that the penny whistle, snare drum, guitar, and trumpet were the only instruments they would use. Katrina told the stage manager that she planned to stand in one place. "No moving about the stage," she said firmly. "And I want the lighting to be simple."

He nodded. "This is your show, Katrina. I just hope you know what you're doing. That's a big stage . . . and you're just one little girl. You might regret this."

"Thank you for your advice." She smiled. "But this is how I want to do it."

When the time to perform came and she was waiting backstage, she hoped she hadn't made a mistake. She had finally moved back to a quiet corner because she was so tired of being asked when she was going to change into her costume for her performance. She was wearing her good green dress with her full Sunday apron over it as well as a Sunday *kapp*. The director had questioned this, worried that her white apron would do something bad to the cameras, which seemed silly. What could an apron do to a camera? But after doing a test, he'd told her it was fine. "That translucent white fabric over the green doesn't actually translate as white," he explained. "It looks more like a pale green, and it's rather interesting." He smiled. "Good luck."

Remaining in the backstage shadows, she was unable to see her fellow contestants, but she could hear them. Breezy had a good solid performance, singing a song about Texas with real gusto and heart. Tyler sang an odd song about a car, but the audience seemed to really like it. And there were lots of other completely different songs—or "totally random," as Breezy would say.

Katrina knew that her performance was last—and that could be either good or bad, depending on the judges, because sometimes they were out of patience by then and sometimes they were in good spirits. But it did give her more time to pray . . . as well as more time to be nervous.

Finally she heard Bruce announcing her name, and she knew it was time to take her place on the stage. It felt so good not to be worried about tripping in high heels or uncomfortable over an overly exposed back, neck, or arms. She took her place in front of the freestanding microphone, waiting for the rat-a-tat-tat of the snare drum and for the lights to slowly come on. Then she began: "Listen, children, to a story . . ." She continued on with all of her ability and all of her heart to the most meaningful line of the song: "'Peace on earth' was all it said." When she finished the song, there was a brief moment of silence, and then the entire auditorium erupted. When the lights came up on the judges, she could see they were all standing too. She took in a deep breath. Perhaps this hadn't been a mistake after all.

"Well, well, well," Ricky said after it quieted down. "Our little Amish girl has pulled off another surprisingly good performance. Nicely done, Katrina."

"Very nicely done," Celeste added. "Although I have to admit you had me worried when you showed up on the stage wearing your little white apron. I thought, okay, it's over now. Katrina is going home. But after I saw the whole thing—the music arrangement, the scenes of your lovely Amish land-scape and children and cows playing on the screen—I got it. Beautifully done, Katrina. You can be proud."

Katrina swallowed hard. Pride was the same as vainglory . . . not an honorable attribute.

"I agree with the other judges," Jack said slowly. "You outdid yourself tonight, Katrina. Your grandmother would be proud too."

There was that word again. She simply nodded, quietly thanking them. But as she was leaving the stage, a couple of cameramen and Brandy stopped her. "Come on over here," Brandy said. "We want to do a quick interview."

Katrina blinked as the bright camera lights came on. "All right."

"Tonight was fun," Brandy said. "We know that you were supposed to sing something that represented you and your values and beliefs. Can you tell the viewers why you chose that particular song? Rather than, say, a hymn or religious song?"

"My friend back home suggested it," Katrina said simply. "It's a song that reflects Amish values because we don't be-lieve in war. It also shows a separateness of two very different sorts of people. Like how Amish separate themselves from the English."

"Well, except for you. How do you explain that?"

Katrina sighed. "It is hard to explain. Even to myself. What I am doing in this competition goes against everything that is Amish. In the beginning I told myself that it was my way of having *rumspringa*, but now I'm not so sure. I even wanted to quit the competition when I felt that I was compromising myself and my beliefs. In some ways this has been a very enlightening spiritual journey. Except that I am still trying to find my way. Who knows? Maybe I will go home tomorrow."

"We know you wanted to win money to help with your father's surgery," Brandy said quickly. "How is he doing?"

Katrina explained that Daed was in the hospital. "I am praying for him always. And if any of the viewers pray, I ask for their prayers too. I know that God will do what is best, but I love Daed . . . I don't want to lose him too soon."

"No, I'm sure you don't." Brandy looked at the camera. "So for any of you viewers who are still on the fence about voting, why not cast a vote for this young lady? I know I don't want to see her going home yet." Brandy thanked Katrina for the interview, and the cameras moved on.

No one seemed too surprised that Katrina made it to the next level. "But I don't know how you're going to follow that up," Breezy said as they went to the meeting room where Bruce Betner was going to give them their next assignment. As they sat down, Katrina spotted Tyler sitting by the windows. Other than a polite greeting here and there, they hadn't really spoken since the night of their love song duet.

Bruce came in and went to the front of the room with a camera crew trailing him as usual. First he congratulated them for making it, reminding them that they were getting close to the top eight. "Now that there are only twelve of you, we want to break you into four groups of three to form trios. Tomorrow's challenge is to sing a song from a famous trio of the past. Maybe it's the Jonas Brothers, or it could be the Bee Gees. It might be Nirvana or Motorhead or even Peter, Paul and Mary." He chuckled. "But I would discourage any of you from doing something from Alvin and the

Chipmunks." He gave them some more instructions, then wished them good luck, and suddenly everyone was moving about, trying to form trios.

Katrina was slightly surprised when Tyler came over, asking if she and Breezy wanted to be in a trio with him. "Sure," she told him, relieved that he seemed perfectly fine, as if nothing was wrong and he hadn't proclaimed his love for her . . . and she hadn't rejected it. Was it possible she had imagined the whole thing?

"I have an idea," Breezy said as the three of them clustered together out in the hall. "Let's do a song from Katrina's grandmother's group, Willow Tree."

"Really?" Katrina was surprised. "You would want to do that?"

"Sure." Breezy nodded. "You got a great response when you did that other song from them. The judges appreciate that your family has a history of music. And I think the voters like it too."

"It's a good idea," Tyler told Breezy.

"Great." Breezy looked at Katrina. "Which song do you think we should sing?"

"After the Storm," Katrina declared without even thinking. She explained how she'd sung it for her audition and how the judges really seemed to like it.

"How does it go?" Tyler asked.

Katrina sang it for them and they both agreed it was a great song. Tyler got the lyrics pulled up on his iPad, and Breezy downloaded the music onto her iPod. By later that afternoon, they had worked out their parts, and it was sounding really good. It was different than how Willow Tree sang it originally, but Katrina liked it.

When it was time to visit the stylists, Katrina knew she would have to have a plan or else risk getting forced into wearing something immodest. So as soon as they were in the suite and before anyone else had a chance to say something, she jumped in.

"I thought that since we're doing a sixties song—and since it's an antiwar song—maybe we could dress like the sixties again. That seemed to go over well the last time we did it. And I can wear my grandmother's dress and boots."

Ronny rubbed his chin. "That's not a bad idea, Katrina. Nostalgia sells. But I'm not sure about you wearing your grandmother's dress again. Fans might not like that."

"It was many days ago," she pointed out. "Maybe they would forget. And I could mention that the clothes belonged to Mammi."

"I like it," Ian said. "Let her wear the old dress, and maybe we can spruce it up with some love beads and flowers in her hair."

"Can you bring us the dress and boots so we can see it and plan for Bekka and Tyler's clothing?" Ronny asked.

"Sure." Katrina nodded eagerly. "I'll go get them now." Relieved that her plan had worked, she hurried out to get Mammi's clothes. As she rode the elevator down, she prayed for God's will to be done during this round. If she could simply make it through one more competition, she would be part of the top eight. Being part of the top eight meant a sure cash prize. After that, it wouldn't matter if the judges or the fans decided to send her home.

As it turned out, it didn't appear that anyone wanted to send Katrina or Breezy or Tyler home following their per-formance of "After the Storm" the next night. Wearing their colorful sixties-style clothing, complete with love beads and flowers, they sang the folk song with a genuine sincerity that brought the house to its feet again.

"You three should consider starting a group when this is all over," Ricky told them when the judging began. "You are that good together. I loved that!"

"I didn't even consider myself a folk music fan," Celeste told them. "But you have made me one."

"I know a record label that would sign you kids tonight." Jack smiled. "But I hope you'll all stick around until the end of the competition."

Katrina only hoped to be around long enough to win some prize money. Despite being told she had a chance at winning the top honors—she'd been told that media sources, whatever that was, predicted that she and Tyler would be the final winners—she truly hoped that the voters would choose someone else.

22

Once again, no one seemed very surprised that Katrina, Breezy, and Tyler made it into the top eight the following day. This meant they had to sign a new contract. Katrina had already signed a contract promising to abide by the rules of *American Star*, but this was something more. According to Breezy, this contract was to ensure that they wouldn't run out during the competition.

"Run out?" Katrina was confused. "What if we are voted out?"

"That's different. The show is worried that the final contestants are talented enough to be offered recording contracts or concerts or marketing endorsements." Breezy held up the paperwork. "This ensures that we stick around until the competition and the show are over."

"But if you don't win? Don't you go home?"

"Sure. But this is mostly for the contestants who will make it to the end." She grinned. "Like you and me. Although everyone is predicting you're going to beat me."

"I do not think so."

"Well, it's going to be a dog-eat-dog world from here on out." Breezy picked up her guitar and started practicing. "I'm in it to win it, and I don't care who knows."

"*Ja.* I hope you do win it."

Breezy stopped playing and studied her. "Are you serious? Or just being nice?"

"You know I don't want to win," Katrina said. "I've told you before, I only want enough money to help Daed."

"But if you won the top prize you'd be set, Katrina. You'd have money and record contracts and—"

"I don't want that."

Breezy rolled her eyes. "I hear you saying that, but it's hard to believe. How can you come this far and not want to go all the way to the end? Can you imagine how fantastic it would feel to be the last girl standing on that stage? Knowing that everyone picked you to win?"

Katrina shrugged, then looked back down at the contract where the line remained unsigned at the bottom of the last page. "You think I should sign it then?"

"Of course," Breezy assured her. "And don't worry. I faxed the whole thing to my dad, and he's an attorney, and he said it's all fair and legal. Just to protect the show. Once the show ends, the contract ends. Besides, if you don't sign, you could forfeit your prize money."

"Oh." Katrina swallowed hard, then signed. She hoped Breezy was right. Aunt Alma had already confessed that it sounded like a different language to her after she'd attempted to read it. Katrina was trying not to worry about Aunt Alma, but it seemed that she became more weary and quiet each day. So much so that Katrina had even suggested that Aunt Alma should go home. "I will be fine without you," Katrina assured her. "It won't be long until it's over anyway. And we have the whole weekend off just to rest up."

"That's good. You need rest. But I am not leaving."

"If you went home, you could visit Daed in the hospital."

Still Aunt Alma had refused. "I will not go home without you, Katrina." She made a weak-looking smile. "Besides, I want to go with you to see Mamm's old friend Larry Zimmerman. Remember?"

"*Ja.*" Katrina nodded eagerly. "I nearly forgot. Jack told me that he has it all arranged. Mr. Zimmerman is back from a big trip, and he has invited us to come to his home on Saturday for lunch."

"Oh, that will be good, Katrina. I look forward to it."

They wore their best dresses and Sunday aprons to visit Larry Zimmerman. Jack had arranged for a car to pick them up. He had explained that he would've gone with them but was worried that it could be misunderstood as favoritism as a judge.

"This is a house?" Aunt Alma said as the car went through some iron gates into an open grassy area where a large stone building loomed before them. "Or a hotel?"

"This is a private home, ma'am," the driver told her.

Aunt Alma giggled just like she always did when someone called her *ma'am*. At first she'd mistakenly thought they were calling her *mother*. Now she knew it was just a word the English used to be polite.

He drove around a circle driveway, stopping by a grand entrance. Then he got out and opened the car doors, waiting for them to get out. "I'll be here when you're ready to go," he told them as he tipped his hat. They thanked him, then went up to the big set of double wooden doors.

Before long a woman was guiding them through the biggest, fanciest home they had ever seen. Not that they had seen many. But this one was beyond Katrina's imagination. Eventually they were taken back outside where some tables and chairs were arranged by a big swimming pool. "This is pretty," Katrina said as she admired the flowers and grass and trees. "Are we having lunch out here?"

"Yes," the woman told them. "Make yourselves comfortable. Help yourselves to the iced tea. Mr. Zimmerman will be out shortly."

They sat down and drank iced tea as they waited . . . and waited. After what seemed an unreasonable amount of time, Katrina wondered if they'd been forgotten and was just about to go and ask, when an elderly man came out.

"I'm sorry to keep you waiting," he said in a slightly gruff tone. "I'm Larry Zimmerman." He shook their hands as they told him their names.

"Jack says you're Starla's daughter and granddaughter?" he said as he sat down across from them, peering curiously at them—almost as if he doubted this.

"Starla was my stepmother," Aunt Alma clarified. "But I thought of her as my own mother."

"My daed is Starla's only son," Katrina explained.

"So you are Starla's granddaughter?" He frowned.

"*Ja.*"

"And Jack says you're a good singer too?"

"Katrina is one of the final eight on *American Star*," Aunt Alma told him.

"I know. And I hear you're making Willow Tree popular again." He coughed. "That might make record sales pick up." He leaned forward, narrowing his eyes at her. "Is that why you're here?"

"What?" Katrina was confused.

"Do you think that you can come collect on Starla's royalties?"

"What?" Katrina glanced at Aunt Alma, who looked as bewildered as Katrina.

"Because if that's what you're up to, you can forget it. Starla gave all that up when she and Willy left."

"I'm not sure what you mean," Katrina said slowly.

"I mean if you came out here looking for money, you are out of luck."

"We do not expect money from you," Aunt Alma firmly told him. "Katrina might win money on *American Star*. But she did not come to get money from you. You can be sure of it."

"All right." He nodded. "As long as we're clear on that."

The woman returned now. She had a large tray with plates of food that she arranged on the table in front of them.

"Eat up," he said as he reached for his fork.

Aunt Alma and Katrina bowed their heads and silently prayed. When they looked up, Katrina was pleasantly surprised to see that Larry had done the same.

"We only came to see you in order to find out more about Mammi." Katrina cautiously picked up her fork. "We didn't know until after she died that she was part of the music group Willow Tree . . . with you. People have said I am like her, and, well, I just have so many questions."

His face seemed to soften now. "You are like her. How she used to look, anyway. She was a beautiful woman." He sighed. "For a short while the three of us—Willow Tree—we were on top of the world. And then, just like that"—he snapped his fingers—"it was over."

"What do you mean it was over?" Katrina asked. "What happened to end it? And how did it begin?"

As they ate, he told them the story of how he and Starla had grown up in an Amish settlement in Holmes County, not too far from Millersburg. "I was disenchanted with the Amish lifestyle. And I loved music. Starla liked music too. And she had the most fabulous voice. We were teenagers and not baptized, so I talked her into joining me in attending a folk festival. We were only going to go for a day. But a day soon became two and then three. During the festival, we met all kinds of musicians. We played and sang and wrote songs, and it was the most amazing time of my life. It was a happy time. Starla was happy too. That's where we met Willy Brown." He shook his head as he wiped his mouth with a napkin.

"Willy had more talent in his pinky finger than anyone I've ever known, and believe me, I've known plenty of musicians. Music just seemed to flow out of him. Almost like breathing. He'd pick up his guitar and start playing a brand-new tune, and then Starla would start singing words—just making them up as she sang—and it would be beautiful. I'd be the one to grab a pencil and start writing the words down, and later on I learned how to write music too—not create it, mind you, but I could write down the notes as Willy played them. I guess you could say I was the one with the business head."

"But you sang too," Katrina pointed out. "I've heard you."

He shook his head. "I was what you'd call a B-rate singer. Willy and Starla were the real talent. But they would never have gone as far as they did without me. Like I said, I was the business-minded one. I started booking us gigs. I kept the wheels greased and rolling. And after a few years, we had a good hit and doors started to open. We got some TV spots and then opened for some well-known bands and eventually got our own big concerts. But I should've seen the writing on the wall." He grimaced.

"What do you mean?" Katrina set down her fork.

"Willy was one of those unfortunate musicians who brought his addictions along with him. Having grown up Amish, Starla and I were kind of innocents. We hadn't seen that kind of thing yet. I mean all kinds of drugs—psychedelics, LSD, marijuana . . . the works. But it was the mid-sixties and we were out here in California doing concerts. It just came with the territory."

"I'm not sure I understand," Katrina said. "Was Willy addicted to drugs?"

He nodded, laying his napkin beside his plate. "Willy probably started out with the mild stuff, but somewhere along the line he became a full-blown heroin addict. I don't know how much you know about heroin, but it's a nasty, brutal drug. And Willy couldn't live without it."

"Oh . . ." Katrina sighed.

"Starla was in love with Willy." He shook his head. "Can you believe it? Here I sit, nearly fifty years later, and it still hurts to remember it. I would've done anything for Starla. I had loved her for most of my life. I even would've gone back to the Amish settlement for her. But she didn't want that. Or so she said."

"Did she marry Willy?" Aunt Alma asked.

"She thought she was going to marry him. That was the plan. But instead of marrying her, Willy got her hooked on heroin too."

Katrina felt sickened. "Mammi used drugs?"

He nodded sadly. "I felt like it was my fault too. I had

talked her into leaving our settlement. I had introduced her to Willy. I stood by and watched it happen. Like a train wreck. A really bad train wreck."

"What happened?" Katrina asked meekly.

"Willy overdosed . . . and died."

"And my grandmother?"

"She disappeared."

"Disappeared?"

"As far as I could tell she just vanished. I tried and tried to find her. I even went back to our old settlement, but she wasn't there."

"Although she wasn't far from there," Aunt Alma surmised.

"I figured she was crashing with some of Willy's old drug buddies, wasting away in some nasty drug house. I knew she wouldn't live long if she kept doing heroin."

Katrina filled him in, as much as she could, as to her grandmother's whereabouts back then. "Then she came to our settlement," she said finally, "married Aunt Alma's father, my grandfather, and she had my daed. His name is Frost."

"Frost?" Larry smiled. "That sounds like Starla. Did she have more kids? She always said she wanted to have a bunch of kids. Sometimes I'd think of her and wonder what it would've been like if she and I had stayed in our settlement, married, and had children . . . would we both have been much happier?"

"She had only one child," Aunt Alma told him. "She told me later in life that he had been a miracle. She thought she was unable to have any children."

Katrina was surprised. She'd never heard that.

"But did she have a happy life?" Larry asked eagerly.

"*Ja*," Aunt Alma assured him. "I think she did."

Katrina told him about the little radio and how Mammi

would sometimes do peculiar things. "Although I don't think of them as so strange anymore," she confessed. "I fear that people will say the same about me . . . when I go back."

"So you are going back?"

"*Ja*. I hope so. My family may not want me, though."

"What about *American Star*? According to Jack, you could win it." Larry studied her closely. "What would you do then? Besides the prize money, you get a record contract. Would you make an album?"

"I don't want that."

"What *do* you want?" He was watching her even more closely now. "An Amish girl competing on a show like *American Star*, singing the way you've been doing—according to Jack anyway. I've been out of the country so I haven't caught up with the show yet. But it does make my head spin. What do you want out of life, Katrina?"

She bit her lip.

"Do you even know what you want?"

"Katrina wants to help her daed," Aunt Alma said. She told Larry about Frost's injured back and recent heart attack.

"That sounds honorable," Larry said, "but that's not the whole story. I know Amish. I grew up Amish. Girls don't just leave and do the things you've done without being tempted into the English world."

"I don't think I care much for the English world," she told him. "I like the people. But the fast way of life . . . the noise . . . the shiny, glitzy shallowness . . . I don't like it."

He chuckled. "I'm sure a lot of English would agree with that."

"Then why do they stay with it?" She pointed out to his fancy backyard. "Why do you?"

He shrugged. "I suppose it's not that different from heroin. It's an addiction."

She suddenly felt sorry for him. "You asked if Mammi was happy in her life. Now I wonder how you would answer that same question."

"Well . . . I made a lot of money. Especially considering I only have an eighth-grade Amish education." He chuckled. "I own my own recording company. Live in a beautiful home. Have lots of impressive friends in the music industry. Happy?" He took in a deep breath, slowly exhaling. "Yeah, I guess so. Relatively happy."

"What about God?" she asked. "Does he fit into your life?"

"That's a good question, Katrina." Larry leaned back in his chair with his hands lying limply in his lap. "Maybe it's something I should give some thought to . . . especially seeing how I'm not getting any younger."

Katrina could tell he was tired, and she suspected this conversation had been draining for him. Aunt Alma looked worn out too. Katrina thanked Larry for his hospitality and said it was time to go. As he walked them to the front door, he gave her what sounded almost like a warning. "I do wonder what Starla would say to you, Katrina. Have you ever considered what sort of advice she might give you?"

As they were being driven back to the hotel, Aunt Alma closed her eyes, but Katrina didn't think she was asleep. More likely she was thinking about what Larry had told them about Mammi. It was shocking to imagine that she'd been in love with a man who was a drug addict and had even become an addict herself. And then to lose the man she loved like that— it was all so sad and tragic. Now things were beginning to make sense too. Katrina understood why Mammi had mostly buried her music, along with her past. It was probably too painful to take it with her. Yet she had still listened to her little radio. As much as she had appeared to despise music, she must have loved it too.

23

When Katrina and Aunt Alma got up to their room, they were surprised to discover that their key card no longer worked. Katrina knocked on the door, hoping Breezy would let them in, but no one answered. They went back downstairs and walked up to the big desk, but even before Katrina could explain, the woman began talking.

"Yes, I know who you are. Katrina Yoder, one of the top eight finalists of *American Star*. Congratulations. From here on out, you and your aunt have a private suite on the thirty-sixth floor. That's just one of the perks of the show. Your things have already been moved up there." She handed her a new packet of plastic key cards. "You're in suite 3620."

"A suite?" Katrina remembered the stylists' fancy rooms. "And you do not mean dessert either."

She chuckled. "A suite is like a small apartment. Very comfortable, with two master bedrooms and a living room and kitchenette. Everything you need for the rest of the competition."

"Oh . . . thank you."

"By the way, Katrina, I noticed that you haven't had any additional expenses."

"Additional expenses?"

"Room charges. You know, for food or the spa or salon or whatever. Your roommate had plenty of charges on her statement. But you don't have a single one."

"*Ja.* That's a good thing."

"No, that's not a good thing. *American Star* is covering the bill for your stay here, Katrina. They will pay for all your food and other expenses. Tell me, have you been paying for your own meals and laundry services and—"

"I do the laundry," Aunt Alma explained. "And I go to the grocery store and I fix our food. Every day I do these things."

"But you don't need to go to all that trouble," the woman explained. "It's all covered by the show. Why not just enjoy our services and give yourselves a break?" She smiled at Aunt Alma. "We have some great restaurants in this hotel."

"Thank you," Katrina told her. "We'll keep that in mind."

"I have something else for you too. The producer wanted to give it to you earlier, but you were out. I'll go get it."

Katrina just nodded, waiting for the woman to return with whatever it was.

She came back with a large envelope that said *American Star* on the outside. "You'll have to sign for it." The woman pointed to a place for Katrina to sign. "Have a nice evening," she told her. "And good luck. I've been voting for you."

"You have?"

The woman laughed. "Of course. You're the best singer on the show. I'm wagering that you'll win. You and Tyler."

Katrina made a stiff smile and thanked her again. Then she and Aunt Alma rode the elevator again, this time to the thirty-sixth floor. When they opened the door to their new room, they were stunned to see that it was as big as a house. "This is like where the stylists stay," Katrina told her as they went in.

"So big." Aunt Alma shook her head. "So extravagant."

Katrina examined a basket of fruit and other food. "Look, this card says it's for us."

"And these flowers too?" Aunt Alma sniffed. "I've never seen such fancy flowers. Have you?"

Katrina was opening the envelope now, removing a letter and what appeared to be a very large check. "Look," she told her aunt. "The letter says that *American Star* wants to pay me for making the top eight. The full amount was fifty thousand dollars, but they've deducted the taxes so it's not as much." She waved it in the air. "But it's still more than enough to pay for Daed's surgery." She was dancing around the room now. "That means we can go home, Aunt Alma."

"Truly?" Aunt Alma's eyes filled with tears. "We can go home?"

"I think so. Why else would they pay me this money now?"

Aunt Alma came to look at the check and the letter. "It says to call Brandy if you have questions."

"*Ja*. I should do that." While Aunt Alma was exploring the rooms, Katrina called Brandy—even using the hotel's phone since everything was supposed to be free.

"Yes," Brandy told her. "We knew how badly you needed the money for your father's surgery, Katrina, so we made an exception to pay you early. You don't need to mention this to any of the other contestants. And we gave you a cashier's check so that you could sign it and send it to your family immediately. Just make sure that you send it registered mail to guarantee it arrives safely."

"But since I am paid, I'd like to go home. Aunt Alma and I want to—"

"Katrina, you can't go home until the competition ends."

"You are not sending me home?"

"No. Of course not. Remember how you signed a contract for the top eight? You are legally responsible to fulfill it. If you don't fulfill your contract, we cannot let you have that money. You do understand that, don't you?"

"Oh . . ." Katrina was trying to grasp this. "*Ja*, I remember now. I was just so excited that my father could have the surgery."

"Yes. We hoped that would please you. We are all so thrilled with your performances, Katrina. This is our way of showing you our appreciation. I'm sorry you misunderstood and thought we were sending you home. Far from it."

"*Ja*. I understand now." Katrina felt like there was a rock in the pit of her stomach.

"I'm so looking forward to seeing your next performance. As you know, from here on out, it will only be solo performances. And I know you'll honor your contract and continue to give us your very best, Katrina. This is your chance to really shine."

"How many more shows are there?" Katrina asked in a meek voice.

"Five more shows. Can you believe it? In less than two weeks, this season will end."

"Two weeks . . ."

"Yes. Well, unless you have any other questions, I should probably take this call that's coming in."

Katrina thanked her, then hung up. "Two more weeks."

"I found our airplane tickets," Aunt Alma said happily as

she emerged from one of the rooms. "They were in my bag, right where I left them." She waved the envelope as she hurried over. "The hotel people put my things in one bedroom and yours in the other. But if we're going home, we won't—"

"You're going to have to go home without me," Katrina said firmly.

"What?" Aunt Alma's smile faded.

"It's all right." Katrina tried to sound happy. "I just talked to Brandy and it seems I need to stay a little longer. But I really want you to go home, Aunt Alma." She handed her the check, making a plan as she spoke. "I need you to get this back home as soon as possible so that Daed can have his surgery. Brandy said I can sign the back of it and it is just like money. But we *need* you to take it there. It would be too dangerous to send this much money by mail."

"*Ja.*" She nodded. "You are probably right. But I cannot leave you—"

"You have to," Katrina insisted. "You know that I'll be fine. I am perfectly safe in this hotel. And *American Star* will take good care of me. Plus, you heard them saying I can eat food at the hotel. They will even do my laundry."

Aunt Alma was not easily convinced, but finally she agreed, and she and Katrina went back downstairs to get help with arranging the airline ticket. After that was settled, Katrina called the Zooks' guesthouse in Cleveland.

"Katrina Yoder!" Mrs. Zook exclaimed. "I am so happy to talk to you. We have been watching you on *American Star*. You have made us so proud."

"Proud?"

"I guess that is the wrong word. I cannot describe it, Katrina. We are so happy. You are like a light shining in a dark place."

"Thank you." Katrina explained that Aunt Alma would be flying home on Monday. "Her flight gets in at night, so—"

"We will pick her up at the airport," Mrs. Zook assured her. "You just give us the time and her flight numbers and we are happy to do this."

"Thank you." Katrina explained how her aunt needed to get home to take the check to Daed.

"We will drive her to wherever she needs to go," Mrs. Zook said. Katrina started to protest, saying it was too much trouble, but Mrs. Zook insisted. "We are so happy to be a part of this, Katrina. You don't understand. And when you come home, we will go get you at the airport too, if that is all right with you."

"*Ja*. I would love that. Thank you."

"And if your family, or your settlement or district—if they do not welcome you back with open arms, we will welcome you, Katrina. You can become part of our family. You and your aunt."

Although it warmed Katrina's heart to hear this, she hoped that it wouldn't be necessary. Still, she didn't know what would await her when she got home . . . if they would even want her to come home. After giving Mrs. Zook the information regarding Aunt Alma's travel to Cleveland, Katrina thanked her for her help and support.

"We are all voting for you," Mrs. Zook told her.

Katrina knew she should feel encouraged by this, but she no longer cared if anyone voted for her. In fact, if people would stop voting for her, it seemed she would be allowed to go home sooner.

Before Aunt Alma left, Katrina asked her to promise something. "I want you to take the check straight to the hospital in Millersburg, where Daed is staying. I want you to pay the people directly for what Daed needs. You do not need to tell my parents where the money came from . . . or even mention my name. I don't want them to refuse it or say that it's not honorable money. Do you understand?"

"*Ja.*" She nodded sadly. "I do."

As relieved as Katrina was to receive the call from Bekka that Aunt Alma had made it safely back home and delivered the check to the hospital, she missed her aunt more than she could have imagined. Rambling around in the suite, practicing the song she planned to sing on Wednesday night, Katrina felt so lonely that she actually called Breezy's room.

"I miss you," Katrina told her.

Breezy laughed. "I thought you'd be glad to be rid of me. I'm sure Alma was happy to part ways with my messes."

Katrina explained that her aunt had gone home.

"Oh, so are you lonely?"

"*Ja* . . . a little."

"Why don't you come visit me?" Breezy told her which suite she was in, and to Katrina's surprise it was only two doors down. When Breezy opened the door, Katrina was so happy to see her old roommate that she hugged her. It was even comforting to see Breezy's messiness again.

"I wanted to go home with Aunt Alma," Katrina confessed as they sat on the big couch together, "but Brandy said the contract won't allow me to do that. So I'm stuck here."

"Until they send you home, anyway."

"I wish they would send me home."

"Me too." Breezy made a sheepish smile. "Sorry, that doesn't sound very nice, but if you were out of the picture, my chances would improve a lot."

"You've been getting better and better," Katrina told her. "I'm not the only one who thinks so."

"Yes, but you're still the favorite. 'The little Amish girl who sings like an angel,'" Breezy said teasingly. "But I should be thankful. My connection with you has probably helped me more than I care to admit." She got a serious expression. "And I should thank you for being kind to me right from the start. You know that first night—when I went out partying and came home drunk as a skunk? I was certain you'd ask for a different roommate, and I even hoped that you would."

"Why?"

"Because I didn't like the idea of rooming with some up-tight Amish chick."

Katrina frowned.

"Sorry. You're not like that. But at the time, when I met you and Alma, I thought someone was pulling a fast one on me."

"What?"

"I figured you couldn't really sing and you were probably just something they'd dragged in to bring their ratings up. And I knew that when the camera crews came to my town, they saw that I was from a good Christian family and that I'd grown up singing in church—so I thought they stuck me with you to make us out to be the goody-goody girls. And that made me want to go out partying, you know, to prove that I wasn't."

"I understand."

"But you and your aunt got me up that morning—or I would've missed the first day and been kicked out. And then I heard you sing . . . and I realized you were going to be my competition."

"Every girl here was your competition."

"Yeah, but I could tell you were really good, Katrina. I knew I was good too, but I also knew I wasn't as good as you."

"I disagree. When you really put your heart into it, you're great. And besides that, you know music. You can arrange it and write it and play it on your guitar. All I can do is learn a song and sing it."

"But when you sing it"—Breezy shook her head—"you really sing it." She chuckled. "That whole Amish bit doesn't hurt either."

"I haven't told anyone, but I think I'm not going to go to the stylists for the rest of the competition," she confided.

"Seriously?" Breezy looked shocked. "That could ruin it for you."

"I want to be true to myself. No more compromising."

"But what if it makes you lose?"

"Then I don't deserve to win."

"You mean you don't *want* to win." Breezy scowled. "I don't get that, Katrina. I mean, you've come this far. You've got voters out there who love you. You can't just roll over now. That seems unsportsmanlike, if you ask me."

"You think I should compromise myself in order to win?" Katrina stood up now, pacing back and forth. "You think I should shave my legs and wear short skirts and face paint and tall-heeled shoes, even though it makes me feel like a liar and a fake? I should turn myself into something I am not in order to win a prize I don't want?"

Breezy's brows drew together as if she was really thinking about this. "I don't know. When you put it like that, I'm not so sure. But you signed on for this contest, Katrina. It seems like you owe it something."

"I know." Katrina sat back down and sighed. "That's what troubles me."

"Why can't you continue to compete without compromising yourself? You can have the stylists help you to find evening gowns like that blue number you wore—"

"With no back?"

"They can make them with backs. And you could wear flat shoes if you want and keep the makeup toned down. Be conservative if it makes you feel better, but at least you'd be fitting in more. And you'd have a chance to win." Breezy got up and started pacing. "Voters expect us to look and act like stars, and that takes a little effort on—" She stopped and smacked herself on the forehead. "I can't believe I'm telling you these things. If I was smart, I'd keep my big mouth shut and just let you go out there in your little apron and bonnet."

She turned to look at her. "But I really like you, Katrina. And I hate seeing you selling yourself short all the time, acting like you're not worthy or like you should go stand in the corner with your head hanging down. You know, I'm not the best Christian—you can certainly attest to that—but I do know this: Jesus said we should be like lights on a hill. You don't put a lantern under a bushel basket. We are supposed to let our light shine before men so that they can see God. And when you perform, it feels like that to me—like you're being a light that points me to God. And others see that too, I'm sure. What is wrong with that?"

"I don't know. Maybe nothing is wrong with it. When I hear you say it like that, it almost makes sense. Yet at the same time it goes against what I've been taught. Amish are different from English. That is how it is. We do not want to look like or act like English. Our ways set us apart, and

that is how we like it—being set apart . . . to serve God."
She bit her lip.

"I guess I don't understand Amish."

"And I don't understand English."

"So, as my dad likes to say, we can agree to disagree."

"*Ja*. I guess so."

"I know you'll do what's right for you," Breezy told her.
"And knowing you, it will probably work out just fine. Even
if you went out there wearing the same dress and apron each
day, you could probably still win this thing."

Katrina stood now. "I should probably go. You might need
to practice or something."

"Before you go, I want to tell you how much I've appreciated your help. I'm not sure I said that before. But I honestly
don't think I would've made it this far without you, Katrina.
It's not just that, though. Being around you has made me
want to get closer to God again too." She smiled. "You've
been good for me."

Katrina hugged her again. "You've been good for me too."

"Good luck tomorrow."

"You too."

24

Katrina thought long and hard about what Breezy had said about being a light on a hill. Katrina had heard that Scripture before in church, but she had always believed that God's light shone through her best when she was serving others in humility and love. She still believed it now. However, if her singing had shone any of God's light onto the TV viewers, she was thankful. Just the same, she decided to wear her own clothes for the remainder of the competition. If the viewers wearied of seeing her in either her green dress or her blue dress, so be it.

For her first solo in the top eight competition, Katrina sang "The Wayfaring Stranger." The lyrics seemed to perfectly reflect how she was feeling at this stage of the competition—as if she too was on a long, hard journey. When she reached the line about going home to see her father, she had tears streaming down her cheeks, and yet she continued to sing—with all her heart, she continued to sing.

"Katrina, Katrina," Ricky began. "You broke my heart with that song, girl. That was so beautiful. I didn't even mind that you wore your little Amish dress again. It seemed to work for you. Really great choice of a song. And you sang with real heart."

"Nicely done," Celeste told her. "But I don't agree with Ricky on your wardrobe choice. I mean, I get that you're Amish, honey, and you don't go for those sleazy, revealing dresses, but you could've picked something more fashionable—more like a real star would wear. You sang beautifully. But I hope you can show up looking more like an American Star next time—if there is a next time. I hope there is."

"That was my favorite performance of the night," Jack told her. "But then I love that song. Even so, not everyone can pull it off. And you did that." He cleared his throat. "As for the Amish outfit, I'm siding with Celeste. This show is called *American Star*, Katrina. If you want to be a star, you have to make some sacrifices."

She just nodded and politely thanked them before she exited the stage—secretly hoping that the fans would react like Celeste and Jack . . . and not vote for her.

As it turned out, the voters continued to support her. The next evening she learned that she had made it into the top six, along with Tyler and Breezy. Her only consolation was to learn that she'd received fewer votes this week than last week. But she was still one of the top three vote-getters that week.

"The voters are sending you a message," Celeste told her. "They want to see you looking like a star, Katrina. Do you really plan to keep letting them down?"

The audience seemed quieter than usual now, as if everyone was waiting expectantly, as if they were hoping that Katrina would agree to play this game according to the English rules. All three of the judges watched her closely, waiting for her response.

"I do not like letting anyone down." Katrina let out a long sigh. "But I also cannot let myself down—and I cannot let God down. I have made a commitment, and I will not compromise. I love God with all my heart and my soul and my strength and my mind. I choose to honor God with how I live my life—whether it's my words or my thoughts or my clothing. If that displeases the voters, they can choose someone else to be their next American Star. I am honored that they voted for me at all." Then she thanked the judges and hurried from the stage.

Fortunately, some outside performers were singing for this show, so following the elimination and her short speech, Katrina only had to sit in the audience and pretend to enjoy the music. Soon, though, with all the pounding and shouting from this rock band, her head hurt so badly that she went backstage to use the restroom. She wanted to remain there until the music stopped, but it would be a very long night. Finally, it quieted down a little, and she emerged from the restroom.

"Katrina." Tyler came over to her with a look of concern. "Are you okay?"

She touched her head. "The music . . . I think it gave me a headache."

He smiled. "Heavy metal does that to me too."

She peered at him. "Are you all right?"

He shrugged. "Yeah, sure, why wouldn't I be?"

She put a hand on his shoulder. "Because I hurt you?"

His expression turned sad. "Well, I guess you might've broken my heart . . . just a little." Now his lips curled up just barely. "But I'm a tough guy. I'm getting over it."

She smiled. "You are a great guy, Tyler. Some English girl will be very, very blessed to get you."

His smile grew wider. "They're already lining up. Even if I don't win *American Star*, the ladies are way more interested now than they ever were before."

They talked a while longer, and Katrina felt relieved to know that he was not nearly as hurt as she'd imagined. Probably not nearly as hurt as she'd been when Cooper parted ways with her. But that was something she tried not to think about. One of so many painful things that she pushed into the corners of her mind.

The next morning, she called Bekka as usual, and instead of complaining like she wanted to, she asked about her father. She knew he'd had his surgery yesterday, but Bekka hadn't known how it had gone the last time they talked.

"Cal said the surgery went good," Bekka told her. "He and Sadie came over here last night to watch you making the final six. Congratulations!"

"Thank you. But Daed—how *is* he?"

"Cal said your daed was up and walking around by the end of the day. That's how good he was feeling, Katrina. Can you believe it?"

"*Ja*, I do believe it. It's what I've prayed for."

"Cal said your parents haven't mentioned a word about the money for the hospital bill."

"So they don't know where it came from."

"Maybe not." Bekka sighed loudly. "But I think they should know, Katrina. You deserve to be thanked for what you've done."

"I don't want thanks. I just want Daed to be well."

"You sound sad, Katrina."

"I am glad about Daed."

"*Ja*, I know. But you sound sad. And you sounded sad last night when you said that about not compromising your faith."

272

"I wasn't sad about that," she explained. "But I suppose I am weary. I want this to be over."

"But you could win even more money."

"I would give it all away. I just want to be done."

"Well, you got fewer votes," Bekka pointed out. "Maybe your time to be sent home is coming."

"*Ja*. Maybe next time."

Bekka laughed. "You are the only one who would be happy to be sent home."

"But I have promised to do my best. I will do that." She asked Bekka if she had any suggestions for her next song.

"'Amazing Grace,'" Bekka said.

Suddenly Katrina remembered the song they'd sung at Mammi's funeral. "*Ja*. That's a good idea. It was Mammi's favorite song."

"When is the next competition?"

"Tomorrow. Then the elimination is on Sunday."

"I can't wait to hear you sing 'Amazing Grace.' It's going to be good."

Despite the judges' warnings, Katrina wore her traditional Amish dress, although she did wear her Sunday apron. She wasn't even sure why. Maybe it was simply because she was singing Mammi's favorite hymn. Before her turn to sing, she took a moment to tell the audience that she was dedicating this song to her grandmother. "Mammi got lost for a while in the English world," she explained, "but she found her way back home, and I think that she understood God's grace in a very personal way."

Then she sang, giving it her all. But before she could finish, she broke down in tears, and unable to sing one more word, she fled from the stage. Tyler and Breezy, who'd both already sung, quickly joined her backstage, hugging her and trying to comfort her, but Katrina could not stop crying. It was as if something inside of her had broken and all of her insides were spilling out all over the place.

"This is too much," Breezy said as Katrina quietly sobbed.

"It's killing her," Tyler said. "She's not made for this kind of pressure."

"Maybe the voters will figure this out," Breezy told him.

"I'm sorry." Katrina stood up straight, using her hands to wipe her face. "I don't know what came over—" Her voice cracked. "I just don't know."

"I know," Tyler told her. "You've reached your end. They should just let you go home."

"I *want* to go home," she told him. "But I promised to do my best and to stay till the end . . . till the voters send me home."

"You've kept your promise," Breezy said.

Soon it was time for the final six to go back out to remind voters to call or email their votes. But when Katrina's turn came, before she could say anything, Tyler stepped out. "I might get in trouble for saying this," he told Bruce, "but I want to tell the voters not to vote for Katrina."

The auditorium grew very quiet, and Bruce looked shocked. "Are you serious? We've never had a situation like this before. A contestant asking voters not to vote for another contestant?"

Tyler glanced at Katrina, then continued. "She is burnt out on this," he told the audience. "You guys saw her fall apart on stage. And she fell apart even worse backstage. I know she won't ask you herself, because she wants to honor the show, but I'm going to ask you. If you care about this girl, don't vote for her. Let her go home."

Katrina was crying hard again.

"Is that what you want?" Bruce asked her.

She just nodded.

"Let Katrina go home." Breezy stepped up to Bruce now. "I'm not saying this because I want to win. I know Katrina sings better than I do. But I love her. She helped me when I was down, and she's down now. She's hurting. You've all seen her doing her best, and she's given up everything to be in this competition. She finally got enough prize money to help her family, and her dad has been through his surgery—and she wants to go home. Even though she's worried her family won't want her back. And I can tell you this." She glanced at Katrina now. "If Katrina wins this thing, if she becomes the next American Star, her family probably won't welcome her back. So if you care about our sweet Amish angel, don't vote for her tonight. Just let her go home."

Katrina wasn't sure what to expect the next evening. Would Tyler and Breezy's plea to let her go home work? Would the voters choose freedom for Katrina, or would they force her to continue singing to them like the bird in a gilded cage? She had heard someone on Breezy's TV saying that this morning. They were comparing Katrina to a caged bird. It was painful to even think about.

To her relief—and the producers' disappointment—Katrina did not receive enough votes to remain on the show.

"You know what that means," Bruce Betner said sadly. "Come on up here, Katrina Yoder. It's time to sing your farewell song to us. I know that a lot of fans are heartbroken to see you go. But it seems your time has come. We're going to miss our Amish angel."

Katrina moved to the center of the stage, taking the microphone Bruce held out to her. "Thank you," she told him. "It's been an amazing experience."

"What are you going to sing for us?" he asked.

The final eight contestants had been told to always come to the elimination shows with a song prepared for their farewell song. She was relieved to finally be able to sing it. "I'm going to sing 'A Simple Song of Freedom,'" she told Bruce, "by Tim Hardin."

He laughed. "Well, that's apropos. You're getting your freedom, so why not sing a simple song about it?"

She put all she could into it. She knew it was an antiwar song, but it felt like a declaration of her freedom too. Not just freedom to leave this show, which had felt more and more like a prison, but her freedom to practice the religion of her choice—to express her commitment to being Amish. And when she was done—she was done!

Katrina could hardly believe it when days later, she was truly going home. She'd boarded a jet in Los Angeles yesterday, arriving in Cleveland last night, and this morning, just three days after being released from *American Star*, she was being driven by the Zooks to Millersburg.

"I don't know why you don't just let us take you all the way home," Mr. Zook said as they reached the outskirts of the town. "We don't mind a bit."

"I appreciate your kindness, but it's what I want," she gently told him. "It's difficult enough that I've been away from home . . . doing what I've been doing. If I come home in an automobile, well, it will only make things worse."

"She's right," Mrs. Zook told him. "Let her go home with her brother. That will please her family."

"*Ja,*" Katrina agreed. "Besides, Cal would be disappointed if I didn't ride with him. Especially seeing how he had to get off work to come and fetch me."

"Will you visit your daed in the Millersburg hospital?" Mrs. Zook asked.

"No. My friend Bekka told me he was allowed to leave the hospital yesterday afternoon. I will see him at home."

"There is a buggy." Mrs. Zook pointed to the dark gray buggy parked by the hardware store just like Bekka said it would be. It was the only one. "That must be your brother there. Nice-looking young man."

As Mr. Zook parked, Katrina peered out the window to see Cal, but to her surprise it was not her brother. Even so, she thanked the Zooks for their kindness and generosity and told them goodbye. She grabbed her bag and got out of the car, hurrying over to the buggy. "Cooper!" she exclaimed.

Cooper's face broke into a big smile as he swooped her into his arms. Hugging her tightly, he lifted her up so that her feet left the ground. "Katrina! It is so good to see you!"

It was a long and wonderful embrace, but suddenly feeling conspicuous as well as curious, she stepped away, smoothing her apron. "Where is Cal? Bekka said he would be here to fetch me today." She assumed it was just a happy coincidence that Cooper was here right now. Maybe he was running an errand for his uncle.

"I suppose Cal is at work on the farm." Cooper picked up the bag she'd dropped on the ground, dusted it off, and placed it into the back of the buggy. "Let me give you a hand."

"You're driving me home then?"

"*Ja.*" He nodded as he helped her up into the buggy. "Unless you have another plan."

"No," she said quickly. "No other plan."

Soon they were driving out of town, and the clip-clop of the horse's hooves seemed like the happiest sound she'd ever heard. Sitting there right next to Cooper was like a dream come true. Or maybe it was like finally waking up after a long, horrible nightmare. Anyway, she was so thrilled she could barely string the words together to speak.

"How did this happen?" she finally asked him. "That you came for me instead of Cal?"

"Bekka."

"Ah . . ." She nodded.

"I used my uncle's business phone to call the Lehmans' the other day. I wanted to find out how you were doing, and when Bekka said you would be coming home soon, I asked her if she could help me arrange to pick you up. And she did."

Katrina grinned and thought, *God bless Bekka!*

"Are you all done with the singing competition now?"

"I am all done. Completely done. Never want to go back again, *done.*"

He let out a relieved sigh. "That is good news."

She told him what she'd found out about Mammi. "It was hard to hear that," she admitted.

"*Ja.* My Aunt Martha told me something like that too. I never would've thought your mammi had been through so much." He frowned. "It made me worry about you, Katrina."

"Oh?"

"I didn't want you to go away and get hurt and not come back. But then my uncle reminded me that instead of worrying, I should be praying. So that's what I did."

278

"Thank you."

"I put you in God's hands." He smiled. "And God carried you back home."

"It was sad to hear Mammi's story, but it was good too. I think it helped to solidify what I already knew."

"What's that?"

"That I am Amish. And that I am happy with my simple life." She took in a deep breath. "I plan to go through baptism."

He nodded with his eyes fixed straight forward. "I do too."

She felt a warm rush surge through her. "That's good."

"*Ja.*"

They rode together in a companionable silence for a while. Katrina's eyes hungrily swept over the landscape that was slowly becoming more pastoral, with red barns and white houses popping up. "How is your apprenticeship going?" she asked.

"Good. Very good. I've learned all kinds of skills already. I love working with wood, Katrina. I love watching how wood goes from being a rough board to something useful and handsome. I think I might love woodworking as much as you love singing."

"I'm not sure I love singing so much anymore." She sighed. "I feel like I'm all sung out, Cooper."

"You mean you won't sing anymore?" He sounded severely disappointed.

"I suppose I might be coaxed to sing if it was for the right reason . . . for the right person . . . not just for vainglory."

"Oh . . . good. That is good." He looked hopefully at her. "Do you happen to *know* the right person? The one you would sing for?"

"Oh, *ja*. I think I do. I have known him for quite some time."

"Anyone I know?"

She playfully punched him in the arm. "I think you know who I mean, Cooper."

He nodded. "*Ja*. I hope so. I hope I do." Then he pulled back on the reins, calling out "whoa" to stop the horse.

"What's wrong?" She looked up and down the road but didn't see anything unusual coming in either direction. In fact, there was no traffic whatsoever.

Cooper climbed down from the buggy and walked around the front, but instead of checking the harness or the horse like she expected him to, he came around and offered her a hand. "Come on, Katrina. Get down from there," he somberly told her.

Holding on to his hand, she climbed down, and once her feet were on the ground, Cooper took her other hand into his. He looked directly into her eyes, gazing at her with such tenderness that a shiver of joy ran from the top of her head to the tips of her toes.

"Katrina Yoder, I am asking you if you will become my wife. Will you marry me?"

"I will gladly become your wife, Cooper Miller." Her heart was pounding and her eyes were filling with tears. "I will happily marry you."

Right there on the side of the road, Cooper leaned down and kissed her, and of course she kissed him back! They both began to laugh joyfully. As he helped her back up into the buggy, she knew there were still some obstacles and challenges ahead for both of them. But she felt confident that with God's help, they would manage just fine.

Melody Carlson is the award-winning author of over two hundred books, including *The Jerk Magnet*, *The Best Friend*, *The Prom Queen*, *Double Take*, and the Diary of a Teenage Girl series. Melody recently received a Romantic Times Career Achievement Award in the inspirational market for her books. She and her husband live in central Oregon. For more information about Melody, visit her website at www.melodycarlson.com.

Meet Melody at

MelodyCarlson.com

- Enter a contest for a signed book
- Read her monthly newsletter
- Find a special page for book clubs
- Discover more books by Melody

Become a fan on Facebook

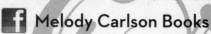 Melody Carlson Books

What do you do when your life's not all it's cracked up to be?
Get a new one.

Worlds collide when a Manhattan socialite and a simple
Amish girl meet and decide to switch places.

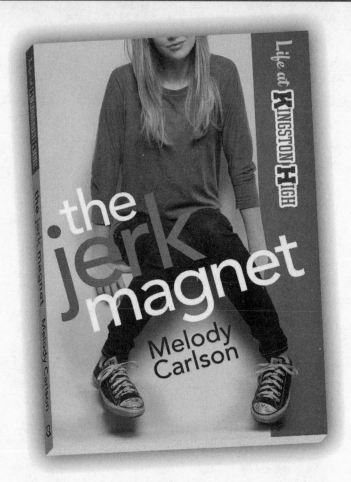

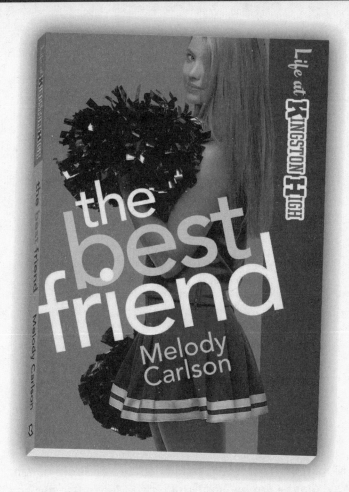

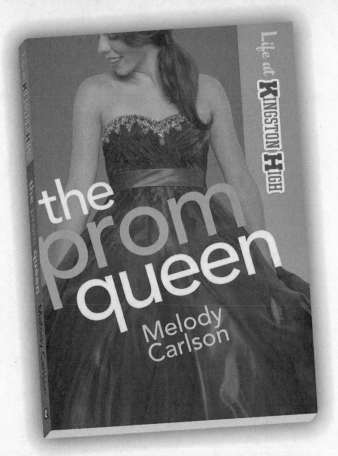

Aster Flynn Wants a Life of Her Own . . .

But will her family get in her way?

 Revell
a division of Baker Publishing Group
www.RevellBooks.com